Other Books by Roger Elwood

Adult Fiction

Angelwalk

Fallen Angel

Stedfast

Darien

Dwellers

Soaring

The Christening

Children of the Furor

Road to Masada

The Wandering

Wolf's Lair

Deadly Sanction

Code Name: Bloody Winter

Without the Dawn

The Blood of Strangers

Dark Knight

Circle of Deception

Juvenile Fiction

Darien's Angelwalk

Terror Cruise

Disaster Island

Nightmare at Skull Junction

The Frankenstein Project

Forbidden River

Sudden Fear

Shawn Hawk

Joanie Loves Chachi (book)

Dukes of Hazzard (book)

The Munsters (book)

Bonanza (book)

Nonfiction

The Joys and Sorrows
   of Christian Mothers

People of Destiny

The Lawrence Welk Story

Blessed by God: Shirley and Pat
   Boone

A Special Kind of Love: Nancy
   Reagan

Golden Paths

The Innocent Sins of Everyday Life

Strange Things Are Happening

Prince of Darkness

A Novel

Riversong

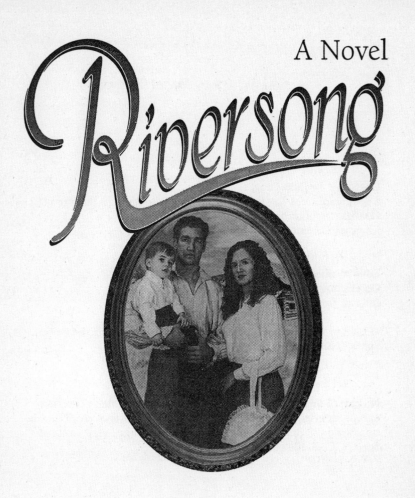

ROGER ELWOOD

Chariot VICTOR
PUBLISHING
A DIVISION OF COOK COMMUNICATIONS

ChariotVictor Publishing,
a division of Cook Communications, Colorado Springs, Colorado 80918
Cook Communications, Paris, Ontario
Kingsway Communications, Eastbourne, England

Designer: Bill Gray
Editors: Sue Ann Jones; Barbara Williams
Cover Photo: Olde Tyme Photography
Interior Designer: Cheryl Ogletree

1 2 3 4 5 6 7 8 9 10 Printing/Year 02 01 00 99 98

To my mother,
whom the Lord chose not yet
to take into His kingdom.

Acknowledgments

Ah, yes! The acknowledgments.

I treasure this space in each of my books, for it represents a chance to show gratitude to some wonderful folks who have helped me along the road to publication, in this case, talented professionals who have been instrumental in helping me to write a novel that has been on my heart for some time now.

I have worked with Cook Communications for the past couple of years because of Karl Schaller and the special qualities he brings to his job. What an absolute inspiration it is to have this principled but not stuffy gentleman as a publisher and editor. Karl Schaller is an extraordinary individual, very much in a class by himself, someone with verve, intelligence, perception, and sensitivity that are exceedingly rare traits in Christian publishing.

Now that Cook Communications has bought Scripture Press, I have also enjoyed working with Greg Clouse, a very talented editor.

I also must thank several loyal and helpful friends: Warren Wiersbe; Bill Petersen, a rock of stability and integrity; Doris and Jess Moody, who are always there when I need them; long-time friends Marion and Harold Lindsell as well as Dorothy and William Conover; and those several other brothers and sisters in Christ who have not allowed my manifold and sometimes infuriating mood swings—a direct result of hypoglycemia—to harm what the Lord has given us: friendship.

And, of course, I include my beloved parents, whom I pray the Lord will allow to stay with me on this earth through the end of this century and well into the next. They are life itself to me, and I cherish our relationship, one that has lasted more than half a century and that will go on into eternity.

Roger Elwood

There is a blessed place,

Where I will live for eternity,

A place of peace and joy,

A place where I will see my loved

ones face-to-face,

And death can never again separate

us.

In honor of

Maggie Engebretsen

Prologue

Oh better than the minting

Of a gold-crowned king

Is the safe-kept memory

Of a lovely thing.

Sara Teasdale

Maggie Engebretsen Stuart was more than ninety years old.

As she considered that notable fact, it seemed at some point that she was not thinking about herself at all but about some other woman, someone far stronger and nobler and smarter than she had ever deemed herself.

Now in her tenth decade of life—more than thirty-six thousand days. So very long to have to face each new dawn, so often to be weary by dusk.

So—

It seemed, to Maggie Engebretsen Stuart and to others of her acquaintance, that she had had enough experiences to encompass several centuries, not just one.

There had been great moments of profound beauty and accomplishment, yes. Moments that were to be treasured, relived through her memories again and again, but along with these, she had faced tragedies of such epic proportions that it was astonishing she had managed to live past the age of forty, let alone more than twice that.

Tired.

Finally, though, life had taken its gradual toll on her, and now she was rapidly fading. As the end neared, people who knew her heard of her nearness to death and began a prayer chain in their own homes, knowing it might simply be the Lord's will that she be taken to Him at last.

Maggie deserved some rest, rest that amounted to far more than a single night's sleep, however refreshing even that might be.

As she preferred, she was alone that last night, a night during which she passed from mortal flesh to immortal spirit, a night of reliving the past and anticipating her future home, for which she had been yearning for a long, long time . . .

When did our love begin?

She asked herself that question with longing, so much longing even after all these years of bringing it to the front of her mind and whispering it to herself as she thought of the man for whom it was intended.

She was an old woman now, an ancient one, a human antique, as it were, who was struggling to relive in a quiet moment by herself the only fulfilling, satisfying romance of her long, long life, the only one that had existed, the only one she had ever allowed herself all those years, though opportunities for others had been plentiful.

Everyone who got to know Maggie Engebretsen Stuart seemed surprised that she could still think in such terms, her expression suggesting as it did the hint of lingering passion.

What she told these people, if they commented accordingly, was a very simple declaration: "Just because there is snow on the roof hardly means there is no fire underneath!"

When did our love begin, my dear, dear Randy?

Randy Stuart . . .

How handsome he was! How strong and yet gentle.

Few people ever knew he had existed, and, now, of those who did, only one woman survived to keep his memory from dying out altogether. But as long as Maggie drew breath, Randy Stuart would not be forgotten.

Still, so many decades later, this old, old woman's heart raced within her chest as she recalled their happy moments together. Even now her breath quickened while she envisioned being held in Randy Stuart's arms, held so close to his strong, muscular body that she found it difficult to breathe but enjoying the warmth of his flesh, the firmness of it, and wanting nothing to spoil such moments as those between the two of them. Still she longed for those moments to be repeated, not in sad little vignettes of senile yearning, but as life had given it, as passion had made it.

Still—

I miss you so very much, she thought. *Without you, Randy, my life is no longer as full as it should be. There is an empty chair at the table of my heart.*

Maggie Engebretsen Stuart was sitting in an old rocking chair on the front porch of a modest, two-story house with a clear view overlooking the Pacific Ocean. The night was beautiful, the air clean, the scent of the surf appreciated even by her aging nostrils, the stars in view across the heavens.

You never made it this far, she thought with almost suffocating melancholic wistfulness, thinking of that special man from long ago. *Yet how much you wanted the two of us to stand side by side on the beach only a short distance from here and feel the cool, salty mist stinging our cheeks.*

Built a dozen years earlier, just before the beginning of the twentieth century, the house where Maggie now watched the pounding surf was surrounded on three sides by the sprawling Santa Monica Mountains. Many years ago the property had been an untamed and utterly wild place entirely devoid of residences.

In those days, rattlers and spiders and coyotes as well as a large population of cougars were persistent threats to the settlers; it seemed to Maggie Engebretsen Stuart that she had had to battle them all more than once over the years.

Still there . . .

The countless number of coyotes had never stopped roaming the area, but the cougars were decreasing in numbers.

Rattlers continued to be a problem, potentially a deadly one, what with the growing number of houses going up and residents encountering them in their yards and outbuildings, looking like forgotten pieces of rope.

But there seemed to be less hysteria now about tarantulas in the midst of growing civilization than in the once-uninformed frontier era, as people realized the creatures were far less dangerous than any of the old myths and their inherently sinister appearance had suggested.

That didn't help me when I fell into a nest of them. I was sick for a week!

A brief smile crossed Maggie's heavily lined face, the pale skin taut against her petite cheekbones, giving her a somewhat haunted look that was not alleviated by the dark, deep-set circles under her eyes.

There was no one health problem afflicting her, merely the accumulating signs that could be expected of anyone who had lived nearly a hundred years.

Every bone in my body seems to know at least a little pain now, she said without speaking the words out loud. *When I saw you in the beginning, you were the one who was in pain. I—I thought you might die then.*

Nearly eighty years ago!

I—I thought you might die then . . .

That image had intruded often, harsh and unwelcome, in recent months when she knew there would not be very many days left.

"Each one brings us that much closer, Beloved," she said out loud. "It will not be long now, my love."

Tears came to her eyes then as she thought of the one man to whom she had ever given herself all the years of her long life.

Randy . . .

That had been a good name for him though no one else had been able to guess the emotional causes of his once-promiscuous behavior. He had been living that sort of life . . . until the two of them met.

Randy . . .

She repeated his name slowly, adding nothing to it, keeping his image in her mind pure and strong as though he were sitting in the chair next to hers, savoring the victory the two of them had enjoyed, the victory over a past that had dragged him down emotionally and spiritually since he was a child.

So tall, Maggie remembered. *Over six feet, broad at the shoulders. I had to stand on my toes to reach your lips . . .*

Instinctively her tongue slowly moistened her lips, and her head fell back against the rocker, a wistful sigh escaping her mouth, that bony old body tensing a bit as she remembered his familiar hands on her flesh.

Your brown hair, Randy, was soft, almost like a woman's.

Maggie's hands opened wide, the fingers outstretched as if to entangle themselves, then closed tightly into a fist.

Your face . . .

It was so clear in her mental vision!

Surely Randy's here right now, and I can—

Abruptly, Maggie Engebretsen Stuart opened her eyes in sudden anticipation, and then that moment ended as it always did, her shoulders slumping, disappointment swallowing her up in its grasp.

A squirrel was sitting on a tree branch to her left, studying her.

"Hello," she said softly, her voice cracking a bit.

The animal scurried down the trunk of the oak tree and onto the porch, stopping just in front of her.

"I have nothing for you tonight," she told it sadly. "I'm just not feeling at all well, dear little friend."

The squirrel hesitated then did something it had always stopped short of doing during the countless evenings that had preceded this one.

It jumped up onto the arm of the chair.

"My! Oh, my!" she gasped with surprise.

The squirrel's little mouth was stretched wide, its teeth clasping firmly something.

A chestnut.

Amazed, Maggie reached out, and the squirrel dropped it into her palm.

"But why, little one?" she asked, touched by what was so out of character for the little creature. "I'm supposed to be giving *you* something."

And then the squirrel was gone, hurrying off into the nighttime darkness beyond the lantern-lit porch.

Maggie looked at the chestnut, puzzled, for several minutes, finally slipping it into a pocket of her simple, floral-print housedress.

In the process she glanced at the empty chair sitting next to hers, a rocker identical to her own, kept there as a lingering symbol of the man she had left behind on the harsh, barren plains west of the Mississippi River.

I'm foolish, she knew as she returned to her endless preoccupation, *foolish to waste time like this, reliving the agony—and yet here I am, continuing on anyway, night after night, talking out loud, as though Randy could hear me.*

She looked up at the sky.

Oh, Lord, how I want my Randy to be there when I enter Your kingdom, she prayed silently but with great passion.

Her grip tightened on the arm of her chair as she stopped the back-and-forth motion of the rocker and just sat there, motionless, scarcely breathing, the sound of waves breaking on the shoreline below the bluff merging with the rhythm of her heart, increasing in tempo as she remembered the answer to her question.

When did our love begin?

That day, that hour, that place, that first touch came back to her in every detail, and she sighed with the joy of it.

Part One
Philadelphia

Never yet did there exist a full faith in the divine word which did not expand the intellect while it purified the heart; which did not multiply the aims and objects of the understanding, while it fixed and simplified those of the desires and passions.

Samuel Coleridge

Tragedies are not always announced in advance, swarming into our lives only after a herald has blown his horn in announcement. They can arrive in an instant, an accident or a heart attack or whatever the case, barging into our inner worlds.

And they can tear us apart, leaving only heartache in their wake.

It is possible that the average person can endure one tragedy and somehow come out of it intact as a human being.

But three at once, each a monumental one?

That has to be much more difficult.

Maggie Engebretsen faced just such an assault on her young life, a life that had known peace and love and as much security as anyone could want.

Abruptly, all this seemed to be ripped away from her.

It is very hard at such times not to stand out under the night sky, look up at the heavens, and demand, "Why, Lord? Why is this happening? What have I done that was so wrong that I needed to be punished so harshly?"

Why indeed?

A question to which there may never be an answer in this life . . .

Cholera.

Whispered and chilling.

A disease from hell itself.

A word spoken in hushed, fearful tones, its implications sending panic racing along every spine.

Some thought it to be a judgment from God. Others believed in a God not capable of anything as cruel as that.

Whatever the case, wherever cholera appeared, devastation came in on galloping hooves, like the Four Horsemen of the Apocalypse, and then the cries of pain and loss and despair rose up and merged together in an unholy din.

Chapter One

Tall, robust, and red-haired, young Maggie Engebretsen worked as a talented nurse in a Philadelphia hospital that housed the biggest contagious-disease ward in the Northeast. Nursing, it seemed, was her life's calling, and she was so good at it, so sensitive to the needs of her patients, that she never seriously considered abandoning it for another profession.

The only matter at issue was where she would continue being a nurse.

Maggie's heart was set on another location altogether, thousands of miles away. But the start of the epidemic had forced her to change her timetable, if not her expectations.

That was what she had been thinking just one year earlier, before cholera had invaded the nation.

Back then Maggie had had no idea that she still would be in that colonial city so many months later.

Why, Lord? she would plead periodically when the pressures were particularly oppressive. *What is Your purpose behind all this?*

And she was not happy because there had been other plans, plans she now thought she might never realize, at least any time soon, needed back home as she was. Her personal dreams, the blatant fantasies that were hers and hers only, would have to wait, because the epidemic was lasting longer and was more severe than anyone in the medical profession at the time had been wise enough to predict. What it would leave in its wake was impossible for anyone to foretell.

I wanted so desperately to leave, she reminded herself during moments when self-pity assailed her. *I wanted to throw myself at the feet of my Lord and venture forth into a land that was new for me, trusting in*

*His constant guidance and protection. But He has seen fit to deny me t[...]
for the time being, and I must not question His wisdom.*

Still, Maggie sighed with great wistfulness whenever s[...] thought of what could have been.

The western frontier.

For a very long time, the possibilities it represented ha[...] intrigued her, and chief among these possibilities was the aspect of adventure, of getting away from what had become a predictable way of life and facing some real danger if need be.

Maggie went on nurturing the hope that somehow, in a year or two or whenever, she might be heading out toward the Mississippi River and beyond!

Perhaps she would be able to serve in one of the many outposts proliferating in that region to meet the demands of settlers reaching into the new frontier, the very words making her tingle with the dreams she had been harboring for a longer period of time than she liked to admit.

"City life is boring," Maggie once had to admit to her mother. "I'm becoming so restless, Mama."

Five-foot-tall, round-faced Natalie Engebretsen was sympathetic.

"I know how you must feel," she said, "because I sometimes wonder if staying here in Philadelphia was what God intended for me."

"But why have you done it then?"

"Safety, I suppose."

"Safety, Mama? But that doesn't seem like you."

"Oh, it may not seem like me. But the truth is, Maggie, I could never come to grips with the danger in any trip westward."

Maggie was surprised.

"It isn't what they say about crossing the Mississippi, is it?" she asked.

"That is a large part of it," her mother had to admit.

Legends about the "Big River" had been entrenched in American culture for a long time, and chief among them was the one called "Riversong."

"It's just a story, I know," Natalie Engebretsen admitted, "but I think there's some truth at the center of it."

Riversong . . .

A mystical call from invisible sirens.

Beckoning, tempting.

Drawing people to the banks of Big River.

And then destroying them in its treacherous waters.

Or if not there, then later across the westward plains, Riversong somehow following after them like marauding demons out to destroy.

"Is it something of real evil?" Maggie's mother mused out loud. "Or just an idle fantasy perhaps?"

"Riversong?"

"Yes, dear. Hearing the stories, I have to wonder, Maggie, is the West you crave a place of opportunity—or perhaps an outpost of hell itself?"

Neither wanted to pursue that thought any further.

his,

ne

d
s

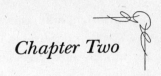

Chapter Two

Philadelphia . . .

It was a nice city although rather stolid in its way of life, digni-
fied, pleasant enough, with a sense of its own importance but not
in any obnoxious way, a city of stability and history, comforting and
serene.

But there was a time when Maggie Engebretsen could hardly
wait to leave Philadelphia, because a city that always remained the
same, however stable, was one that bred restlessness and boredom.

She would have been vastly more tolerant of the place except
for the fact that it was also terribly unexciting for a vibrant young
woman such as herself, in her early twenties, someone who had
heard romantic stories of frontier life and found herself enticed by
them, the promise of adventure in a rugged new land holding far
more appeal than staid, very old-fashioned Philadelphian, stories
that ran counter to everything that Riversong embodied.

"It's going to be soon," she had remarked to her sister, Roberta,
those months earlier. "I can feel it. I really can."

Roberta was a little older than Maggie, and though she also
had her own private hopes for the future, she unhappily was
forced to sublimate them, remaining in the background as her
baby sister became more or less the focus of attention within the
family circle and, in fact, for anyone who happened to meet the
two of them.

Maggie seemed to have the greater sense of excitement about
her, a charisma Roberta lacked, and both were fully aware of that
imbalance.

"We don't always get to do what we might want," Roberta said
during that same moment with Maggie, sighing with resignation as

her forthright admission triggered some wistful images that had been repressed for years, images that carried with them a touch of resentment since it seemed that Maggie, not Roberta, was the likelier one of the two someday to do anything as exciting as joining the ever-expanding flow of northeastern adventurers who had decided to pull up their roots and head west.

I've read about the Rockies, you know, and seen in my mind their snow-capped peaks. They must be so beautiful, Maggie, Roberta said in imaginary conversation.

You didn't know that I ever think about places like that, did you?

I seem to do my work endlessly, day after day, always without complaining, and yet I wonder, oh, dear, dear sister, I do wonder: What would it be like to stand at the very top of Pikes Peak and look for hundreds of miles in every direction, as God Himself must do over the whole earth from His vantage point in heaven?

She caught her breath.

To glance down, down, Maggie, can you imagine doing that, down on a patch of pure white clouds to the north, and feel your body tingle with the thrill of that matchless moment? They say the air is very, very thin up there, and maybe my lungs couldn't endure the strain for long. But if only I could see that view once . . . just once—

The two of them had been standing in the family's large kitchen, often the center of much discussion as they shared the various cooking duties, getting the evening meal ready that day, the menu including succotash with roast duck, the different aromas combining to form an enticing overall aroma.

"This is what I do," Roberta went on. "Maggie, listen to me, please: I get up in the morning, and help Mama and Papa, and then I take care of the house while they're working at the restaurant. You're always at the hospital. I just stay here, you know. But I see no need to put up a fuss. It is my destiny, I suppose, nothing more, nothing less.

"Maybe I'll never leave, Maggie. It's possible, you know; maybe that's going to be my destiny, to rarely go beyond the boundaries of this house, and never beyond this city. Wouldn't that be something? Wouldn't that just be something—to actually leave?"

Maggie reached out and put her hand gently on her fragile-looking sister's thin shoulder.

"Go with me," she said quite earnestly. "Drop all this, leave it behind you. The two of us will head west, Roberta, you and I; maybe we'll buy one of those covered wagons and make a real adventure out of the trip. There would be so much for us out there. Listen to me, please: You know I'm telling the truth."

Roberta put down the stuffing she had been preparing for the duck.

"What would happen to Mama and Papa—and the restaurant?" she asked honestly, with some fear showing on her face. "They are not about to hire someone else to help them, even if they could afford anybody. You know that, Maggie. Our family business surely would go down the drain."

The Engebretsens ran a thriving restaurant just at the edge of Philadelphia's rough-and-tumble wharf area, which seemed to bustle with activity twenty-four hours a day, and they did so with such decency that they were respected by social giants and low-class scoundrels alike.

Reports of the family's extraordinary generosity toward men who were down on their luck had spread quickly throughout the area, and the hapless vagabonds were often given meals at no cost. For many of them, it was the only way they survived.

"What we do, we do to honor our Lord," the girls' father, Lars Engebretsen, would tell anyone who seemed amazed at his kindness. "We do nothing whatsoever in our own strength but it is the Holy Ghost who takes over and compels us to feed those unable to take care of themselves."

At the beginning, the hardened wharf types would accept food but retain their cynicism over why it was given.

"You get nothing out of it—is that what you're sayin'?" one man after another would remark. "I can't figure you out."

Lars would respond in a typically kind manner.

"You don't have to, stranger," he said. "I'm just doin' what Almighty God has always done for me—and for you."

Most Philadelphians at first resorted to laughing behind Lars

Engebretsen's back, but in time, this stopped altogether and citizens at every level of the social order seemed somehow to realize that Lars and the other members of the family were never less than serious, committed to feeding the hungry for no reason other than the remarkably simple fact that it was what they all felt Christ wanted them to do. Thus it was something they did freely, without thought of gaining any kind of favors later on.

At one point, several of the vagabonds had pooled their limited resources and bought the family a leather-bound Bible. On the first page was an inscription: *FROM THE WHARF RATS—We love you, as you first loved us.*

The restaurant was a spiritual blessing for the family as well as their financial livelihood. Yet it was a time-consuming business, one that required long hours of work by the parents, who were now in their late fifties.

The elder Engebretsens were usually quite weary by the time they arrived home each evening, but they had been devoted to that sort of daily routine without interruption for more than two decades and had grown accustomed to conducting their lives in no other way.

Roberta was silent for several minutes as she continued on with the monotonous stuffing process.

Finally she spoke again, though with some obvious reluctance.

"Why didn't you go to the restaurant and help them?" she asked, a touch of bitterness in her voice. "Why is it that everything like that seems to fall on my shoulders? They really aren't that strong, you know."

Roberta was right to a real extent.

After the first decade and a half of her life, Maggie had allowed her attention to be shifted to nursing and away from the restaurant. She no longer assumed that her future was to be tied up entirely, or at all, in the family's business, no matter how successful it was.

"I am a nurse," Maggie replied. "There's never been any surprise about what I wanted to do with my life."

"Doesn't your family mean more to you? Shouldn't you help

them before you go on to other people?" Roberta pushed.

Maggie hesitated, not wanting to say anything that would stir up her sister's feelings any more.

The two of them had had this same discussion, or one similar to it, more than once over the past several years, and it invariably concluded in the same way as the latest one.

Maggie always hesitated to say anything further because Roberta seemed to possess a special knack of knowing how to make her feel quite guilty, and unreasonably so.

"You get to do what you want," Roberta went on, some passion in her voice making it a bit unsteady, "but not your dear sister. Why does it always turn out that way, Maggie? Why has it never been any different for me?"

Apart from the demands of nursing, Roberta's attitude was the other cause of Maggie's postponing her dreams of going west.

"No more, Roberta," Maggie begged, "please, don't let there be any more of this kind of talk between us."

"That's only because you know it's wrong. Isn't that it? You can't justify leaving this family behind you!"

"It's not that at all. It's—"

"It's what? What can you say? There's—"

Roberta bit her lower lip while an all-too-familiar frown showed in deep lines across her pale forehead.

"Sorry," she said. "I know you're doing what you think is right. It's just that I get so tired. I look at these same old walls, and my mind goes beyond them to the places you'll see if your dreams come true, as they usually do."

A cabin on the prairie.

Cattle spreading out in several directions.

A giant of a man as her husband, his strong arms holding her close to him. Children running to and fro—

Tears began a journey down Roberta's cheeks, reaching her lips and then continuing on to her chin.

Maggie noticed this was happening and walked around the table to the other side. She hugged her sister, not a forced gesture but a genuine one.

She suddenly had cause to wonder if she had done enough of that over the years or had taken everyone in her life for granted just because they were always present and apparently would never leave her.

"I wish you the best. I truly, truly do," Roberta told her. "Oh, Maggie, forgive me for acting like this over and over again. You must want to give up on me. I love you so much, and yet I seem so bitter, so spiteful, so jealous of you."

. . . so spiteful, so jealous of you.

Maggie had to admit that she felt this way too, periodically, though she tried her best to fight any such impulses. At the same time, she had to admit that the idea of helping others through nursing had shifted her attention away from her loved ones.

"Forgive me for putting my desires above everything else," Maggie replied. "Maybe I should be staying right here, pitching in like I used to do. Maybe—"

"No!" Roberta declared, pulling away, her eyes widening. "I'm all right; I just have to rant and rave now and then. God's hand is on you, Maggie. He's going to bless you in a way that's beyond my tight little imagination, and I shouldn't resent you for welcoming that challenge into your life."

Her tone seemed especially poignant, no real anger in it but some regret that she had not been given what she thought was a better chance in life.

"Why do you think that?" Maggie asked, genuinely puzzled. "God has His hand on all of us."

"I just know," Roberta replied. "I just know these things."

Maggie felt melancholic herself then, her own mind and not the Lord taking control of her and bringing on a wave of sorrow so strong it affected her the rest of that day and well into the inhospitable night.

Later the same evening, nearly midnight, the four of them sat around the dinner table, sharing their impressions of the events of the day as the flickering candlelight played over their love-filled faces.

And, afterward, before they left the table to do the dishes, Lars

Engebretsen told them about the rats.

"They've always appeared around the wharf, but now there has been an invasion of them, it seems," he said intently, though trying not to alarm his family more than necessary.

"Here, Papa?" Roberta asked, immediately picking up on what her father had said.

"At the docks."

"More than usual?"

"Many more, dear girl."

Roberta settled back against her chair, pondering the rather sinister implications of what she had learned.

Maggie, ever the vigilant nurse, spoke up and asked her father, "What is being done about them?"

"Everything possible, I assume."

"Any likelihood of disease?"

As usual, Maggie was getting right to the point. While her father admired this quality in his daughter, he was feeling increasingly uncomfortable that it required of him a certain candor that was at odds with the need for maintaining calm within the family circle.

"A very real one," Lars Engebretsen replied.

Maggie sat back in her chair, her mind racing ahead to what might happen. This was a tendency she had, thinking of something that had not come about as yet, and worrying herself incessantly over whatever it was.

"Any clues as to where they came from, Papa?" she asked. "I understand that there is cholera now in the Caribbean."

Her father was silent for a moment.

"We are being so gloomy," he said gamely. "I shouldn't have said anything. It probably is unimportant."

"All those rats?" Maggie replied incredulously. "How can anything like that be unimportant, Papa?"

She had studied enough of the available medical texts of the time to learn just what infected rats could cause in a community, a country, or an entire continent.

Something as painful—and as deadly—as warfare, something

destructive enough to wipe out entire families, villages, racing across country after country and leaving unimaginable chaos in its wake.

Bubonic plague.

Especially vivid in her mind were gruesome stories of the nightmarish plague outbreaks throughout Europe in the 1300s and for several centuries thereafter. And now cholera was out there, lurking at America's edges.

Knowing how severe an outbreak could be—and how easily rats could carry the germ aboard ships that arrived at Philadelphia's harbor from all over the world—she had petitioned the city government to maintain vigilance about rat infestations. Yet the mayor and others seemed lackadaisical, at least at the very beginning, and this had annoyed, frustrated, and alarmed Maggie. The problem was that she was a woman, and the men of politics paid women no attention.

But Lars Engebretsen listened to her, and he was as disturbed and frustrated by the city fathers' inaction as his daughter was.

"But what can we do if the authorities won't take action?" he asked her, feeling quite powerless in the face of coming catastrophe. "God help us! Our elected representatives do not seem inclined to do anything at all!"

"I think we should pray right now," Natalie Engebretsen said quietly, with her usual wisdom. "Let's join hands and pray."

Her family members did as she suggested, praying for God's help in overcoming the rats, which were even then scampering throughout Philadelphia and the surrounding countryside, carrying with them the beginning of a nightmare.

Chapter Three

Dark and mysterious.

They were that, these things of darkness.

They hid as though waiting, whether along the wharf or in alleys or wherever they happened to be.

Always, they were present in scenes that seemed perhaps ripped out of a medieval play, with the odors and the sounds of another world altogether.

Scurrying creatures.

Dirty and smelly and contaminated with all manner of mischief . . . and disease.

Creatures with tiny, blood-red eyes that pierced the darkness, pinpoints of crimson that, in themselves, sent tremors of fear through any who happened upon them.

Rats.

Ordinary, filthy, furtive rats—carriers of great calamity, carriers of the deadly bacteria that, unknown to early Americans, contaminated the water supply and thus killed hundreds.

And then thousands.

Children liked the dank, intrinsically creepy harbor area of Philadelphia. In the shadows of the big ships rocking restlessly at its piers, they found some of the scary appeal of a haunted house but without the supernatural ramifications.

Mysterious and alluring . . .

That part of the famed colonial city had never seemed less than another world entirely.

It did not look the same as the rest of the city.

It did not smell the same.

And the people working there were a rough crowd, often profane and vulgar, brutal, scarred men from faraway countries, coarse individuals accustomed to living harsh lives like the rats, alternating between the dark and musty holds of ships to the bright, wide-open places, lured there by promises of intrigue and adventure.

Yet the harbor area was essential to the survival of not only the city of Philadelphia itself but a large part of the East Coast region, because it was a major entry point for imported goods from Europe and South America.

And children could not resist its allure . . .

They were constantly devising clever ways of thwarting their parents' unmistakable wishes that were squarely against the children's going there, sometimes getting together in groups to figure out yet another deception so that bunches of them could sneak around the docks and warehouses when they should have been at school or at their chores.

A place of dreams, the wharf was for them.

For them the hulking ships, straining at the ropes that linked them to land, held a certain mystique, representing strange ports in exotic places and promising big adventures to be lived.

Young stowaways were always a problem, a critical one for the shocked loved ones who were left behind as well as for the shippers themselves, forcing upon them extra responsibilities when intruders were not discovered until the ship was well on its way to a destination that often was thousands of miles away.

More than a few children tried to stow away on their quest for adventure, having convinced themselves that facing the unknown was worth whatever danger might confront them.

"To live in the jungle!" one ten-year-old boy had exclaimed just days before he disappeared. "I want to do that so much I dream about it at night."

He lowered his voice in disappointment.

"But Mama and Papa think I'm foolish," he added. "You know

what? I won't let that stop me. I won't!"

Four days later . . .

It was only four days after he spoke that the ten-year-old was gone.

And his frantic parents did not hear from him ever again, never knowing if their son had been kidnapped by rascals at the harbor and perhaps sold into slavery in some foreign land or if he had simply embarked upon the vision that had taken hold of him so early in life, taken hold and would not let go.

A few years later, the father committed suicide. The mother took her own life just six months after that. Neither could endure the loss of their only child.

The call of the harbor . . .

Groups of children would congregate on the weathered docks, watching with fascination the many boats come and go, smelling the distinctive odors that drifted in from the river and the ocean beyond, playing games like tag and three blind mice and some trying their hands at fishing. They were enjoying that period in the midst of their childhood when they could have a good time being what they were.

So much fun all this was, until the first encounter with what would prove death in a small, too-young body . . .

One of the little boys somehow caught a rat in a crate, intending to train it to do tricks as his secret pet. Gradually, he tamed the creature—at least enough to eat from his hand and endure his stroking the rat's fur. The other lads marveled at how the once-hated creature had become a friend.

A few days later, the illness struck suddenly, without warning. One morning the boy awoke as usual, full of energy and mischief. And by evening he was wracked with stomach cramps, weakened and dehydrated. Soon it became apparent to his parents—and to the doctor they quickly summoned—that the little boy was deathly ill. And he was not getting better.

In less than twenty-four hours, the youngster had become very weak and pale, losing control of his natural functions, thrashing about in his bed with pain, and shaking violently with chills until his anguished parents were nearly beside themselves. The doctor had been summoned again and again throughout the day and the night and now into the next day, and his face never changed as he listened to the boy's weakened heartbeat and felt his cold, wrinkled skin. On his last visit, he pulled the father aside.

"I've . . . I've done all I can do," he said quietly into the taller man's ear.

"You're giving up? No! No! Don't leave us! There's got to be something . . . " the hysterical father argued.

"I won't leave you until . . . The lad's not got much longer, only an hour perhaps, Mr. Armbruster, if he's lucky," the doctor continued in his quiet, humble voice.

The stunned father looked at the doctor as though he were an angel of death. Peering into the physician's solemn eyes, the father's mind wandered to a time—could it have been just the day before?—when little Tad had gleefully jumped off the steps to greet him as he had come home from work. Then, only a few minutes later, the boy had doubled over with the first signs of distress—terrible, wracking stomach cramps. The dehydration had set in quickly and then the anguishing chills. All through the night the little boy had fought the invader, fought to live. But now, less than twenty-four hours after the first signs of the illness, the mother's low, aching heart cry from his bedside told the father and doctor the boy had died.

His death sent his mother into a prolonged fit of hysterics that threatened her own health and her sanity.

Not a minute of the last few hours of his life had been spent without pain, pain that spread throughout his frail little body, causing him constantly to moan or whimper pathetically.

First, the rats.

And then this boy.

Virtually unnoticed at first was this one dead child and a few rats, hardly the ingredients of anything that required special attention or that threatened the fabric of local society.

In some respects, cholera seemed almost innocuous—as odd as that thought was for anything so dreaded, so deadly in the manner in which it worked itself through a community, a land. As though acting according to some feral plan, at first it destroyed only one isolated victim at a time, in this case one lively and mischievous little boy. His death was sad, yes, but hardly cause for widespread panic. That was why cholera was often overlooked at first, considered a fluke illness, perhaps, causing one fatality—a tragedy to the individual's family but not a calamity with dire implications for the society at large.

Or so it seemed . . . until others became ill, eventually hundreds of men, women, and children, not just in Philadelphia but in scattered cities and isolated outposts across the growing nation.

Hundreds, then thousands.

The epidemic had started.

Part Two
The Nightmare Begins ...

God planted fear in the soul as truly as He
planted hope or courage. It is a kind of bell or
gong which rings the mind into quick life
and avoidance on the approach of danger. It
is the soul's signal for rallying.

Henry Ward Beecher

Cholera . . .

Historically it had been confined to India and other Asian countries where sanitary conditions were minimal and all manner of diseases flourished.

Apart from the bubonic plague, which killed a third of the population of Europe after its first outbreak there in 1347 and subsequent outbreaks of plague over the centuries that followed, cholera was the most feared of all epidemics.

Cholera.

While the virulent and devastating plague had apparently vanished from the world scene, there was no such cessation as far as cholera was concerned.

Not surprisingly, portions of the United States of that time, especially its cities with their primitive living conditions, fell victim to the effects of inadequate sewerage facilities along with an abundance of diseased rats and other carriers that could spread the disease rapidly.

Especially Philadelphia . . .

Chapter Four

Maggie Engebretsen had been warned, but after her parents became ill, she had little choice.

The ward where everyone who had cholera was quarantined.

"You don't want to be assigned to that ward, Maggie, if you can avoid it," another nurse, tiny, short-haired Amelia Rutledge, had told her, not realizing that as the epidemic's victims multiplied, more and more hospital space would have to be allocated to cholera patients and a greater percentage of the staff would have to put their own lives at greater risk.

At that point, Maggie hadn't ventured inside that part of the hospital; no one except essential personnel was allowed.

But there had been stories coming from the ward, and Amelia wasn't the only nurse telling her some of them, stories that mimicked the horror of some medieval nightmare.

"It's awful," the other young woman was saying as they sat outside on the steps leading to the hospital's rather dreary colonial-style entrance. "The patients become so . . . so . . ."

Amelia started shivering as she recalled what she had had to face since early in the fast-moving epidemic.

"They're so . . . pitiful," she managed to say, "not much more than skeletons with skin stretched so tightly over them. And the skin itself is cold and withered, Maggie, even before they die.

"And their ribs, you can see their ribs, like the poor souls have died in some terrible famine in Africa or Europe, not here in the United States of America, the land of plenty!"

Amelia looked straight at her friend.

"But it's what I don't see that's maybe even worse, Maggie."

"What do you mean?"

"They know what must be done to their bodies after death finally releases their poor souls from such torment!"

Black smoke.

It could be seen periodically during the day, rising like clouds of doom, always reminding them of what was happening, filling their minds with horrible images of corpses disposed of en masse.

Maggie knew about that, knew about the ghastly clouds of black smoke that could be seen drifting up from the place, miles away, where the bodies were taken. No one said anything about this, not even the grieving survivors, as though by ignoring the reality, its full impact somehow would be lessened.

"I try so hard to help them," Amelia added, "but then I find myself becoming resentful when they can't hold anything down and they get sick all over me. There have been many times lately when I have asked myself what I am doing there."

"You're there because you know it's where God has put you," Maggie told her. "It's where He wants you."

Amelia smiled a bit as she considered that thought.

"You know, when they're dying, some of them look up at me, the ones who aren't in comas, and they grip my hand real tight and whisper good-bye. They're the patients I've managed to talk to about Jesus . . . those willing to listen."

. . . and whisper good-bye.

Maggie had seen that or something like it with a few of her own patients. She remembered especially the man who had had a stroke and was almost completely paralyzed.

He had been like that for a number of weeks.

She was the one who had taken care of him—feeding him, washing him, taking care of his needs.

"I loved him," she said out loud.

"Who was that, Maggie?" Amelia asked.

"Oh . . ." Maggie replied, suddenly realizing she had spoken only those three words without verbalizing the rest of her thoughts. "This middle-aged man, Amelia. I was with him so much the last few weeks of his life."

She hesitated, rolling her head around for a moment, trying to rid herself of a headache that had gripped her temples.

"Before he slipped completely into a coma, he was able to talk just a little. The paralysis made speech very, very difficult for him, but I could hear him if I put my ear right next to his lips.

"One of the last things this man said to me was simple, Amelia, so very simple, and yet it meant an awful lot to me at the time, and you know, it still does. Yes, it still does."

Her emotions were nearly overcome by the memory.

"He just said, 'Thank you,' didn't he?" Amelia finished the thought for her friend.

Maggie turned, surprised, and glanced at Amelia.

"How did you know?" she asked.

"You're newer to this than some of the rest of us, Maggie. You've not had as many patients die on you as some of us have.

"But most of my patients in the cholera ward do die. The ones who are at peace in their spirits seem able to break through their terrible pain, maybe just once, maybe not more than that final time, and that's what they always seem to say: 'Thank you . . . thank you for caring . . . for trying to help me.' But there's more to it than that."

Amelia cut herself off, fighting back tears before she added, "It's to me and to you, Maggie, that they speak when they say what they do, but I think it's also to the Lord—most of all to Him, because . . . because it's usually not long after that that He chooses to call them home."

"Have they ever . . . have they—?" Maggie tried to say.

"Have they ever what?" the other asked.

"Sorry," Maggie said. "It's that same man I was mentioning. I was beside his bed, tucking in the sheets after putting on a fresh set.

"Suddenly he sat up straight and looked around, smiling from ear to ear.

"He said, 'Thank You, Jesus!' and then, just as abruptly, fell back on the bed. He had died in that instant, Amelia."

The two of them sat there in silence for the next several minutes. Maggie had begun to wonder how long it would be until her family was affected, for she had to acknowledge that everywhere she turned, so many others were being dragged into the nightmare.

"You and I have been spared so far," she said out loud. "We must consider how gracious the Lord is."

Amelia turned her head sharply.

"That's the wrong way to look at all this," she said, her voice stern. "That is the wrong way indeed!"

"I . . . I don't understand," Maggie admitted.

"That sounds like the Pharisee praying about how good he was and how fortunate that he wasn't like the beggar nearby."

Maggie was becoming angry, especially since such a judgmental comment was coming from someone she considered a friend who knew her well.

"I don't think I meant it that way, Amelia."

"But that's how it sounded. Are none of the dying and none of those who have already died Christians? If any are Christians, does that mean the Lord is being kind to you and me but not kind to them?"

Maggie fought the impulse to be angry at what her friend had just said, fought because there was an edge of truth—real, deep-down truth—to Amelia's words.

Finally she had to admit this.

Amelia started crying then.

"What's wrong?" Maggie asked.

"All this," the other woman remarked. "All this pain. It's just getting to me, Maggie. I pour out my love, my hope, my prayers every day."

Her cheeks were becoming red.

"Sometimes I feel so tired I start thinking I have no love left, no hope, that my prayers don't get above the ceiling. And now here I am, being hateful to you when you don't deserve it. You don't deserve it at all."

She leaned forward, into her friend's arms.

"It must have been from the Lord," Maggie said softly. "If that is the case, how can I feel hurt or angry or anything of the sort?"

Amelia pulled away, wiping her eyes.

"Do you really mean that?" she asked.

Maggie nodded.

"Thank you, dear, good friend," Amelia spoke with real earnestness, openly relieved. "Thank you for saying that."

She stood, ready to go back inside, then noticed an odd expression that had settled on Maggie's face.

"Are you all right?" Amelia asked, deeply concerned.

"I just need a couple of minutes," Maggie told her.

Amelia smiled then disappeared into the hospital.

It was not the simple, caring question from a friend that had lodged painfully in her mind. It was another question altogether, nudged upward from her subconscious perhaps, a question that undoubtedly had been present for quite a long time but one that Maggie had been able to ignore until just then.

How much of my faith means nothing more to me than a convenient shield against encroaching adversity?

It was a question Maggie Engebretsen would not answer fully until early in the next century.

When Maggie got home, she found Roberta sitting in the dark on an old, rusty-chained swing that hung from the thick branch of an ancient oak tree. She was humming peacefully to herself as Maggie slid into a second swing next to Roberta's.

"We did this as kids," Maggie said, "and we're doing it now. I suspect these swings will outlast us both."

Roberta's face froze as her sister said that, and she stopped humming.

"Still thinking about that dream that bothered you a couple of nights ago?" Maggie asked, knowing her sister so well.

"Yes," Roberta acknowledged candidly, but with regret that it was so. "I can't get over this feeling."

It had not let go of her.

A dark vision, a chilling one, bleak and scary, with echoes in some far-off place, a place of barrenness and death and despair, an unholy dread of

it following her even after awakening.

"Can you tell me more about it?" Maggie asked, more deeply concerned than she was letting on.

"I—I was all alone in this dream. Mama and Papa were nowhere around. That was the first part, Maggie, and that was why it was so scary. They weren't there. And neither were you."

Roberta was shivering slightly.

"I had never felt so alone before," she added.

Her eyes were shifting from side to side as though she feared something from the night around her.

"It was such a dark place," Roberta continued, a rasp of hoarseness edging her voice. "And there was only me in all of it."

Alone.

She had never liked being alone. The darkness seemed smothering to her, an enemy always.

"Was there anything else in the dream?" Maggie asked, wondering if her sister was holding anything back.

"Just that . . ." Roberta told her. "I am grateful, you know, grateful that there wasn't anything else."

She stopped swinging and brought one hand to her mouth as her face dissolved into a tearful grimace.

"It seemed so vivid, Maggie."

How vivid it was, a dream with the sense of reality, a dream so real that she never expected to awaken from it, expected it to stay with her, imprisoning her in its bleakness . . . and it did.

"I walked and walked and walked," she recalled, "but there was just that terrible nothingness."

She jumped off the swing and stood in the middle of that familiar old yard, looking up at the sky.

"I wonder if the Lord was trying somehow to tell me that I would have to get used to being without anyone at all, getting used to being terribly alone. But, Maggie, I just don't think I could handle that sort of life. I just don't!"

Maggie slipped out of her swing and stood beside her sister.

"I'm suspicious of dreams," she said. "Either they mean nothing, or we give the wrong interpretation to them."

"Maybe so," Roberta replied, clearly not convinced.

Just then their mother called them into the house for dinner, an especially delicious one of trout with raisin sauce that she had begun hours earlier as part of the restaurant's fare for the evening.

Despite the death and dying in the city around them, these were good days for Maggie and Roberta Engebretsen. They joked and laughed and enjoyed their moments together. Even Roberta, normally a melancholic personality, seemed to be lifted out of her gloom.

Maggie was the last to go to bed that night.

She walked out on the front porch for a moment, soothed into peacefulness by the crisp, clear air. The sky was dark that night, no moon at all, only a thin sprinkling of stars.

"Thank You, Lord, for the joy in my life, even in the darkness," Maggie prayed with great feeling. "Thank You for every bit of this life of mine."

As she was going back inside, she jumped as she felt somebody unexpectedly touch her shoulder. She swung around abruptly.

No one.

She shrugged, blaming her imagination and thinking nothing more of it, wanting instead to have the warmth of that evening, the love of it, last as long as possible.

Chapter Five

The plague hit the Engebretsen family hard. Both parents as well as Maggie's sister had to be hospitalized, and it seemed all three would surely die . . .

Roberta Engebretsen.

A precious member of the family circle, appreciated for the joy she had brought her parents and the companionship that meant so much to her sister.

Yet she nevertheless had not always felt as loved and needed as in truth she was, because as matters invariably turned out, her younger sister Maggie ended up getting the greater degree of attention.

I am just so useless and weak, she said to herself more than once. *What good am I?*

Roberta was neither, of course, but she had convinced herself that this was so, and she acted accordingly.

The process of dying made her something else altogether, for she showed real courage, inspiring those around her.

And she was conscious longer than many other patients, so much so that the normally rather jaded doctors and the other nurses marveled.

"I never thought . . . of myself . . . as strong," she said ironically. "I looked . . . at myself as . . . the family weakling."

But Roberta was far from weak.

And she declared her intention to live.

"I must!" she declared to Maggie. "I must survive in order to help you . . . and Mama and Papa . . . get the business back in shape. After the epidemic passes . . . it will be a terrible time. . . . They will need all the help they can get."

Maggie could only nod when Roberta said such things, smiling reassuringly at her sister while silently anticipating her death. And as her sister lay dying, Maggie Engebretsen felt her world collapsing.

Every available corner of the hospital's cholera ward was jammed.

Eventually the administrators had found it necessary to expand the space allocated to epidemic victims.

Soon there was no room left anywhere in the hospital, and another, makeshift, facility was set up on a large farm on the outskirts of Philadelphia to take care of the massive overflow. Now Maggie rushed from one location to the other, trying to meet the demand for her services at the main hospital then hurrying to tend to her family, who had been admitted to the temporary facility.

For nearly a week, she was forced to take her family's horse and buggy between the two institutions and then back home, with little more than moonlight available to light her way, driving herself because there was no one else to ask.

A disastrous situation.

As she hurried on her way one night, Maggie could see the faint outline of colonial-style houses on either side of the road.

It was a dry time of year, with a major drought in the making, and the horse's hooves continually kicked up dust that caused Maggie to periodically rein in the horse and erupt into a siege of coughing.

Each time she arrived at the temporary hospital where her parents and Roberta were being cared for, she approached the door, wondering if this would be the time when she would walk in and be told one or more of them had . . .

I wanted to avoid considering their deaths as long as I could, and now here it is, wedging itself into my mind again, she said as the carriage rolled up to the hospital entrance. *Just a few days ago, I looked at my parents, so healthy, and thought that they would live another twenty or thirty years and that I would have a family of my own before they were dead.*

The word hit her hard.

Dead.

Would it be her hardworking father, a tough, broad-shouldered man who was capable of the sweetest tenderness? Or would it be her mother, a short, frail-looking woman who, despite her size, possessed more endurance than others who had twice her bulk?

Or Roberta?

Dear, dear Roberta.

The sister she loved more than life itself. Roberta, who was sometimes jealous, but in the end never less than loyal, never less than loving.

Because they had been admitted separately, over the course of a day and a night, her mother, father, and sister were in separate rooms of the farmhouse hospital. At least they're not in the barn with all the most recent admissions, Maggie told herself as she glanced toward the huge, drafty structure across the barnyard. Before the previous owners themselves had died of cholera, they had provided for their property's use in such an emergency.

Twenty-four hours . . .

What a change so short a passage of time could bring!

The night before, Maggie had stood next to Roberta's bed, with the coughing, moaning, and crying of several other patients in the same room creating a backdrop of misery. Tied around Maggie's nose and mouth was a cloth mask that had been routinely dipped in alcohol.

Roberta was conscious but gave the impression that this could change any minute because the cholera had drained so much of her strength.

She lifted her hand slightly.

"Forgive me," she said.

"For what?" Maggie asked.

"For ever criticizing you as I did, for ever saying that you had so many privileges that I never did, for—"

Roberta began to cough violently and nearly passed out, her

bloodshot eyes rolling back in their sockets.

Maggie started to bend down, to take her sister's hand in her own.

"No!" Roberta said as she pulled away, her voice strong, the word not at all muddled by the effects of the disease.

"But I want to touch you," Maggie begged.

"You mustn't. You mustn't do that at all! Surely you know how much danger you're in even being here like this."

"But I'm a nurse."

"A nurse who wasn't assigned to the cholera ward in her own hospital until it was absolutely necessary. Why do you think that was the case? I've talked to the administrators, Maggie. They think you're the best. They don't want you throwing your life away during the next few months. Other patients with other problems need you, patients who—"

Roberta couldn't continue talking in such a streak of words. There just wasn't any strength left in her body.

Maggie noticed that a bluish tinge had appeared on her sister's lips, which were pressed tightly against her teeth.

"I'm so cold now, Maggie," she said. "First I'm burning up, like every inch of my skin is on fire and now—"

Her body was visibly shaking.

"—this awful—"

Abruptly that spasm stopped, and there came to be a strangely peaceful smile resting on Roberta's face.

"The Lord knew I wasn't able to do what you do," she said. "The Lord is so wise, Maggie . . . so very wise."

She passed out then.

Panicking, Maggie thought her sister had died that instant, but it was not the case. Not yet.

Earlier, Maggie had been to see her parents. Both had slipped into comas by then. They looked so pale, so thin.

Once so strong, so vital, she thought, sadly scanning their cold, shivering shapes. *Now weaker than young children!*

She reached down, touched her mother gently with two fingers on the forehead, intending a kind of kiss.

How many times did you stand by my bedside or by Roberta's side when either of us was ill as children? How many times did you both lovingly nurse us back to health, no matter how little sleep you got, no matter how—

Maggie knew she was on the verge of tears.

"Oh, Mama," she said out loud, "I feel so helpless. I . . . I am helpless, Mama. You gave me this life of mine. You helped sustain me again and again by your love, your care. And now I can do nothing but—but watch you—"

. . . slip away.

She was glad she had been able to stop those two words from escaping her lips. To have said them would have been admitting to her mother how hopeless her situation was.

How could she admit that?

Her mother always had seemed so strong, as though propelled by an inexhaustible reservoir of energy that astonished those around her.

Next Maggie turned to her father, who had been moved to the next bed.

He was only in his late fifties. But he seemed so old now, his face deeply lined, streaks of gray appearing throughout his ample hair.

Whenever Roberta and I had a problem, a question of some sort about life, anything that concerned us at all, we went to you as much as to Mama. You always had time for us. You put everything else aside, and we became the only other people in the world because you blocked everybody else out so long as we needed you.

Just then her father's body went through a series of spasms, and his nose started to bleed. Another trickle of blood appeared at the corner of his mouth.

"Help, someone!" Maggie screamed. "He's hemorrhaging, he's—"

Another nurse ran into the room just as Lars Engebretsen grew quiet again.

"Good Lord!" she said, then she uttered something that sounded like "Forgive me for saying that" and left the room.

"Where are you going?" Maggie demanded.

"I have other patients."

"But what about this one? What about my father?"

The woman hesitated, her face contorted with disgust. It was obvious that she had never faced such an extreme case before, and she was abruptly realizing that she simply could not cope with the escalating demands of attending to someone whose death was coming in such ghastly stages.

"I'm sorry. I'm very sorry," she said, "but I . . . I just can't—"

In an instant she was gone.

Maggie took off her shawl and laid it on a bureau a few feet away, the personal furniture a reminder that the building had once been a home.

Gently and lovingly she undressed her helpless father and threw the soiled bedclothes in a bucket sitting near the door.

Then, in the hallway, she found a small basin and a pitcher filled with water; she pulled towels and a clean nightshirt out of a linen closet and returned to the ward to bathe her father. As gently as she could, she wrestled the clean nightshirt over his head and over his bony torso, quickly re-covering him with the blanket in an attempt to stop his shivering. Then she rested him back against the pillow and settled into a high-backed chair between her parents' beds.

Maggie was holding her father's hand and humming his favorite hymn when a doctor entered the room.

"Are you insane?" he asked, astonished. "You shouldn't be here; you shouldn't be touching these patients. You aren't allowed here."

"I'm a nurse."

"Then get back to your own patients, wherever they are. There may still be some hope for the others. Spend your time with them."

"Sir, these are my parents, and the only way you will get me to leave them is to pick me up and carry me away, but you will not find this an easy task, for I shall be fighting you every step!"

The doctor bowed his head, understanding the extent of both Maggie's grief and her persistence.

"I'm very sorry," he said, "very sorry indeed."

The doctor moved on to the other patients in the room and eventually left, turning down the lantern as he passed through the door. Maggie sat in the straight-backed chair, alternately reaching to touch her mother then her father.

An hour passed, and finally exhaustion set in. Maggie became aware that she had yet to return home and get some sleep before her morning shift began at the other hospital. She carefully adjusted the blanket over her mother, then her father, leaned down to kiss one forehead, then the other, and finally stood, not wanting to leave but knowing she had to.

Maggie had stepped out into the hallway when she thought she heard a sound in the room, not just a voice, because there were three other patients inside as well, but a voice that was strikingly familiar.

She turned and looked back.

Her mother!

She thought she saw her mother move a bit, then those familiar blue eyes opened and looked at her, and a smile crossed her mother's face, the smile she had shared often over the years, a smile filled with unselfish love and abundant joy.

Mama, are you trying to tell me something?

Had she heard her mother whisper something to her? Had she seen those familiar lips move ever so slowly and—?

Then that moment passed, or perhaps it had never happened at all. Natalie Engebretsen was once again quite still.

Two days later . . .

It was just a simple dinner, but it was also a miracle of sorts. The Engebretsens—all four of them—were sharing a humble meal no one had dared to think possible just forty-eight hours earlier.

The parents were still very weak, and so was Roberta, and their chances of recovery were still slim, though they were all hanging on, however tenuously. But none of that mattered at this moment; nothing mattered except that they were all together on the porch of the farmhouse hospital . . . sharing a tiny meal, perhaps for the last time.

"There are some who would say," Lars Engebretsen began slowly, "that our situation proves the truth of the adage 'Eat, drink, and be merry, for tomorrow we die.'"

He grinned feebly as he added, "But that is not the Christian way; therefore, that is not our way, my dear family."

The four of them sat quietly on the front porch rockers and enjoyed the familiar camaraderie they had shared so frequently.

"Are we too much concerned about tradition?" Lars mused unexpectedly.

Natalie was caught by surprise.

"Why, I've not thought about it," she admitted. "Are traditions so bad?"

"What if all but one of us is taken by the cholera? What good would our traditions be then? Yet we have inculcated respect for them into both of you girls. Would that leave Maggie with a twofold responsibility—struggling to survive on her own and struggling to maintain the family's traditions?"

Maggie considered that for a moment.

"Papa, may I respond?" she asked.

"I was looking forward to hearing what you think," he assured her, pushing the words out in a rush so he could draw in a new breath of life-sustaining air.

"I would either find our traditions an anchor, not as much as our faith in Christ or—"

"Sorry to interrupt," Lars spoke, "but consider this: Is that faith not one of those traditions?"

They were free enough with one another to allow for interruptions that were not designed to be impolite but helpful instead.

"It could have been," Maggie ventured, "if that was how you and Mama had raised us."

"Please explain," he said.

"For some, going to church and Bible reading are rituals. And aren't traditions merely rituals handed down from generation to generation?"

She was hoping for her father's encouragement, that her thinking was on the right track, and he gave this to her by smiling rather broadly.

Encouragement it was!

"But you instilled in Roberta and me not a faith of repetition of ceremony and rituals—of traditions," Maggie continued, "but you gave us the heritage that was your own, a living faith."

"Tell me, please," Lars asked, "what is a living faith, as you call it?"

"It comes from the center of my soul, from the center of Roberta's. It is not something spoken merely from the lips on Sunday as prayers are repeated, as hymns are sung. But it flows from the part of us that will always be eternal. We take our faith with us to the grave, and it stays with us as we ascend to our Heavenly Father."

Lars was very pleased, but he wanted to hear more, as though to be reassured that he and his wife had engrained in their daughters these most-important values.

"You know what has been concerning me about faith?" he asked, looking at Roberta this time.

"I am not sure, Papa," she said, far less confident in verbalizing such matters than her sister was—and far weaker physically.

"Here in the hospital, I've heard some of the nurses and the patients talking about faith. And I shuddered to hear their words!"

"What upset you?" Roberta asked her father.

"The issue of faith was put on the level of regular church attendance, saying grace, that sort of thing, you know, being even-tempered toward one another, charitable to the poor, the homeless."

"Yes, Papa, I see what you mean. The dying are often given false security by people who tell them if they've gone to church every Sunday, asked a blessing on each meal, refrained from engaging in foul talk, and so on, that that is all God cares about."

Lars Engebretsen nodded his head weakly, closing his eyes as though relieved at what he heard.

"Exactly," he said softly as Roberta's pale, drawn face creased into a smile. "How many souls are in hell this very moment because of such well-meaning but misinformed people?"

The thought was a startling one.

"Here, so much attention is paid to easing the dying patients' physical suffering," Roberta said, "and saying whatever soothing words came to mind, that their souls are ignored altogether."

Natalie finally added her voice to the discussion.

"But some of the nurses are not Christians," she pointed out. "Could they be expected to say the right thing under such circumstances?"

Lars acknowledged that his wife had a point.

"Then it is the continuing obligation of those who are Christian to try and enlighten those who are not. Am I correct?"

Everyone agreed he was.

"And failing that, to go directly to dying patients with prayers that their souls might be saved in time, yes?"

Again there was agreement.

He turned to Maggie, and suddenly she felt the enormous pressure of that moment.

"What . . ." Lars' voice was giving out. He moistened his lips and drew in a breath. "What have you been able to accomplish in this regard?" he asked.

Maggie cleared her throat nervously, because witnessing for Christ was such a natural, instinctive action on her part that she did not keep tabs on every individual with whom she had shared the Good News.

Interestingly, Lars would not let her speak without first saying, "Let me make it easier for you."

She was glad for her father's willingness to help.

Lars said quietly, "Heaven's streets may be crowded because of you, my dear Maggie."

"Why, Papa? What do you mean?" Maggie asked, surprised by her father's statement.

"I've overheard tidbits of discussion about your sharing the Gospel with those who were dying."

"You have?" she said, eager to hear what he had to say.

"Yes. I heard how strong and how enthusiastic your witnessing was—and there was more than a little of it, from what I heard."

"You heard this from the patients?"

"Yes, and the nurses too, but they weren't the only ones."

"Who else, Papa?"

"Dr. Bowder."

"He—!"

"Indeed he did."

"Was Dr. Bowder upset with me?"

"Oh, no, Maggie, he was pleased. That man was pleased you would go beyond purely caring for the bodies of the patients, trying to get them well so that they could leave the hospital—and probably continue lives that were displeasing to the Creator."

Maggie felt tears starting to trickle down her cheeks.

"I never knew he was concerned about their souls. I never had the slightest hint, Papa."

"Oh, he is, Maggie, he is. Dr. Bowder just doesn't have your gift of witnessing, of teaching, of sharing. But he will be greeting you in heaven someday, be certain of that."

Roberta leaned over in her rocker and put a hand on her sister's arm.

"I was preparing to welcome you to heaven, myself," she confessed. "I was getting ready for the Lord to take my soul—and wondering if Mama and Papa and I would go together and wondering how . . . how you would get along without us."

Chapter Six

Traveling even a short distance was a chore in those days.

Harnessing horses and hitching carriages could be time-consuming and irritating. And driving the horse-drawn carriages to one's destination was a physical struggle, especially for many women, whose arms ached with each tug of the reins. But it was a way of life, and most people accepted such delays as something that could not be wished away.

Maggie paused outside the farmhouse hospital, tempted to go right back in, whatever the protests from those in charge.

"You are working so very hard already," one of the doctors cautioned her. "You are the best nurse we have. If you fall, that would be a serious blow. We cannot afford to lose you, Maggie. Get some rest, please."

If she were not so tired, she would have resisted the order. But she relented, knowing that the doctors were only concerned about her health and strength.

It was only a few hundred feet to where she had tied up her horse and carriage, but she had to pass by the barn once again.

Dear Lord, she prayed, *give me the strength. I have so little of my own, and I feel very weary right now.*

An especially large barn, this one, long and wide though not much taller than others in the vicinity.

Every bit of interior space was being used as a cholera ward, with a degree of crowding that doctors found necessary but unfortunate.

A simple barn. So commonplace in normal times, especially on the edge of Pennsylvania farm country.

Not anymore.

Now it was a place to die, a place to spend whatever days or hours of mortality remained, and then—Maggie hesitated as she walked directly in front of the dimly lit, disease-filled structure.

Someone died just now! she exclaimed to herself, intuitively sensing what had happened. *How could I know that?*

This was not the first time Maggie had felt such intuitions. Others had grabbed hold of her senses even during less tragic times.

My heart beats faster when it happens, she thought, *and I find breathing more difficult. Sometimes when it's over, I am elated; other times I must fight against the most overwhelming depression. Have they gone to heaven, Lord? Or is it hell?*

Flickering lantern light could be seen through the uneven slits in the large double doors at the barn's entrance.

And sounds.

Oh, those sounds!

Moaning continued ceaselessly from the suffering cholera victims, a large number of whom would die within a matter of days.

"But not all," Maggie said aloud as she stopped walking for a moment. "Why not all? Why is it that some are stronger than others? Is God's hand perhaps on them more completely than the rest?"

That question stayed with her more than she would have liked.

Never in her more than two decades of life had she questioned anything about God, and she never wanted to start. She had seen too many lives ruined for time and eternity by going down that road.

She walked up to the barn and peered through a crack between the boards.

A scene from hell . . .

A place of last resort for dying citizens who simply had nowhere else to go.

Candlelight reflected off their waxen faces, their pale, white forms. Hands reaching out into the air then falling back.

Their cries!

Out of pain. Out of fear.

They cried as if they were being thrust into the maw of death, and especially for those who were not Christians, it was a horrible end to a living nightmare.

And the odors . . .

The odors of death, not completely describable but there nevertheless, thick and nearly palpable.

And soon, she thought, *their lifeless bodies will be lifted onto . . .*

She turned away from the barn and continued walking toward the carriage, suddenly seized with a compulsion to return home as quickly as possible, to close around herself its familiar, once-comforting walls.

Not quite halfway home.

That was how far Maggie Engebretsen had traveled on her journey when, near midnight, her life was changed forever . . .

The roads were generally safe, everyday life around Philadelphia having evolved from the rugged colonial days when everything was difficult to a much easier existence after the War of 1812. Yet, there were real but rare episodes of danger—the sudden appearance of highwaymen who would seize valuables and then be off, a traumatic act but not one customarily accompanied by brutal violence.

Nevertheless, the outbreak of cholera had created a legion of people who were literally not in their right minds, adults and children who, once having decided that they would rather die at home than in any impersonal hospital ward, surrounded by the rising misery of others like themselves, would use any means at their disposal to resist. Just before they lapsed into comas—though some remained relatively alert until the last moment—they were subject to psychotic behavior, behavior fueled by metabolic changes that were devastating.

These were the circumstances of the heavyset middle-aged man who stepped in front of Maggie Engebretsen's buggy that night, causing the startled horse to rear back and the carriage to sway just enough for her to tumble off the seat and onto the ground.

"It's the nurse from the hospital!" the man exclaimed, somehow recognizing her. "Thank God!"

She hesitated, thinking perhaps she could do something for him, perhaps help him get to the hospital she had just left.

"Thank You, God! Thank You, God! Thank You, God!" the man repeated in a babbling and erratic manner.

He was only a couple of feet away from her when she saw the wild look on his face, the spittle dribbling from his mouth.

She scrambled to her feet, intending to run. He was faster.

Grabbing Maggie roughly, the man pushed her back down to the ground.

"A nurse, yes—a very pretty nurse," he said, chuckling.

Just as he was bending over to kiss her, the man cried out suddenly, his body shaking with great violence as though he were experiencing a convulsion. He grabbed his head with both hands, screaming.

"The voices! The voices tell me to do this!" he cried out. "How can I not pay heed? How can I just turn away from them?"

He became ill then, a wave of nausea gripping his stomach.

Maggie nearly blacked out, the odor of the man overpowering. As he was heaving some more, she managed to push him to one side and then ran toward the buggy, amazingly still standing in the same spot. She was about to climb up to the seat when there was a sharp pain in her right shoulder.

A knife!

He had stumbled toward her and stabbed her in the shoulder with a long-bladed knife that was slightly curved at the end.

A wave of dizziness swept over Maggie, but she managed to scramble onto the seat and across to the opposite side of the buggy then jump out, stopping just short of unconsciousness as she hit the ground.

Straight ahead was a thick section of trees and growth.

Maggie headed toward it, sounds coming to her of the man behind her snarling and spitting and moaning like a rabid beast.

She tripped, then got to her feet and continued running without having any real idea of where she might be heading, knowing only that she had to get away as fast as she could, wherever "away" was.

Light.

Ahead.

Light . . . and help!

Thank You, Jesus!

She saw a farmhouse, much smaller than the one that had been converted into a makeshift hospital.

Maggie hesitated only a second as she heard her pursuer still thrashing through the undergrowth behind her.

Her shoulder and back felt wet, sticky. The pain was beginning now in earnest.

Lord, Lord, Maggie prayed in panic. *I could bleed to death, Lord, I—*

She was very weak and could hardly breathe.

A window.

She looked through it.

Candles were flickering in their brass holders. But she could see no one, no one at all.

Oh, Lord, her mind screamed. *Where? Show me where to go!*

Another light.

In the barn.

The entrance was open, and surrealistic, flickering light was dancing out from the large, open double door.

She hurried toward the barn.

Suddenly the crazed man burst into the clearing in front of her.

Confused, she looked at him, her eyes wide with terror, not seeing that it was her attacker.

"Please!" she screamed. "I need help, Mister! Someone—!"

Then the man was upon her again, and she fell beneath him to the ground. This time she saw the knife and tried to deflect it, but her strength was failing, and he was about to plunge it into her chest.

His face began to fade in her vision as a wave of darkness swept over her, and she prepared herself for death, something that seemed unavoidable at that moment, in that place, lying under a maniac's weapon.

Someone shouting.

The man's weight was suddenly jerked off of her.

She heard the sounds of a frantic struggle.

And then a sudden cry of pain, not her own.

Seconds passed.

Hands touched her, gently this time.

Nevertheless she screamed and screamed and screamed.

"He's dead," a voice informed her coldly. "You have nothing to fear from me. I'm going to take you inside."

She felt herself being lifted up.

Then being put gently on something quite soft.

Goose down, she thought idly. *I do believe it's a goose-down mattress like the ones Papa made. There's a certain smell. Yes, it's goose down.*

"I'm going to have to clean your wound, bind it up," the voice said. "Let me give you some good old Kentucky bourbon to ease the pain."

She started to mumble a protest.

"You're wearing a cross, I see. So, I can understand how you feel; I really can. But you need to drink it, Ma'am. You're not consuming anything that wouldn't be considered medicine just now. Go ahead, please."

He lifted her head up, and she forced down some of the liquid he offered, gasping a bit as the fiery liquor passed down her throat.

He was right.

The bourbon helped, but even with it in her system—and no matter how gentle the stranger tried to be—taking care of the wound caused the most intense pain Maggie had ever experienced: sudden, sharp waves of it.

Pain that seemed to be threatening a longer hold on her than she could bear.

She fainted.

But just before that happened, her eyes fluttered open for a second or two, and she caught a glimpse of the most handsome man she had ever seen: dark, brunette hair framing his head in arched waves that seemed to form an angel's strange halo over his strong, dimpled face.

Chapter Seven

I don't know what is happening, dear Lord. I am frightened, and I feel so very alone. Please, let me understand . . .

Suspended.

She seemed to be suspended in a place that might have been called Nowhere, for it was dark and soundless and—

Am I dying?

Strangely, Maggie felt no real fear as that question formed in her mind.

A part of her brain assumed that could be the sole explanation, death claiming her after seizing so many of her patients.

Dying . . . yes . . . that has to be it!

She tried to convince herself that she was ready for it, ready to embrace the eternal.

And who was that man I saw? Please help me, Lord!

Sound at last.

Faint, but there, something to sense, to—

And a smell, yes, she could smell something.

The sound of flames crackling and the crisp odor of wood burning stirred her attention first as she felt the warmth of a fire; then she noticed a gathering of various other scents, long familiar—in fact, familiar since those happier days when she had often settled in front of the fireplace at home with her parents and her sister. Such moments had long ago become a treasured family ritual on cold winter evenings as they played games or just talked or sometimes sang songs, including a few hymns.

Something soft underneath her body.

And with it she felt a sense of wanting to reach out and touch whatever it might prove to be.

Something soft and thick and warm covering her completely. She opened her eyes.

A young man was sitting in a chair a few feet away. He had dozed off, with his head tilted slightly forward.

She didn't feel threatened, but still she was nervous.

What happened while I was unconscious? Maggie wondered tensely. *Where have I been brought?*

She tried to move.

Pain.

A jolt of pain made her nauseous.

The stranger stirred, looking up, smiling as he saw her.

"You were out for quite a while, all night in fact," he said. "I suspect it was from more than just that knife wound. You seemed to have no energy left."

. . . no energy left.

She chuckled a bit.

"I'm not surprised, Sir," she told him with candor that surprised her. "I've had a heavy workload for weeks now."

"At Philadelphia Memorial?" he asked.

"Yes! And how would you know that?"

"I was there to see a friend. But they wouldn't let me in. I noticed you out of the corner of my eye as I was leaving."

"And your friend?"

"She died of cholera a few days ago."

"I'm sorry," Maggie remarked, embarrassed that she had dared pry into such a personal matter at all.

I should have known better, she scolded herself.

He rose from his chair and walked over to her bedside, sitting down beside her.

"The man who attacked you," he said. "I had to kill him, you know."

Maggie tried not to gasp but failed.

"It was self-defense," he commented wisely. "I am quite sure the Bible allows for that, doesn't it?"

She nodded though she was still startled.

"Some would say no. Some would say that no killing is permissible, that taking a life for any reason is a sin."

"The Quakers?"

"Yes."

"There are a lot of them around here, especially further inland."

Maggie studied this man as he talked.

Handsome he was, this one, with that brown hair and those sparkling blue eyes that reflected the fiery light, strong cheekbones and very wide, wet lips that—

She blushed as she turned her eyes away from his mouth.

"I would be happy to take you to the hospital now," he said.

"It's a long distance," she reminded him.

"Being in the company of a beautiful woman is hardly a chore," he said, grinning, an expression that turned Maggie's palms sweaty.

She tried to move off the bed and stand but couldn't.

"So weak," she said. "I don't think I can make it."

"Why don't you stay here for the night?" he offered with complete nonchalance. "You can have my bed."

She turned apprehensive at that suggestion.

He laughed.

"You can have my bed, but I'll stay out here," he added. "I put you here by the fire to keep you warm until you regained consciousness. Now's the time to be in bed, with lots of covers piled on top of you."

Once again she felt awkward.

"Forgive me, Sir," she said. "I didn't mean to suggest anything."

"I won't forgive you if you call me Sir again," he joked. "My name happens to be Randy . . . Randy Stuart."

"I'm Maggie Engebretsen," she said a little sheepishly.

"I'll be as gentle as I can," he replied as he started to pick her up.

His breath close to her ear.

His unshaven cheek momentarily brushing against her own.

His strong arms around her, his body warmth curiously reassuring, Maggie had to admit to herself, though somewhat uneasi-

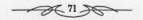

ly, that the experience of being carried by this man named Randy Stuart wasn't altogether unpleasant.

After losing consciousness following the attack, Maggie was surprised that she slept through the night and most of the next day.

"Rest . . ." she heard the stranger say softly to her. "That is what you need most."

. . . no energy left.

For long months, even before the epidemic, Maggie had worked very hard, even to the point of endangering her own health, for she was convinced that the profession would not tolerate any halfheartedness on her part, and she had committed herself to whatever it took to be a nurse, a good nurse.

"I have to do it this way," she had told her mother, who was greatly worried about her. "What if I hold back, what if I do not give nursing whatever I am capable of, and someone dies because of me, someone who would have been saved? I could not live with my conscience after that. I would want to die myself."

The epidemic was an unnerving crash course, showing Maggie what being a nurse would really demand of her.

At home, Maggie had been blessed with a rather clean, orderly existence, from the early years of everything being provided for her and Roberta to the more recent, relatively independent period when she left her family during the day and worked at the hospital.

Even now, after completing her training and working steadily at this job she had chosen, she sometimes seriously wondered what in the world she had gotten herself into; sometimes she tried to visualize continuing in nursing for the rest of her adult life—and couldn't conceive of wanting to do so.

Her primary job was patient care: keeping patients clean, giving them medicines according to a physician's authorization, and otherwise being at the beck and call of the patient or the doctor.

But as challenging as routine patient care could be, nothing compared to what she had to help with in terms of operations,

given the requirements of primitive surgical methods at that time.

Painkillers were limited in number and effectiveness, and diethyl ether and chloroform were the only available anesthetics. Both caused side effects: With chloroform, the margin of safety was extremely narrow indeed, and improper dosages of it could be fatal; and even in proper dosages, it could cause heart, liver, and kidney damage as well as general poisoning in some patients. The situation was so bad in terms of chloroform's toxic quality that many patients had opted to go into major operations without taking a chance on anesthetics of any kind save simple hard liquor.

One of the main risks of using the other available anesthesia, diethyl ether, was that it was highly combustible, and there were numerous instances of operating rooms bursting into flames as a result.

So, as a new nurse, Maggie had been forced to get accustomed to a variety of situations, none of which was easy to take.

Often as she was falling asleep at night, incidents replayed themselves across her mind in a montage. Again and again she relived the one surgery-room fire she had witnessed, when the sheet covering a middle-aged man had ignited and the flames had quickly enveloped the rest of the room, almost causing that entire part of the hospital to burn to the ground. Other nights she would dream again of standing beside patients who would die during surgery, gasping from the poison in their systems, poison in the form of chloroform that continued to be given for many years because of ignorance over the cause of their deaths.

I felt so helpless, Lord. They died right before my eyes, and I could do nothing. I was their nurse, and I had no remedy. I had nothing to offer.

Now she lay in a stranger's bed, exhausted and wounded and . . .

Just before sleep did come in that unfamiliar house, she heard Randy Stuart moving around in the next room, and though she once again disliked the admission, she could not ignore the fact that thinking about the very handsome stranger who had befriended her made Maggie Engebretsen feel a little less troubled as she closed her eyes and wrapped herself in the peace of that still, quiet night.

Breakfast.

The aromas helped wake Maggie up, reviving her with a familiar blending of the scents of coffee, fresh-baked bread, poached eggs, and sausage, a standard breakfast for her family at home.

At first she doubted that such a man could cook anything worthwhile, then she started eating.

And she was amazed.

"You are actually a very good cook," she told him, surprised that he was able to do anything of the sort.

He seemed almost to glare at her.

"*For a man,* isn't that what you mean?" Randy kidded her, though that remark was not entirely in jest since it was assumed in those days that cooking was entirely the province of womenfolk, and a man in the kitchen was out of his element, except for those hardened settlers who had to cook their own food or die of starvation.

She seems nice enough, he thought, *but a little haughty, I would say. I'll get rid of that trait but quick!*

He wanted to see how alert she was after her ordeal, and while his attempt was a rather lame one at best, it did seem to work.

"What's that?" she asked, not sure what he meant. "I don't know how you meant that, Mr. Randy Stuart."

"You called me a good cook."

"That I did."

She wanted him to know that she really had enjoyed the poached eggs, country sausage, and hot bread spread with fresh preserves, but she was beginning to resent the fact that he seemed intent on turning her comment into something else.

"You are indeed," she repeated. "These are wonderful sausages, cooked just right, and the eggs are . . . done very nicely too. You may not know that my family and I have a restaurant and I happen to know about such things, even though I am only a woman."

He started with a little chuckle then, which grew into an episode of rather boisterous laughter.

"Why are you—?" Maggie spoke, more irritated than she should have been under the circumstances.

She finally saw what he meant, and her face reddened.

"I didn't mean it that way," Maggie remarked quickly. "I never really think like that."

"I didn't either. Just kidding, Maggie Engebretsen."

She paused for a moment, glancing at this handsome stranger and trying to analyze him in an instant.

"Anything wrong?" the stranger asked. "That's a strange expression on your face."

"Not everyone pronounces my last name correctly."

"I have some friends who are Scandinavian. You hang around them enough, and you pick up little clues about things like that."

She sensed something then, something that was present for only a moment then was gone nearly as fleetingly.

A certain melancholy . . .

There seemed no good reason for her to pick up on that, because there seemed no good reason for it to exist. Everything about Randy Stuart appeared to be happy and robust, not the sort of personality that would serve as a breeding ground for melancholy.

Then, almost immediately, she realized how dumb it was that she had looked on the outward appearance, with no clue, really, as to what was going on in the man's mind.

By now they had finished their breakfast and had moved to the rough-hewn stone fireplace, and though Maggie had not asked, she could well imagine that Randy had built it himself since he had the obvious body for such hard work.

She was sitting on a chair, with Randy on the floor near the hearth.

Normally Maggie would not in any way pry into a stranger's privacy, especially one who had saved her life, not to mention her virginity. Even though she had told him about her own circumstances—how her parents and sister were near death in the temporary hospital and how lost she felt in accepting the inevitable—she knew she had not earned the right to ask anything significant about the man. She knew it would be terribly forward of her to ask him any questions of real intimacy.

Nevertheless, despite the circumstances, Maggie felt a curious need to know a little more about him. Before she knew it, the first question had slipped out.

"Do you live here alone?" she asked, taking a sip of tea to help her *appear nonchalant.*

"Sometimes," he replied.

"Sometimes?"

"I have friends over every so often."

"Oh . . ."

He seemed reluctant to go beyond those few words, and she decided it would be unwise to press the matter.

They sat in silence for the next several minutes. Maggie had the impression that Randy was a bit offended by her tentative probe into his personal life.

"Are you upset with me?" she asked.

He looked up at her suddenly, genuine surprise registering on his handsome face.

"Not at all," he told her. "Why do you think that?"

"You became so quiet so quickly."

He turned away from her and faced the fireplace, which still had some glowing embers left from the night before.

"People," he said cryptically.

Maggie wasn't sure what he meant by that, but she was determined not to be nosy again.

A minute or so passed.

"People enter your life for a while, and then they're gone," he said finally. "You get used to them. You learn to like them. Some—"

He hesitated, bowing his head for a moment.

"—you might even love. And then they leave or are taken away."

"But having them in our lives, however briefly, can prove to be a blessing," Maggie said despite her resolve to keep quiet.

"But is the blessing worth the pain of saying good-bye?"

He stood, paced the floor.

"Is it worth the pain of knowing, in some cases, that you'll never see them again? That all you have left are the memories?"

He stopped in the center of the room.

"And what about those you thought were friends and it turned out that they were not friends at all but instead were just using you, that all they wanted was your—?"

He was more emotional than he intended to be in front of this beautiful stranger, and that annoyed him greatly.

This must stop, Randy told himself. *She will have no respect for me if I continue on like this.*

He broke off, and she saw him trembling.

"Are you ill?" she asked.

"Ill?" he said as though studying that single word. "Not of the body, Miss Engebretsen . . . surely not of the body."

He excused himself and went outside briefly.

When Randy returned, he acted in a manner that seemed cooler toward her, distant, though never less than polite, and Maggie regretted this abrupt change in him. Indeed, she regretted it very much.

Randy Stuart initially didn't talk much as they rode to the hospital in Maggie's own carriage, which he found not far from where she had been attacked, the horse waiting faithfully for her to return.

"How are you going to get back?" she asked him.

"I'll manage," he said.

"It's a long trip. I regret your inconvenience."

"Don't worry yourself."

Maggie studied his face without being too obvious about doing so.

The good looks were there, almost to perfection, but something else clouded his features, something that came from his eyes and the general set of the dimpled jaw, a weariness, an emptiness,

a lack of joy so intense that she felt well-nigh compelled to probe and find out what was wrong. Yet she was restrained from doing so by the fact that she had no right to pry, and she didn't want to bother, at least any more than she already had, this man who had been kind to her, had saved her life in fact.

On their way back into the city that morning, Maggie could see people on their horses or in their own carriages or working in their fields, as neighborhoods came to life on the outskirts of Philadelphia.

Normally at that hour she would have been hugging her parents and her sister, saying good-bye to them for the day.

Nothing would ever be normal again. She knew she would soon have to say good-bye to them forever. Few who contracted cholera survived its ravages.

"Oh . . ." she gasped out loud, not intending to do so but unable to rein in her emotions, which were so strong at that moment that she couldn't help herself.

"Miss Engebretsen?" Randy asked, breaking his silence.

She could not answer immediately.

"Thinking of your parents?" he added.

She nodded.

"You can cry, you know," he told her. "That won't embarrass me. I've seen lots of women cry before."

Maggie did just that, sobbing so hard she caused herself deep and wrenching pain, in her chest. He pulled over to the side of the dirt road, and she fell into his arms as the tears kept coming.

"I'm . . . so . . . sorry," she said, "putting . . . you . . . through . . . all this!"

"It's fine," he said, patting her gently on the back. "Let it all come out, Maggie. I don't mind at all."

"There'll be . . . be no funeral, really. Their bodies will be tossed . . . into that . . . that awful . . . that awful pit!"

She couldn't bring herself to say it, to describe the giant pit that consumed hundreds of bodies in the inferno at the bottom.

It seemed like a human copy of hell itself, bodies thrown over the edge into the consuming flames, a few not dead but snapped out of comas and trying to crawl desperately back to the surface, but none of them able to, none of them—

"I've had to put some people into it myself," Randy said suddenly.

Maggie pulled away so she could look at him; seeing his own eyes cloud up, she read in them memories as vivid as her own fears for the future.

"It may be the worst thing anyone has to do, and when it's a loved one . . . " he said. "The first to go was my brother. I didn't want somebody else doing it. Only I had the right. Only—"

It had been done at night.

Clouds of smoke had reflected the fire.

Randy hadn't wanted to let go, had tried to hold his brother's body, cradling it in his arms. But knowing the disease it contained, he eventually relinquished it—opened his hands and said goodbye.

The sides of the pit sloped to the fire at the bottom.

And the bodies were supposed to tumble down into it. But some stopped partway and had to be prodded with long poles.

That was what happened as he finally dropped his brother's body and it—

He shook the images out of his head as a chill grabbed hold of every bone in his body, and he hugged himself feverishly for several moments.

"I'm supposed to be giving you comfort," he said ironically. "Please forgive me for failing in that."

She reached out and touched him on the cheek, gently, and he leaned his head into the warmth of her hand.

After he had walked her to the door of the hospital and left her horse at the livery stable, Randy Stuart left without delay, saying nothing else.

A short while later, learning that her wound required no further work because it had been treated so expertly, Maggie inquired about her benefactor's whereabouts and was told that no one had any idea where he was.

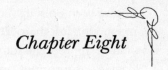

Chapter Eight

Dr. Morgan Bowder.

He was an exceptional doctor, both in his knowledge gained from many years in his profession and in a massive presence that was commanding if only for its sheer bulk, a presence that he was not reluctant to use to get what he wanted in any professional situation.

Philadelphia Memorial Hospital's veteran executive director and a man respected across the United States as a talented surgeon, he knew well the effect he typically had on people, even those better known than himself who would often come to him as if they were fortunate enough to have an audience with some legendary king—and, when he wanted to do so, often used this effect like a weapon.

This was one doctor who could give any underling what amounted to a nervous breakdown with just a few words spoken by a voice that seemed suited for the baritone role in a tragic opera.

Maggie did not have a great deal of contact with this bearlike Dr. Bowder, in part because she had invariably allowed herself to be as intimidated by him as everyone else who came in contact with the man, quite apart from the fact that he routinely discouraged any kind of personal contact with the hospital's large staff.

So it was unusual when he asked her to come to his office, doing so directly rather than through an assistant.

"Miss Engebretsen," he said after they both had sat down, Dr. Bowder behind a desk that seemed to match his own size, Maggie in front of it, "I want you to listen most carefully to me. Will you do that, young woman?"

"Of course, Sir," she replied, "of course I will."

"You've been working very hard," he said, his round face devoid of any emotion just then. "Despite the conditions facing us, I think it would be appropriate for you to take a few days off."

Maggie was surprised, and this registered on her face.

"I know that sounds unusual, coming from me," Dr. Bowder admitted, "but, you see, I have to hold in my emotions as much as possible, I mean, given the administrative position that I have."

His expression showed his weariness with the kinds of pressure that his responsibilities imposed.

He swung around and faced her again.

My family!

That word ripped across Maggie's mind.

They're—

"Miss Engebretsen, I am sorry to have to tell you this, but your father, your mother, and your sister are all—" he started to say.

Dead . . .

The three of them were gone!

"I saw them yesterday!" she cried out. "They seemed a little stronger. I thought . . . I thought they might make it."

"Cholera weakened your father's heart and your mother's," he told her carefully. "We cannot be sure just why your sister died. But this is typical of the disease. I have seen similar circumstances frequently."

Maggie tried to stand but couldn't; the room was spinning.

Something wrapped around her abruptly.

Strong arms.

Dr. Bowder's.

Hugging her, holding her gently but firmly so that she would not fall and hurt herself.

No! her mind screamed. *They can't be dead. You would not allow this to happen, Lord, You would not—*

Just before she lost consciousness, she heard him yell as though someone had suddenly punched him in the stomach. In that instant, his rigid, highly professional manner disappeared.

Dr. Bowder arranged for a makeshift bed to be set up in his office and stayed with her until Maggie regained consciousness.

She felt as though there was no strength whatsoever left in her entire body, for she could just barely open her eyes.

"I feel so weak," she acknowledged.

"You don't have cholera," he told her. "When I suggested that you needed a rest, I was quite sincere."

"But I don't need—" she started to say.

My family! Sweet Jesus, help me! My family is gone!

For a moment, the shock of this knowledge forced her into a kind of temporary amnesia. For a moment Maggie had forgotten. Then the news came rushing back into her mind, and she began to cry.

"No!" she said loudly. "I don't want to go on living. How can I? I—I have no one left!"

"I too am alone, Maggie Engebretsen," Dr. Bowder said with great sympathy in his voice. "I know how you feel."

Words left her, and she sobbed so hard she was soon choking.

"I know, yes, I know very well, but you're dying right now; that mustn't be!" Dr. Bowder told her after he had wiped away tears from her face. "You probably feel, now, like joining your parents and Roberta and forgetting this life altogether. You just know you can't spend time in that familiar old house alone without going quite insane."

He lowered his voice to a near whisper.

"Do you not realize that all of us here at this hospital have felt precisely the same way at one point or another in our lives?"

Maggie hesitated, astonished to hear her thoughts being verbalized as accurately as Dr. Bowder had succeeded in doing just then, and she wanted to stop the man, wanted to shout to him that he must not go on saying such things, that facing the truth so harshly was intolerable for her.

"I can't listen!" she tried to tell him. "I can't do this."

He was pushing her too hard, expecting too much.

"Please stop!" she begged. "Please—!"

But he paid no attention.

"You will listen, Maggie Engebretsen; you will listen to me. Are you going to allow this monstrous disease to be responsible for wiping out your entire family as though it had never existed in the first place, even the many precious memories gone because there is no one left to treasure them?"

Maggie's eyes grew frightened, darting from side to side.

"I am alone, Sir," she said, weeping. "There is no one left. And now I shall have to stand by that awful pit and watch their bodies being consumed by the flames. How can I stand that, Sir? Tell me, how can I?"

"I've taken care of it," he said.

"But how?"

"Not every body is to be disposed of in just that manner. For some, there are a few other choices."

"To be burned to ashes on individual pyres, is that what you're saying? Is that so much better, Sir?"

"For people with money, it can be different, Maggie."

"But my family's not wealthy. We don't have the—"

"But I do," he interrupted. "And it's being arranged."

Maggie fell silent briefly, still very much confused, not fully aware of what he was telling her.

"There is a process," he said slowly.

Then he paused, looking at her and trying to gather precisely the right words.

"And this process involves having the cholera victims' bodies treated with certain substances then wrapped in canvas and sealed in airtight coffins. But it's very expensive. You're right about that."

"And . . . and then they can be buried rather than burned?" she asked tentatively.

He nodded.

"It is a privilege that has to be bought, as I have inferred, and so I would not want to make any kind of public announcement about my role in view of the resentment it would stir up in the populace. I hope it helps you in some way."

Maggie fell back against the mattress, her mind whirling with the news that Dr. Bowder had provided.

"But why?" she asked. "Why are you doing this?"

"Someday I may be able to tell you," Dr. Bowder said as he

stood, his great bulk straining a bit. "Right now just call it something personal. Yes, call it that, something too personal for me to express to you as yet. Will you let me leave it at that, Maggie Engebretsen?"

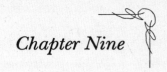

Chapter Nine

The funeral was in a church more than a century old.[1]

It was the church the Engebretsen family had attended for many years, a large colonial-style building with thick columns across the front and massive double doors at the entrance.

While the family had been exceedingly popular in the community, only a handful of people, the ones trustworthy enough to keep the circumstances confidential, were told and invited to attend.

Unlike the Engebretsens, those with huge sums of money didn't care who knew about such matters, their wealth giving them an arrogance that superseded any sense of wondering about the community of which they were a part. If lower-class citizens were bothered, that hardly concerned them—only the full exercise of their economic power mattered.

A rush of jumbled thoughts raced nonstop through Maggie's mind as she sat and tried to listen to the eulogy without making a fool of herself.

They lived their lives as a strong witness to You, Lord, but now there is only secrecy because of the way I've chosen to bury them! They wouldn't care at all what happens to their bodies now, because they're already inhabiting heaven with You, Lord! What have I done?

She felt ashamed then, ashamed that she had invoked special privileges in dealing with the deaths of these three who would have never allowed it in life.

---

1. Not as many of the old colonial buildings have remained over the years as there should be. Other countries—particularly in Europe—typically do a far better job of preserving the remnants of history than the United States does.

The poor who die from cholera are thrown one after the other into one of those pits. But here I sit before fine, polished-wood coffins, dressed in my best clothes, with the only people I can trust never to tell any of it, for if anyone did, the jealousy would spread, and there would be ugly words spat out behind my back.

She glanced about guiltily, as though the coffins were accusing fingers pointing straight at her. The average Philadelphian was not nearly so fortunate.

Dr. Bowder, sitting beside her, noticed. He reached over, placing a hand on her shoulder as he whispered, "It is your gift to those you loved so very much, my dear Maggie. If there be any sin in it, realize that Christ's death brought forgiveness for all sin, even that which is much, much greater than today's."

Tears were trickling down Maggie's cheeks as she looked at him, appreciating what he was trying to do but realizing that pride, as much as love, was at the center of what she had done.

There was no way she could have allowed her father, her mother, and her only sister to be shoved into a common fire pit with whores, beggars, scoundrels, and others. So had she gathered together a small, tight group of friends, sworn everyone to secrecy, and held this formal funeral instead, paid for with Dr. Bowder's generous help.

Minutes later, as though in oddly timed confirmation of what she seemed to be hearing from that still, small voice within her, Maggie saw that even her attempt at discretion had fallen into pieces at her feet.

As the coffins were being carried outside to be buried in the church cemetery, a woman whom she vaguely remembered from the hospital came bursting into the sanctuary.

The woman had caused quite a fuss at the hospital, Maggie remembered, though she could understand why she was so upset. The nursing staff had refused to let her see her loved ones for fear of contagion, and this had angered her greatly—and understandably.

"How prideful you are!" she screamed at Maggie now. "My parents were turned to ashes by a raging fire. But you have placed these folks on a pedestal and given them the burial of royalty. How can you call yourself a Christian? You are—"

Dr. Bowder approached the woman, trying to calm her.

He failed, and she spat at him, yelling a profanity at the small group of mourners, then at Maggie.

"You couldn't get your dainty hands dirty, could you?" she kept on. "Me, I had to watch. I made myself watch what was happening. And I will be haunted by what I saw for the rest of my life.

"But you! Not you, Nurse Maggie. No, never you! You had no courage. You could not bear to see them slip down into the fires along with a hundred others. Be honest with yourself. You're weak. You'll never be anything but weak. And you think your money makes you better than the rest of us."

"I did it out of love," Maggie protested. "I did it because—"

"You can't fool me," the woman spat out the words. "You wrap around your arrogance the banner of love, and that may fool these others but not me. It had nothing to do with your parents, and you know it. It has everything to do with your position in society. You couldn't possibly get your hands dirty, could you?"

"That is not true," Maggie tried to tell her, hoping to get through the other woman's grief. "You just do not know what you are talking about."

"But I do. I know about your kind. You think you're so special, and people like me are dirt under your feet. You—"

Maggie felt a strange lack of anger, something resembling pity taking its place along with a dawning sense of awareness.

"Did you love your parents less than I did?" she interrupted.

"No!"

"Did I love them less because of what I did? The answer too is no. I don't know why it turned out this way. I think maybe it's because you're right. God in His great wisdom knew I was weak.

"God understood that I couldn't endure doing what you did. That's when He stepped in and gave my mother, my father, my sister this burial instead. I praise Him for it. I give Him the deepest gratitude I can feel."

"Your sister?" the woman said. "Your sister's gone too? Roberta?"

Maggie nodded slowly.

"We were friends," the woman told her sadly. "We were—"

Her eyes widened suddenly, and she turned quickly, heading for the front door, yelling, "Please forgive me! Please, please forgive me!"

Maggie felt a hand once again on her shoulder.

Dr. Bowder.

"I know her," he said with a tenderness that belied his bulk. "She's an only child. For that woman, it's worse, Maggie, if you can imagine it. She too was devoted to her parents, but unlike you, she remained at home with her mother while her father left the house and worked. Her home life was the very center of her world.

"If you had been the one to die along with your mother and father, and Roberta had survived, your sister might have reacted similarly to that woman. Because you and your parents were the very center of Roberta's world too, Maggie."

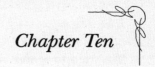

Chapter Ten

The obligation she had dreaded since the epidemic had struck was now nearly over, but perhaps the worst part had yet to be played out.

The coffins being lowered into the ground.

The dirt being thrown in the graves until there was nothing to be seen of the coffins.

Better than the alternative she would have had to face, better than what the poor endured, but still a good-bye, still a—She did her best.

And she thought she would make it through the ordeal well enough, but she was wrong, terribly wrong.

Yet how expertly she deceived Dr. Bowder and the handful of others, thanking them for attending, a slight, grateful smile bending her lips. Then only Dr. Bowder remained behind with her. After she paused again briefly at the grave sites, he drove her back home, her face devoid of emotion during the ride, no real conversation occurring between them until they reached the Engebretsen residence. Then there was another thank-you for his kindness, a kiss on her cheek, and then she was inside the empty house, a house so big now, bigger than it had ever seemed before. Walking through it, smelling the familiar scents, hearing in her mind the voices that were now gone, gone for the rest of her life, she sank to her knees in the middle of the parlor.

It was merciful indeed that she passed out a few seconds later.

Answer the door, Maggie! Please answer the door!

The distant sound of someone shouting and pounding on the front door pulled Maggie Engebretsen back from the total darkness into which she had slipped.

It can't be important. I won't pay attention, and it will go away, and I shall remain here until I too am dead.

She tried to ignore it because oblivion, however temporary, somehow seemed far more desirable than returning to life itself.

Knock-knock-knock-knock—

Again and again.

Why don't they stop? Why can't they understand that I just want to stay here, unaware of anything but—?

A voice.

Quite familiar. Begging her to answer.

Amelia!

Her nurse friend from the hospital.

I've got to answer. I've—

Maggie struggled to open her eyes.

So weak . . .

The piano appeared across the room then faded into blackness and then came back into focus. The old chair Lars Engebretsen had enjoyed so much. The knickknack-cluttered mantel above the fireplace.

Finally her vision returned fully.

I still can't move. I—

Seconds passed. The knocking became more frantic.

Maggie's legs could not support her, but she managed to pull herself along the floor toward the door, nausea washing over her.

"Amelia!" she cried. "I'm very sick. I—"

Maggie came close to passing out again, but that moment went by, and she somehow remained conscious.

She managed to get herself to a kneeling position.

The bolt on the door hadn't been swung straight across but just far enough to keep the door from being opened.

Finally Maggie was able to slide it back and get out of the way as Amelia turned the knob and the door opened.

Her friend's eyes widened as she saw Maggie's condition.

"What happened?" she said, astonished.

"I think I was trying to die," Maggie replied, her voice quite weak, raspy. "I think that's what it was."

Amelia managed to lift Maggie enough to pull her down the hall and onto a bed. Then she helped her slip out of her dress and into a clean nightgown.

"I shouldn't have put you through this," Maggie said. "I'm not worth it. I'm not worth much of anything."

"You must never say that," Amelia retorted. "How can you throw those words into the face of our Lord?"

Maggie bowed her head.

"It's so hard to let go," she said. "I feel as though—"

Maggie started coughing then, and soon another clean nightgown was needed.

"You've got to go to the hospital," Amelia insisted as she searched for a clean towel in the washstand.

"No! I . . . want to . . . stay here. . . . I *will* stay . . . here!"

"I won't allow you to commit suicide, no matter what other label you might attempt to put on the act."

Maggie raised up off the bed and held her head at an odd angle as though listening to a strange sound and, unable to identify it, suddenly leaned to one side and fell from the bed, nearly hitting the floor before Amelia could catch her.

Maggie's recovery did not go nearly as smoothly as Morgan Bowder had hoped it would, despite the efforts of everyone at the hospital who knew her and others who did not.

The doctor had expected her to be devastated by the deaths of her family members, but he was surprised that she found it as difficult as she did to bounce back from that tragedy, knowing what he did about her apparent stability, clearly shown as she had nursed some of the other dying patients at the hospital.

A few days after she was admitted to Philadelphia Memorial, he decided to join her on an outside walk, noticing that her steps were still slow, even wavering.

"You cannot go on this way, Maggie," he told her honestly as they walked a pathway through some autumn leaves. "You cannot pretend that life has stopped for you as well as your parents and

sister and that only your heart is beating while nothing else works."

She stood for a moment under a large oak tree.

"Roberta and I have swings hanging from a tree like this one," Maggie recalled. "They're still there, you know. We would swing back and forth, sometimes talking, sometimes just being silent together, thinking as we went back and forth, back and forth, a gentle breeze blowing across our cheeks."

She reached out and wistfully touched the thick trunk of the tree.

"It will be right here, I suppose, a century after I—" she started to say it but couldn't get the words out.

"You are wondering, now, how you can face the next half century or longer without your parents, your sister," he said. "Isn't that the case, Maggie?"

She swung around, her eyes filled with tears.

"It is," she said. "It is!"

Dr. Bowder spotted a bench some few yards ahead.

"Let's sit down," he told her. "My weight means I tire out more quickly. I've been meaning to do something about it, you know. But I just keep putting off the ordeal."

She nodded, and they walked toward the bench, not noticing at first the nurse who was coming toward them.

As they were sitting down, the nurse approached the two of them.

"Miss Thompkins," Dr. Bowder said, puffing a bit as he looked up. "How can we help you, my dear?"

"It's Maggie," she replied. "Someone's asking for you. A new patient, here for a little more than an hour."

"Who is it?" Maggie asked, wiping her eyes quickly with a frilly pink hankie.

"He's delirious," the nurse answered. "But he did have some papers in his possession."

"Come on, Miss Thompkins," Dr. Bowder said a bit impatiently. "What is this gentleman's name?"

Miss Thompkins was blushing.

"What in the world is going on?" Dr. Bowder asked sternly while rather enjoying that particular moment.

"Well, Sir, he's quite, uh, handsome."

"His name, please, his name!"

"Randy, Sir. His name is Randy Stuart. All the nurses find him very, well, attractive. But he's got a terrible reputation."

"You know this man?"

"We all know about him."

Maggie spoke up then.

"I don't," she said quite innocently.

Miss Thompkins blushed a deeper shade of red this time.

"He's . . . he's not the . . . type of man you should . . . should . . . ever be interested in," she said self-consciously.

"Perhaps our coworker here is paying you an awkward compliment, Maggie," Dr. Bowder remarked, "but a compliment just the same."

He saw Maggie's expression, saw that the tears had stopped, saw that her own cheeks were turning pink.

"Maggie, why don't you visit with this Randy Stuart?" he suggested rather mischievously.

"Sir," Miss Thompkins interrupted. "Forgive me for interfering, but, you see, he's . . . dying of cholera."

"Oh!" Maggie caught her breath, suddenly understanding who the man was.

Dr. Bowder misunderstood her reaction and instantly regretted what he had said, knowing that Maggie Engebretsen was hardly strong enough at that point to handle a relationship with someone who might not survive the next twenty-four hours.

But he also noticed Maggie's reaction to the news, for in an instant, her manner changed.

"It cannot happen again," she said, her voice strong.

"What is that?" Dr. Bowder asked.

"I cannot allow that disease to take anyone else from me."

"How well do you know this man?"

She told them what had happened.

"I see," Dr. Bowder said, rubbing his chin. "But, Maggie, he's too far along. I don't mean to be unkind, but you're now grasping

at straws. And with this situation the straw will only break in your hands, Dear."

"I must try," she protested. "He will die if—"

"He will die anyway. You can do nothing that the other nurses are not equipped to do," Dr. Bowder replied. "It is a vicious enemy, this cholera. It operates in virtual secrecy. Perhaps someday it indeed will be brought down, but right now we are nearly helpless."

"Nearly helpless—isn't that what you just said?"

"Yes, it is, but—"

"But some patients do survive, don't they?"

"That's right, Maggie, but—"

"Do you know why?"

"It's a mystery, I admit."

Maggie knew she was being difficult, contrary to the way she generally acted, but this time she could not control herself.

"Then Randy Stuart could become one of those survivors."

"That's possible, Maggie."

"But he won't, Sir, if he doesn't have the will to live, if all he wants to do is lie there in his bed and let the disease consume him."

"How do you know that about him?" Dr. Bowder asked.

"I know," she replied. "I know."

I know . . . I know.

Indeed Maggie did.

Randy Stuart had sent out signals about himself, probably without ever intending to do so, a weariness about him beneath the well-bred politeness.

He wants to die, she thought as she, Dr. Bowder, and Miss Thompkins walked back into the hospital. *For him, a fatal sickness is nearly always a kind of answer to prayer. Life has lost its meaning. It—*

"How is it that I know so much about Randy Stuart, that I feel so much?" Maggie speculated out loud.

They were inside, Miss Thompkins having gone off on her rounds, and she and Dr. Bowder were standing in his office.

"I don't know," he replied, "but I just cannot see how I can allow you to go into that ward, Maggie. It has only a handful of nurses to tend to scores of patients. We don't want to risk contamination among the staff any more than necessary. It's pointless to add yet someone else to the list, and wasteful too."

"Wasteful?" She repeated that last word as though it was something that tasted bitter. "Don't you see how I am? Don't you see that—?"

"I know what you are implying, Maggie, and it's wrong, terribly, terribly wrong. Do you think that God will honor such an outlook? He alone is to be our strength, our refuge. Once we give over any significant portion of that to another human being, we are risking His rebuke."

"But is God standing around just waiting to add pain to our lives, waiting to send judgment if we stumble and fall from time to time?"

"Of course not, Maggie. He is forgiving by His very nature. But there comes a time when He is compelled to act, when He doesn't stop forgiving, but with that forgiveness He must send to us a message, sometimes a message that is a very hard one, to be sure."

"I know He didn't take my family from me as any kind of judgment upon me," she said. "I know that deep down inside me. But I also know that I have to have someone, Dr. Bowder.

"After all those many years of being only with my loved ones and now, returning to an empty house, it's . . . it's more than I can stand. Maybe this man will die. Maybe he's not the one to fill up my life once again, but if I don't reach out, I'll never, ever know."

Several of the nurses and doctors had gathered nearby. As Maggie stopped talking, they broke out into spontaneous, collective applause.

Dr. Bowder looked at the others then at Maggie.

"Remarkable," he said. "You are quite remarkable, Maggie Engebretsen. But then I always knew that."

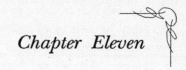

Chapter Eleven

Randy Stuart looked completely helpless.

The man who had rescued her from what seemed certain rape or death now appeared like a child, a child reduced to being utterly at the mercy of those around him.

You seemed so strong just a short while ago, Maggie thought. *Now you are like a newborn baby. How you must hate being like this!*

She somehow sensed what he was thinking as she began to clean him up, a constant need for cholera victims. He groaned as he was moved, and to her he felt more like a lifeless lump of clay than a living human being.

You are almost as perplexed by your embarrassment as by your pain, she continued thinking. *You could endure the one much more stoutly than the other.*

Ironic.

It was that, every bit that.

A man who had bragged about having no ties and needing no one was suddenly dependent upon others for everything, for his very survival.

It's as though God is using this nightmare to humble you, Maggie thought as she sat by his bed during the first of what would evolve into several quite awful visits. *Now you know that you need others no less than the next man. But you are afraid of admitting it because that would mean you owe a debt to others.*

Randy seemed as far gone as did other cholera patients in the final stages of the disease, but somehow Maggie saw in him a special helplessness that was so much in contrast to the way he had conducted himself when she first met him, when he had stepped in and rescued her.

Am I only now to sit here by your bed, unable to do anything for you, she asked herself, *except hold your hand and let you know you're not alone, let you know that whatever happens, I care? At least I care.*

Maggie knew that she might have been throwing her own life away by entering the cholera ward. Nurses frequently did come down with the disease, which was why the staff was quite limited, confining exposure the only real precaution that could be taken in those days.

Every so often Randy would regain consciousness, look up at her, and smile sweetly . . . then drift into unconsciousness again. He was able to speak only twice during the early part of the time she spent with him.

"Go away," he whispered. "There's no point in your dying as well."

"Not everyone gets the disease," she told him, even though she knew of few natural-immunity cases.

Randy had an answer for her.

"Not everyone gets this close to someone who is dying," he remarked.

"You won't die," she said though less than confidently.

He sneered a bit.

"You mean God won't allow it?"

Maggie ignored his cynicism.

"Yes, that's exactly what I mean," she replied sweetly.

"When did He tell you this?"

Randy tried to smile but was too weak, and then his eyes closed and he lost consciousness again.

Maggie was standing out in the corridor, taking a break, when Amelia came by to say hello.

"How are you feeling?" Amelia asked.

"Lonesome. I feel as though everybody is avoiding me, not because of any worry about catching cholera but because I decided to show some kindness toward Randy Stuart."

"I can understand how the others feel. But I am not about to stay away from a friend because of him!"

"Bless you. I need your company just now, Amelia. God must

have heard my little prayers a few minutes ago.

"Why are you doing this?" Amelia asked. "You risk yourself for someone who is little more than a stranger—and a stranger with a disturbing reputation at that! As nurses, yes, we have to do that, but in your case there seems to be something else involved in what you are doing."

"He needs someone."

"You hardly know the man."

"That's true. But how many of your patients do you ever really know, Amelia? Are any of them dear friends?"

The other woman seemed to be lost in some swirling thoughts for a moment, and Maggie could see that she was struggling.

"Please, Maggie, anyone but Randy Stuart," she finally said. "Anybody but him."

"But why do you say that?"

Amelia was feeling increasingly awkward, cornered into a spot where she was not comfortable at all, and yet she could not simply turn and walk away.

"Everyone knows about Randy."

"And what do they know?"

"He . . . he goes after any skirt he can."

"He likes women then? Is that what you're saying?"

"It's more than that. He seduces them, Maggie, that creature does, and then throws them aside, like trash."

"Rumors, Amelia, rumors," Maggie replied.

"No . . ."

"No what?"

"It's the truth," Amelia said as she started to turn away.

Maggie touched her shoulder.

"Were you one of those he mistreated?" she asked gently.

Her back still facing Maggie, Amelia nodded just once and then quickly walked away.

Oh, Lord, Maggie said prayerfully. *Can this be the man in the next room? Can this be the one You want me to—?*

She heard a cry.

Randy Stuart.

It was loud, and there was pain in it.

If I could only have held Papa's hand and Mama's and Roberta's as they died . . . Lord, would that have been too much to give me . . . to let them know that I was by their side when Your angels beckoned them into Your heavenly kingdom?

That thought would stay with Maggie Engebretsen, fresh and accusative, for many months after her family died.

She had not been with either of her parents or her sister when they went to be with the Lord, and she regretted this. But she sensed that it was going to be different with Randy Stuart. She could feel his life slipping away from him, along with any coherence that he had possessed even a few hours earlier.

"I . . . I . . . I'm sorry . . . for . . . how . . . how . . . how I treated the . . . the . . . others."

He would say that over and over, each time his voice a little harder to hear, the words less and less distinguishable.

Randy Stuart had regressed another level and was now totally helpless. After a short while, Maggie elected to take care of him directly, relieving the other nurses of that responsibility.

"No hope . . ." he mumbled. "Just . . . let . . . me . . . die. . . . I'm . . . so close . . . now. . . ."

His eyes opened briefly, looking at her.

"I . . . don't . . . want . . . to . . . live . . . " he told her.

"You will live," she said, raising her voice more than she had intended. "You will not give up!"

Randy wrapped the fingers of one hand around her wrist and kept them there, his grip featherlight.

Nurses came and offered to take Maggie's place periodically, but she would not allow it. She found herself talking to Randy even when he was unconscious, hoping somehow that her words were getting through.

"I know how you feel," she would tell him. "Until yesterday I didn't want to live either. I had nothing to live for. The center of

my world had been cut out and cast aside. And I returned to a house that seemed nothing more than an open tomb that was just waiting to claim me."

She would go on like this for quite a while, until she tired, until the hopelessness of the situation became overwhelmingly apparent. Then she would stand and walk away . . . only to come back and sit by Randy Stuart's bed and talk some more.

Once, as Maggie started to leave, she heard a voice, and thinking that it was his, she turned quickly.

It wasn't.

Someone else.

Another patient.

A man in his late fifties.

She walked over to his bed.

"I've heard you," he said. "I've heard you talk about living in a kind of hell. I've been there, Miss. But Christ lifted me out of the pit I was in, and I shall soon take His hand as we walk together into heaven."

He was smiling amidst his pain as Maggie held his hand.

"Miss?" he asked.

"Yes?" she replied. "What can I do for you?"

"Mention our precious Savior, our precious Lord, when you talk to that man. Maybe it will help you both."

She thanked him, walked out into the corridor adjacent to the ward, and leaned against the wall, her eyes shut, a headache pounding.

. . . maybe it will help you both.

She asked herself if he could be right, if she had given Christ a sufficient place in her prayers since tragedy had struck her life.

Have I let You down, dearest Lord? she prayed. *Have I innocently and with no deliberate intent ever turned my back on You?*

Was she so overwhelmed by the need to be with someone—and a seemingly inappropriate person at that, a man who was not much more than a stranger to her—that she had perhaps pushed the Lord unceremoniously into the background?

How can I expect to give him comfort when the Source—?

She opened her eyes.

The corridor was deserted, dark, smelling of antiseptic, and chilly.

But that wasn't why she was shivering just then. She sensed it again . . .

Three of the patients had perished in that instant. She knew it before she could return to the ward and confirm it.

A fourth would die soon, the one who had spoken to her about Christ.

Abruptly, the man called to Maggie as she stepped back into the ward.

She walked over to him.

"The Lord . . . spoke . . . to . . . me," the man told her earnestly. "I really felt His presence so strongly."

"What did He say?" Maggie asked, trying to conceal her skepticism.

"That your male friend's going to make it."

She couldn't hold back a chuckle.

"That would be wonderful, Sir, but he's very sick now. Cholera is predictable in its impact. After a certain progression, it—"

She stopped short, realizing she was also talking about the man himself.

"But, even so, not him," the other said. "That one will survive cholera's worst attacks, and yet he will not accept—"

The man started coughing violently.

He was dead less than ten minutes later, never completing his prediction.

After his body was taken away, Maggie returned to Randy's bedside.

"Did you hear that?" she whispered. "He thought you would pull through this. I hope he's right. Randy, that would make me very, very happy."

She touched his forehead. It seemed warmer. Perhaps cholera's violent chills, a result of the severe dehydration, had eased their grip.

Maggie kidded herself for thinking that, for trying to rationalize what could surely be the only outcome, however harsh it might be to even think it.

Then a bit of moonlight caught Randy's face.

After so much agony so quickly, how can you seem so handsome as you do, lying there in that deathbed of yours?

She found herself looking at his cheeks and his lips, still full and healthy-looking somehow, sighing as she envisioned what could never be, those lips touching her own and great passion working its way with them both.

"Good night, sweet prince," she whispered. Then she returned home to the big, empty house.

Maggie was afraid to go into the hospital at first the next morning. She couldn't face the news that surely would be given to her.

Lord, even with You at my side, I am unable to endure this, she prayed. *Don't expect it of me, Lord, please don't.*

Dead.

Maggie knew that was what she would be told. There was no way around a fact as harsh as that.

"He died last night," Dr. Bowder would say soon after she arrived. "Nothing else could be done for him."

"I know that!" she would scream in despair as she tried to keep from collapsing. "I was just hoping—"

Then, undoubtedly, Dr. Bowder would say something else, attempting to be profound in her presence.

"We should never wrap around ourselves anything that amounts to a futile sort of hope, Maggie. That is only the spirit of delusion. The Lord wants us to face life fully, without being foolish in such important areas as life and death. He is the spirit of truth, and it is truth that He wants us to—"

Finally shutting off the imaginary scenario that was playing through her mind, Maggie got out of bed, washed, twisted her hair into a knot, and held it in place with a tortoiseshell hairpin, dressed, and went out to hitch up the carriage.

From the street, the hospital seemed so familiar, as it should, and yet so forbidding, like her first visit to some massive fortress.

And dismal.

Yes, it looked more dismal than ever.

As Maggie pulled up in front, the horse's hooves stopping their clatter on the cobblestone street, she hated getting out at all, hated the thought of going through the familiar front entrance of a building that, in the midst of the epidemic, seemed like entering a giant tomb. Each time she walked through the door she felt the place closing around her so tightly that she worried she might never leave, trapped there like so many dying, pain-wracked victims.

Autumn made it all seem worse somehow.

After an attendant took the horse and carriage, she walked among thousands of fallen, multicolored leaves.

They look almost prettier now than in life, she thought idly. *How opposite they are to human beings. As leaves drop and die, they inspire beautiful poetry, wonderful art, the fondest memories. But for the rest of us—*

Maggie bent down, picked up one particularly fine specimen of brilliant autumn hues, almost artificial-looking in its sublime perfection. But it was notably dry, this leaf, and it crumbled in a few seconds.

She watched the pieces, some like fine dust, slip through her thin fingers, and she was overwhelmed with sadness again, not because of a single leaf but what it seemed to symbolize in her life.

She turned and glanced at the hospital.

"I can't do it!" she said out loud. "I can't go in there and walk down that corridor and look at that empty bed or see it taken by someone else."

She looked up at the overcast sky.

Lord, spare me that . . . as You did with my family.

When she was a child, she had often heard her parents talking about death. And it had filled her with great fear. She started having nightmares. In one of these nightmares, she would be standing before coffins containing the bodies of her mother and father. She would think how nice they looked—pale, yes, but otherwise seemingly in the grip of a deep and gentle sleep.

Every night while her parents were alive, they would come into her room, bend over her bed, and kiss her on the forehead. In that terrible, terrible dream of hers as a child, she would bend over her mother, so still in that cushioned box, and kiss her on the forehead—and then pull back instantly. *You're so cold, Mama,* she would think, *so cold!*

And then she would go to her father and hesitate, expecting him to open his eyes and comfort her as he had done so often while alive. But he would remain quiet, unmoving, even as she kissed him on the forehead. And again and again, the cold was there, like a block of ice, and she would pull back, and think, *Cold, Papa! So cold!*

The words weren't sequestered only to that moment of melancholy nighttime fantasy; she would invariably end up blurting them out as she awoke from the dream, screaming those words into the darkness of her room until her parents came running to her and held her and whispered their comfort, always at her side, always, always.

No more . . .

It was quite early now.

There was no activity outside the hospital.

A breeze that had commenced now stirred the dead leaves, their movement mocking life.

She saw a single squirrel scampering past.

Otherwise she was alone.

She sank to sit on the cold stone steps.

There is no strength left within me, dear Lord. I cannot even bring myself to go into this building and face the bed of a man who is little more than a stranger to me. But I must do it, Lord. I must do it somehow. Please, Father, please lift me up; please pour just a measure of Your strength into this weak vessel.

She jumped as she felt a hand on her shoulder.

Dr. Bowder.

"I saw you out here," he told her. "I thought you might be ill.

Are you okay, Maggie? Can I help in any way?"

She nodded gratefully.

"May I walk inside with you?" he asked.

"Yes . . ." she said weakly, not loud enough for Dr. Bowder to hear. "I need you next to me."

"What did you say?"

"Yes," she repeated, louder this time.

"Good, good."

The two of them walked together up the steps to the front entrance as though in slow motion.

As they approached the steps, Maggie began to feel like a rag doll with all the stuffing coming out of her.

"Lean on me," Dr. Bowder whispered. "Lean on me, dear Maggie. Let me be your strength now."

Finally they were inside and starting down the long corridor.

"No," she said. "No, I cannot do this."

"Yes, you can, my dear Maggie. You can indeed," Dr. Bowder said as they stopped at the entrance to the ward.

"He's gone, Sir," she said, her voice trembling. "I know he's gone, and I . . . I cannot bear the sight of seeing—"

Dr. Bowder was smiling.

How can you smile, knowing—? Maggie asked herself. *How can you possibly act that way now of all times?*

"You're right, Maggie," Dr. Bowder said. "The young man named Randy Stuart is not there."

She started to cry.

But her mentor placed his fingers under her eyes and wiped away the first few tears.

"Rest easy, Maggie. He's in the recovery ward," Dr. Bowder told her. "Last night the chills broke. Randy Stuart's going to be one of the handful who will pull through!"

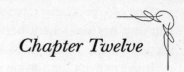

Chapter Twelve

Maggie decided not to go in to see Randy Stuart immediately, though at first that was all she wanted to do.

I want to make sure how he is doing, she thought. *Nobody cares as much about him as I do. Maybe no one else cares at all.*

It was Dr. Bowder's idea for her to wait.

"You're too emotional now," he said. "And this Randy Stuart who has so captivated you is still a very sick man, my dear. Let it pass for the rest of the day. Make it tomorrow . . . in the morning."

The expression on her face told him a great deal.

"I know what you're thinking," he added. "How in the world are you ever going to wait? Isn't that it?"

As usual, he had spoken bluntly but with great accuracy.

Maggie nodded.

"The Lord will provide," Dr. Bowder said, smiling.

Fine for you to say, she thought somewhat irritably, thinking how easy it was for people like him to dispense ever-so-handy spiritual platitudes. Then she felt ashamed of herself, since Dr. Bowder had proven again and again to be a man of depth and sincerity.

"I'll manage," she replied in tight-lipped fashion.

"I know you well enough, Maggie. It'll be a rough few hours. You'll have to prepare yourself for that."

His face was intent as he spoke.

"Dr. Bowder, have you now taken on the role of my substitute father?" she asked with utter gentleness.

He winced a bit, but then his face settled into a half-smile.

"You could say that," he remarked.

Maggie was physically much better, virtually recovered in fact. But her emotions proved to be the problem.

That afternoon she returned to the cemetery where her parents and her sister were buried and spent more than an hour there.

It was difficult for Maggie to leave, for in doing precisely that she was once again acknowledging that she was alone, that she had to survive without her family by her side, without the strength they provided.

"What would you have thought of him?" she asked as she stood before those three fresh graves. "Roberta, you would never admit it, but you would have found Randy charming and wonderful, and you would have started dreaming about him, dreams that would have made you blush if you'd ever told anybody about them."

Speak for yourself, Maggie scolded herself, *don't try to put your own words in Roberta's mouth when your sister's no longer around to defend herself.*

She turned toward the other two plots.

I wonder if you would ever have approved, she mused while being convinced of the answer. *I think you might have taken one look at his reputation and then told me that I shouldn't even be near the man, let alone fall in love with him and wish I could spend the rest of my life in his arms.*

Fall in love with him . . .

Maggie had never quite admitted that to herself before then.

She might have harbored feelings of that sort toward Randy, but she simply had not been willing or able to recognize them as such, because that would have meant taking a step, a rather large step in her life, and she had little confidence she was ready for that.

Oh, Lord, I have to admit my weakness. I have to admit that I'm scared, scared over what has already happened, and now over what might be right around the corner . . .

Randy.

Even the mere thought of his name, with Randy himself miles away in a hospital bed, even that made her face flush and her pulse quicken.

Yet how could she consider giving over everything of a personal nature in her private world to anyone right now, particularly to a man who was little more than a stranger in her life?

And now the thought of marriage had even settled in, surrounded by a mountain of misgivings. She wondered if she had what it took to be anyone's proper wife.

Wife.

Mrs. Whoever . . .

"Foolishness," she said, suddenly dismissing the very idea at this stage in her life, what with the turmoil of the past few weeks and all the uncertainties that seemed to be blocking her way. "I'm not about to get married to someone like Randy Stuart!"

"They tell me you want to head west," Randy was saying as he sat in a wheelchair on the lawn outside the hospital. "I've been there, you know. Can I tell you anything about the frontier?"

Maggie nearly laughed out loud at such an understatement.

"Yes, that happens to be one of my dreams," she replied as she sat on a stone bench in front of him.

"Why haven't you done it? I mean, why haven't you gone ahead and grabbed hold of that dream, Maggie, and made it a reality?"

It was a very direct question about something very private, and she was struggling to give Randy a proper response.

"I . . . I couldn't," she said lamely, wishing her tongue had not chosen that moment to become tied up in knots.

"Why not?"

"Because . . . because it would be—"

"Disloyal to your parents?"

She did not acknowledge at first that he was quite right, marveling at how expertly he had gotten into her mind after so short a time, pulling out thoughts that made her notably uncomfortable.

Her silence concerned him.

"Forgive me if I got too close there, Maggie," he said, looking at her intently. "Impudence does seem to be one of my many rather serious and unbecoming traits."

"It's all right," she told him.

That was the first time he had called her Maggie. Before it had been Miss Engebretsen. But not Maggie.

"You used my name finally," she pointed out. "You've not done that until now."

Randy smiled as he replied, "We've been through the Valley of the Shadow together. I figured it was time. Have I offended you?"

She shook her head.

"You haven't," she remarked.

Maggie meant that, truly.

The past few days had involved moments of warm and tender intimacy. She had been both nurse and friend to him, rarely leaving his side. Still with little strength of his own, he had to lean against her to keep from falling.

There is little between us that could be offensive now, she thought honestly.

While Randy would remain quite weak for many days, the worst problems had passed, and getting out into the fresh air that day was a particularly momentous time for him.

"I took it for granted," he told her.

"Life, you mean?" she asked.

"Parts of it, I guess."

Occasionally Randy Stuart bordered on being a bit inarticulate, and Maggie had needed considerable patience as he had tried to explain himself to her. This time was no exception.

"The air, I think," he went on. "Breathing it in, enjoying the bracing feel of it against my lungs."

He reached out and clasped her hand.

"Having someone like you," he added.

"Me?"

"Yes, someone who . . . who—"

He pulled back, trapped by a host of thoughts that were proving awkward for him, odd thoughts for such a man to hold, thoughts almost impossible to express, particularly to a woman like Maggie.

But then the words came, like a tornado, tearing through

Randy Stuart and leaving more than a little emotional devastation in its wake.

"You had never met me before that night," he said. "And even now you probably don't realize who my parents were."

Maggie shook her head, admitting that she had no defensible reason to give the matter any thought.

"They were very wealthy," he continued. "They—"

"The Stuarts?" she exclaimed.

"Yes, the Stuarts. But don't let your eyes light up, Maggie. I have not been blessed with any of their money."

She knew he was teasing, so she took no offense at such words.

"They disowned me," he said. "They kicked me out. When they died, their fortune was willed to charity. I was left out in the cold, as the expression goes."

"But why? How could they do that to their own son?"

"Because I hated them. I despised what they had done to me."

To Maggie, he was not making much sense at that point. But she had to admit that she enjoyed the mere sound of his voice. So she chose to continue listening.

"Until I was well into my late teens, they dominated me," he went on. "They kept a strict leash on me."

"What were they afraid of?"

"I was the only child they had left. I suppose my parents could never have faced having anything happen to me."

Maggie was comparing what Randy was telling her with the childhood she herself had had, a fulfilling period of her life that she would always enjoy returning to in the privacy of her mind during quiet moments.

Not to have that foundation, she thought. *How devastating! When Randy recalls his own childhood, there's only—*

Bitterness.

"When other boys were going out, I had to stay home," he said. "They didn't want me to get involved."

"Ever?" Maggie asked impetuously.

"I began to suspect that they considered contact with other people, especially attractive girls, to be some awful kind of malady,

perhaps like scarlet fever or even cholera. It was certainly to be avoided, they thought."

"Your father felt that way?"

"I never knew what his feelings were about much of anything at all. My mother ran the show, Maggie."

They were quiet for a bit.

From where they sat they could see new patients being helped into the hospital, a large percentage of them apparently suffering the final stages of cholera.

"They wait so long," Maggie remarked. "It's as though they expect some great miracle from God, and then they give up and seek help from other mortals."

"You're a Christian, and you don't believe in miracles?"

"I do, yes, but when you're a nurse, you realize that a miracle is a miracle, that it doesn't happen very often, and that most people who contract cholera die. And the ones who survive, well, I don't know which ones do so from a miracle and which ones would have made it anyway. That's impossible to tell."

They looked at the sad parade for a few moments more, and then Randy spoke again. "When the epidemic started, I found myself hoping that I would contract the disease and die. I was convinced that this was the only way I could escape from how I had been living, if you can call it living."

He repeated those last six words.

"You may not be able to imagine what it was like, Maggie, sitting at home, listening to my father's many recitations, his opinions, often quite lame. He would talk on and on about any number of world events, like the War of 1812 or the growing antislavery movement in this country.

"It wouldn't have been bad at all if he knew or cared very much about any of this. These tirades were, however, simply snippets of knowledge that he used to impress people around him. His ideas never got below the surface, for that was the kind of man he was, all surface charm and no depth whatsoever."

He was trembling with repressed anger.

"Then too my grandfather had participated in the American

Revolution, and I constantly heard about all the battles he fought in, never knowing what was truth and what was empty bravado.

"At first, I'll admit, this was quite thrilling stuff, Maggie, but after years of it, after wishing I was outside, with other children my age, I began to hate every last word of anything my father happened to be saying."

. . . outside with other children my age.

She could see in his expression years of compressed longing with an overlay of bitterness.

"Finally, though, I had had enough. I ran away to . . . to . . . " he stuttered.

"To what, Randy?" she gently prodded.

He chuckled as he said, "You may not believe this, but I joined the circus."

Maggie started laughing.

"You're right," she admitted. "It is hard to believe."

"But true," he assured her.

"Tell me about it."

"It was small, really, a few animal acts, jugglers, clowns, that sort of ragtag collection."

Randy tilted his head back slightly, the memories strong, the sights, smells, and sounds still vivid in his mind.

Some of his circus friends were tragic figures, he remembered.

That little dwarf!

The tiny man had tried to appear happy to the circus people and to the audience members who paid to see his clown act, but those who knew him well saw the core of melancholy that seemed to dominate the very center of his being.

Randy went on to tell her about the variety of people he had come to know, a quite earthy group of gypsies, it seemed, men, women, and children who genuinely enjoyed the constant travel, abhorring the idea of putting down roots in a single location. Eventually, in his descriptions, he got around to mentioning the dwarf clown.

"I felt some kind of harmony with him," Randy admitted.

For Maggie, that was extremely difficult to comprehend.

Randy was the most handsome man she could imagine ever meeting, a man other men could envy, a man other women could dream of being with. She knew of a dozen men who would sell their souls if they could be remade to look like Randy.

"His name was Girulf," he went on. "In the original French, that meant wolf or spear, something sleek and powerful and fast. That seemed all the more cruel since Girulf was always quite chubby, which only emphasized his deformity. Girulf lived for the laughter of the crowd. He reveled in hearing them chortle over his pathetic antics."

"But they were laughing, really, at his condition," Maggie added. "Isn't that it, Randy? He was making fun of himself. And they were callously laughing at that poor man's misery."

Randy sighed as he told her, "That was what I decided, namely, that I was overwhelmed by the sadness he experienced. I wonder how many people even thought of him as a man. Were they looking at another human being or simply a pathetic freak who was making a fool of himself?"

He cleared his throat nervously and squeezed the bridge of his nose, perhaps to hold back tears, Maggie guessed, or maybe just to clear his thoughts.

She knew soon enough.

"But the circus people themselves were sincere and more genuinely caring, I think, than any people I had ever known," he recalled with some wistfulness. "Yes, I admit that they were a rather vulgar bunch at best, but I always knew where I stood with them every minute of every day. They were incapable of pretense."

His enthusiasm was becoming even more evident.

"Something else!" he exclaimed.

"Tell me," she said, still wanting to hear more of his voice.

His eyes seemed to glisten as he continued.

"They had no one fencing them in. Think of that, Maggie! These people could go anywhere they wanted. At one point, we even entertained settlements west of the Mississippi."

Maggie's eyes widened in an instant, and blood rushed to her cheeks. She could feel her body temperature rising.

"I knew that would get a reaction from you," Randy said mischievously.

"What was it like?" she asked, trying not to appear as excited as she actually felt at that moment.

His answer disappointed her.

"Not good, Maggie, not good at all. The settlers are often quite hungry. Out on the plains, it's cold enough in winter that many of them die of exposure despite their best efforts to keep warm. The Indians are always hovering—"

"So the Indians are as dangerous as the reports indicate?" Maggie interrupted impetuously, fascinated.

"They are; they are. Marauding bands sometimes come out of nowhere and wipe out entire settlements."

Maggie's heart started beating even faster.

"Does that discourage you?" Randy asked.

Not sure how she felt about that aspect of frontier life, she ignored this as she said, "The West Coast . . . did you ever make it all the way to the West Coast?"

"No, I didn't. But I can tell you it's true that you have to go through an earth-bound hell to make it to the Pacific, Maggie, and I didn't get that far. The conditions were far too rough for me, frankly."

"All of it was like that?"

"No . . ."

Randy's normally strong voice grew softer, lower, until he was speaking in not much more than a whisper.

"I admit that there are also some beautiful places out West, Maggie, very beautiful places that take your breath away."

"Tell me about them!"

He seemed to be growing tired.

"Not now," he said. "Maybe later."

And she knew that that was the end of it for the day.

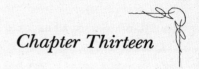

Chapter Thirteen

It turned out that Randy had one relapse of startling consequence, so strong that he seemed to be close to dying again but, in
the end, he survived.

Cholera was like that, haunting survivors with the possibility of
recurrence for days, weeks, or even months. Fortunately, Randy's
second bout was over rather quickly, but its severity was perhaps
worse than the earlier episode, deep and dark and awful.

Maggie was with him during that entire twenty-four-hour period, though Dr. Bowder not unexpectedly protested, telling her she
had simply been lucky the first time around.

"Lucky, Sir?" she said. "Is that a word any Christians should ever
fall into using?"

"I accept the correction," he went on, "but I must point out that
being a Christian doesn't guarantee any of us unlimited freedom
from suffering. Most of the apostles who stood with Christ Himself
died painfully, as martyrs, but I am sure you know that!"

"I'm going to stay with him," she repeated.

Dr. Bowder was frowning.

"But will he stay with you, Dear?" he asked pointedly.

She was certain that Dr. Bowder was referring to Randy Stuart's
acknowledged reputation as a womanizer.

"I think it's going to be different with him from now on,"
Maggie replied. "I really do believe that."

"You deserve better," Dr. Bowder said in a sigh. "But if any
woman can make a better man of him, you're the one to do it."

After Maggie had left his office, Dr. Bowder opened the center
drawer of his desk and pulled out some sheets of paper.

On them were written statements from various women with

whom he had spoken over the past week. All had been talking about Randy Stuart; all had told him the same thing.

Dear Father God, he prayed after bowing his head, *she just doesn't know how much she will need You as time passes. Change her, Lord, or change that man. Amen.*

Dr. Bowder stood then and walked over to a full-length mirror on a closet door in his office, looking at his very large frame, not large with muscles, not well-developed and strong, but large with fat, layers of it, a body he wished he had the discipline to change but which had remained much like that for most of his adult life.

If only I were different, Maggie, he thought. *If only I looked less like this and a little more like Randy Stuart . . .*

Surviving what only a few cholera victims ever did, Randy Stuart was finally able to go home, though he would have to rest for a week or so, his rundown body needing that time to recuperate.

And he would still need sustained nursing care.

He will need help for the full time he spends recovering, Maggie told herself.

Maggie hurried to Dr. Bowder's office and volunteered to help.

At first there was resistance from the man.

"Do you think that is quite proper?" he asked as he sat at his desk, his large hands folded on top.

"Is it quite proper to leave Randy to fend for himself until he is completely well?" she retorted though without any real anger, for she was not ungrateful to learn of Dr. Bowder's continuing concern. "Without him, I would not be alive. He has earned my help if only for that reason."

"But there is another reason, is there not?" Dr. Bowder asked pointedly, his gaze so intent that she blushed a bit.

"You do answer my question, you know," he added, "without so much as opening your mouth."

Maggie tried to smile, to be as nonchalant as she could manage.

"You worry about Randy's intentions, don't you?" she asked.

"And your own."

Maggie turned away, trying to be angry at him, trying to pretend she shared none of his anxieties.

Dr. Bowder stood and walked around the desk to stand next to her as he put his hand on her shoulder.

"Maggie?" he said, dealing with his own uncertainties. "I . . . I care about you. I don't want you to be hurt."

She faced him again, tears flowing freely.

"I know that," she said, turning her back to Dr. Bowder. "But I happen to be alone now. I have no mother, no father, no sister. They've been ripped right out of my life. And you are saying that that leaves me with a choice? I can take a chance and pray that Randy is the one man with whom I should share the rest of my life. Or I can stay quite safe, can't I, and live with no one. Yes, and I can surely shrivel up and die that way."

Maggie's expression was one of pleading.

"Which is better?" she asked slowly, with great affection, now facing him. "To live in what amounts to certain despair, knowing that I shall always be alone? Or to trust the Lord and pray it is His will that I spend my days and nights with the man who protected me when I needed him so desperately?"

Dr. Bowder wanted very much to protest, to come forth with some reasoned argument about the course of action that Maggie had set for herself. But the look on her face silenced anything he might have said along those lines.

"This is the first time in weeks that I've seen you—" he started to say, instantly wishing that he hadn't.

"—anticipate happiness," she interrupted, putting her finger gently on his lips. "Isn't that it, Dr. Bowder?"

"Yes . . ." he admitted with some reluctance. "It is, Maggie. It truly is. Your eyes are sparkling; your voice is—"

He was now the one to turn away.

"If that man does anything to hurt you, if he . . ." Dr. Bowder mumbled, his voice trembling as it trailed off.

"If he does, you'll be there, I know," she told him, genuinely touched. "Look at me, please."

He did so.

"Will you be there in my joy also?" she asked.

"The wedding? Is that what you mean, Maggie?"

Her smile indicated that it was.

"And more," she added. "Our first child, a second perhaps . . . all of that. Will you be my friend throughout whatever lies ahead?"

"Oh, Maggie, I—" he tried to tell her how much he would hate letting go, but he had no right to do that, no claim whatever on her. So he finally added, "Yes, I will. You don't have to worry. I could never desert you. How could I ever do that, my dear?"

There was no doubt that Randy found it difficult to acknowledge that he would need to depend upon any woman, for they had been altogether disposable components of his life for so long that falling into that pattern of behavior with Maggie would have been routine for him.

At first, after he had fully recovered, that was precisely what he intended to do, whether he admitted this to himself or not—use her in every way he could and then leave.

After all, Maggie Engebretsen had served an immediate purpose, and eventually she would have to go, just as the others had!

It was an awkward moment for him . . . thinking he didn't need her anymore but having feelings for her that he knew he could not easily ignore. He had become a victim of the promiscuous lifestyle into which he had fallen. All the other women had been trophies of a sort, put on some mental shelf and ultimately forgotten. And yet here was someone who had cared for him, bathed him, fed him when he could not feed himself, and now knew him more intimately than any of those other women who had shared his bed.

Maggie, he thought, *you are making this so difficult without ever knowing what you have been doing to me.*

He told her he wanted to talk with her, and asked if she would be willing to take a walk with him. But she had just finished cooking dinner and was concerned that the stew not grow cold.

"You don't like it at all when it's cold," she reminded him.

"It'll be fine," Randy said, smiling with a cheerfulness he didn't really feel.

She wiped her hands, and the two of them walked outside.

The surrounding countryside looked especially fine that time of year, the leaves of a thousand trees blazing with the colors of fall.

"So clean, so pure," Randy said as he stood and looked at the familiar sights. "I've seen all this for a long time, and yet it overwhelms me each year, as though I am seeing it for the first time. That doesn't make any sense, does it, Maggie? Be honest, now!"

"I can understand what you mean," she replied, her chest strangely tight as she sensed something in Randy's manner, something about which she prayed she was going to be wrong. "The air is laced with a hint of winter and—"

She turned suddenly, interrupted herself, and asked, "You're not becoming ill again, are you, Randy?"

He shook his head, and she felt immediately relieved.

"Thank God!" she said.

"Maggie?"

"Yes . . ."

"I'm not much of a Christian, you know. I've been to church as an adult fewer times than I can count on the fingers of one hand."

"The Lord can change—"

"No, Maggie, that's not going to happen to me. I've done too much that you would call sinful. I've—"

He stopped, saw the totally faithful, trusting, and by now familiar expression on that soft, thin face of hers.

"You make it so tough to . . . to—" he started to say, but the words stuck somewhere between his vocal chords and his lips.

"Tough, Randy?" she asked. "Tough for what?"

Maggie had no idea what was coming, but she sensed it would be painful.

She had grown so fond of Randy Stuart. She had dreamt so much about this one man. She had secretly spent many hours planning a lifetime between the two of them and, therefore, anything that caused him some distress caused her distress too. Yet now she could not help him because she did not know what was bothering him.

"Is it talking about Jesus as we sometimes do? Does that disturb you?" she probed. "I can't stop that, Randy. He's my Savior and—"

"—you want Him to be my Savior as well!" he blurted out. "But that's not the whole problem, Maggie. Actually it has very little to do with the way I feel now. If you were not a Christian at all, I would still want to . . . to—"

He saw that expression, now so obviously troubled, now anguished because of him and yet still submerged in the sweetest trust he had ever known.

She thinks I will do nothing to hurt her deliberately, Randy told himself. *How little this beautiful young woman knows about the way I am, the way I act sometimes beyond my control.*

"I really think you and I should stop—" he said, making a genuine attempt to force the words out one by one.

I can't, he thought. *I can't do it. Anything I would say would destroy her. How can I do that? How can I harm this beautiful—?*

Maggie indeed was that, five feet six inches tall, shimmering red hair, sparkling blue eyes set in a thin but not bony face.

He reached out and ran a finger gently over her lips.

"I think I love you," he said, surprising even himself by uttering words he had not intended minutes earlier. In fact, he was saying altogether the opposite thing of what he had planned, and yet saying the words seemed so natural, so right for that moment. The other words, the words of rejection, of turning his back on her, were strangely pushed aside, discarded at least for the moment as he gave in to the passion that he suddenly felt for her.

"I want you with me," he said, ready to kiss her.

Maggie blushed.

"And I want you," she said.

"Now," he said, "let's go back inside—"

"I've wanted to tell you that I love you, Randy," Maggie interrupted him. "I guess I also tried to pretend that I didn't feel that way at all. I tried so very hard to deny any such feelings that I might have had for you."

"Because you had no interest in ending up like all the others," he offered, resigned to what he considered the obvious response.

"Yes, yes, that was it, I think," Maggie admitted. "I'm naive in a great many ways, I suspect. I mean, you could use me; yes, you really could fool me all the way, and if you tossed me aside, I—I don't know what I would do, Randy. After Mama and Papa and my sister, I don't think I could bear losing someone else who really mattered to me. I just couldn't."

"But you aren't afraid to tell me now," he pointed out.

"Because it seems right. It seems now that I must, Randy. Aren't you here to tell me too? Isn't that what you wanted to talk to me about?"

He turned away from her.

She's making it so hard to say. She's—

Maggie touched him on the shoulder.

"Is that what you wanted to tell me?" she asked. "Turn around, Randy. Go ahead and tell me straightaway."

He faced her again.

"Maggie, I think we . . . we should—" he stuttered.

Then he reached out and took her hand in his own and added, "Maggie, I want to be your husband."

The words seemed to sweep through every inch of Maggie's young body, tingling nerve ends in a way she knew was possible but had never experienced until then.

"And I want to be your wife," she said

Despite the skepticism of Dr. Bowder and quite a few others, especially those who had known Randy Stuart far longer than she had, Maggie Engebretsen found that she was happy with the man, that she completely trusted him in everything though she knew she would have to be patient because the jam-packed emotional baggage from his past was more substantial than she had suspected.

It seemed apparent to Maggie that Randy was dealing with

invisible phantoms, phantoms that had haunted him since he was quite young, making a mockery of his childhood years. He had decided a long time before to avoid dealing with them, to simply pretend they had never occurred.

But Maggie helped him. Oh, how she helped him day after day without ever feeling put-upon. Instead she was happy that she could contribute to the life of another human being, which was exactly the reason why she had become a nurse in the first place.

I care what happens to him, she told herself, *and I care because . . . because I love him, though maybe I shouldn't.*

With Maggie by his side, Randy gained new strength and a surprising new desire to banish those phantoms. And in doing so, he knew a commitment was being forged with her that had every chance of lasting a lifetime.

They became husband and wife, married in a fine old church located near Independence Hall in Philadelphia. Every detail of the ceremony and the reception that followed were planned with the help of Dr. Bowder and Maggie's other hospital friends as well as neighbors elsewhere in the community.

"We probably won't have very many guests, despite all the invitations," Dr. Bowder warned Maggie. "These are such awful times, and everyone seems to be staying home, away from large crowds."

"That makes sense," Maggie said in agreement.

But both were wrong.

The attendance was massive.

Uninvited women who had "known" Randy came to the wedding out of skepticism and curiosity, ready to gossip behind his muscular back and Maggie's veiled head, but they ended up doing little of that, quietly exclaiming instead that they could see a difference in Randy that seemed to be genuine, not just a performance.

At the reception, held on the estate of a family whose members all had miraculously survived the cholera epidemic, one of those women approached Maggie and Randy. She was probably quite young, but the sort of life she was leading had robbed her features of any appearance of youth, substituting instead dark circles and a troubled look in her eyes, eyes that seemed incapable of looking directly at them.

"I envy you," she said to Maggie. "I envy you so much that I can taste it. I loved this man; I loved him more than anyone I have ever known."

She bit her lower lip nervously.

"But I was never the woman who could help him," she said softly, with regret underlining every word. "And now I have no one. I am so very lonely."

She looked at Maggie.

"Treat him well," she said. "Be patient. Love him with all your heart. If you do, if you break down those barriers he has built up over the years, he could become the greatest lover, the finest friend, any woman has ever known."

Maggie gasped at her boldness as she turned and walked away.

Surprisingly, though it was relatively close, Maggie and her family had never been to the New Jersey shore.

"I am landlocked," she told a friend a couple of years before the cholera hit. "I am eager to see the Pacific Ocean nearly 3,000 miles away, and yet I've never been to the edge of the Atlantic Ocean just 60 miles away!"

She puzzled over why that was the case and came to the conclusion that she was stuck in the midst of a tyranny of responsibilities that kept her where she was.

"No matter . . ." she would say when questioned about this, but it was becoming more of an issue to her than she seemed willing to admit.

Thus, their honeymoon was spent on the South Jersey oceanfront.

Randy was not ignorant of the fact that Maggie had been raised in a strictly moral family environment.

His own caprices made him directly the opposite of her, for he had lost his own virginity at the age of fourteen, and almost from that day on, Randy Stuart must surely have been one of the most sexually active males in the entire state of Pennsylvania, at least that was how his reputation painted him.

A search . . .

For Randy, sexual conquest had been a search, and ironically before he had even kissed Maggie, he had found the woman he really needed, had found the many answers he had searched so desperately for during the past ten years. Everyone who knew her, including Dr. Bowder, came to her over the next few years and remarked about her astonishing ability to tame this wild man.

But on their honeymoon there was still enough wildness about him that made their first night together one that exceeded anything either of them had dared to dream about.

Later, as they rested side by side in the darkness, Maggie could not speak for a while, overcome with the amazement of it all. She reached out across the narrow space, closed her hand around his own, and wondered if life could ever be better for her than at that moment, in that bed, beside a man, a husband, such as Randy Stuart.

Gradually, over the course of the next year, Maggie shared with Randy her desire to leave Philadelphia and journey to the western frontier. Since he already had been west of the Mississippi River, he tried repeatedly to warn her that the real conditions made the romantic visions painted by fiction writers seem rather empty-headed and utterly false. But she was not to be persuaded to give up this dream of many years. Eventually, instead of turning Maggie around and away from it, Randy himself became infected by her enthusiasm. And since he wanted to please Maggie as much as he could, he gave in and said that they would go, that he would give up the cabinet-making business he had started and they would sell the restaurant Maggie's parents had started. The two of them planned to liquidate everything but Maggie's heirlooms and mementos and use the money to buy the best and biggest covered wagon they could find. Then they would start out for the frontier that had proven so alluring to Maggie for so long.

Dr. Bowder and others tried to persuade them to change their minds, but they would not ignore Maggie's dream any longer . . .

Five years later . . .

Even among the staid environs of Philadelphia, the two of them were finally being accepted as an authentic and happily married couple, despite Randy's earlier reputation.

Even Dr. Bowder seemed to have changed his opinion.

"He is a very good man," the doctor told Maggie one morning. "I think we all were extraordinarily wrong about him."

So they had become a part of the community in a real way and were happier than they would have ever thought possible.

But now it was nearly time for them to begin the journey westward, to leave behind the only life Maggie Engebretsen Stuart had ever known.

"So many times you and I started to plan this, my darling," she reminisced one evening, "only to be distracted by something else."

How true that was. More than once they had delayed or canceled their odyssey because of a reluctance to leave the security of a community in which they had become deeply involved.

But the lure of the frontier was undeniable.

"People out West call it the song of sirens," Randy had told her. "Riversong is the name they use for it, the call of the West."

"Riversong . . ." Maggie had answered pensively. "Mama told me about Riversong. It has to do with Big River, doesn't it?"

"The Mississippi," Randy replied. "It has an almost mystical image among those who feel its pull. For the pioneers moving westward, crossing the Mississippi represents a change, maybe you could call it a rebirth, a chance to start over again in a new land. The idea of crossing the Big River takes hold of some folks and won't let go. It changes them, Riversong does, because normal folks would never brave the perilous Mississippi unless they were willing to risk up everything they had to build a whole new world for themselves somewhere on the other side."

"Maybe that's what's happened to me," Maggie said in that same pensive tone. "Maybe it's been Riversong that's kept alive my dream of going west."

Riversong . . .

A beguiling force that caught one's longing and held it captive like a hypnotist's pendulum swinging endlessly in the mind, its fascinating appeal too strong for many adventurous travelers to resist.

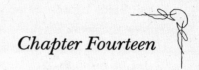

Chapter Fourteen

Maggie had expected Randy to steer clear of the cemetery where his parents were buried and take an altogether different route out of Philadelphia.

Not so.

He chose the road that went directly by the church.

As they approached, she thought he would hesitate only for an instant, wanting to stop but going on quickly anyway. But she was surprised.

Randy pulled back on the reins and stopped the horses just in front of the cemetery's ornate iron gate.

He paused for a few seconds, and she could see that he was undergoing a real struggle within himself.

"I don't know, Maggie," Randy said, his voice calm despite the emotions that registered on his face. "It's so morbid. I should just walk away and not turn back at all.

"I shouldn't be doing this. It's not the right thing. They're not there anyway. I know that, Maggie, I have always known that. What good will it do for me to stand before two impersonal granite markers?"

"It's not morbid, Randy," she replied. "It's a cleansing you need to go through. You cannot merely walk away from what this means to you. You have to go through with it, Beloved, purge yourself at last of the awful hurt and anger you've held on to so long."

"I've been emotionally gutted for a lot of years. I need to get away, not go back now. Don't you see that?"

"You need to confront their hold over you. Nothing is more important than that. Otherwise you will carry the burden for the rest of your life," she answered.

"Their hold? I gave that up years ago, Maggie. Where in the world have you been?"

He cringed at the sharpness in his voice.

"Sorry. It's just that—"

"As long as you think about your parents the way you do, as long as you wake up in the middle of the night, your whole body trembling, they do still affect you, Randy. You have to be willing to acknowledge that. Anything else is wrong, plain wrong."

He smiled as he said, "What a mess your husband is."

"We're rebuilding, aren't we?" she said. "We two are rebuilding everything in our lives, aren't we? Stone by stone."

"God help us!" he blurted.

She leaned forward, putting her arms around him.

"I feel so weak," he said. "I feel so—"

Though they had shared just about everything since their marriage began, Randy knew that there continued to be dark corners in his own life about which Maggie had no hint whatsoever, and he dreaded having to tell her any more than she knew already.

"You do have strength," she reminded him. "You have the strength that is promised in the Scriptures."

Randy looked at her solemnly, an expression she would not know the truth of until many years later.

"If only . . ." he started to say.

"Yes, my love?" she asked.

"Nothing," he said. "I'll go in there, Maggie. I'll do the best I can. I have to make the break, and I have to do it now."

He climbed down out of the wagon and headed for the gate. As he swung it open, he turned and looked back at her.

"I love you," she told him. "You take my love with you . . . remember that."

He nodded.

The gate creaked shut behind him.

Randy stood before the two tombstones.

How can I love you both so much and yet hate you all at the same time? Randy thought. *How can that be?*

Tears ran down his cheeks.

You destroyed the years that mattered the most.

His face twisted in a momentary expression of rage.

You took them from me and laid them as waste at my feet!

And as a result he had tried to enjoy a certain kind of revenge by sleeping with every woman who would have him!

Randy fell to his knees and then onto his face. He started pounding the ground with a reaction bordering on hysteria.

There was in his mind just then a transient memory, a memory of one afternoon when he was ten years old and was standing on the front porch of their home, looking at a group of boys gathering to play a roughhouse game in a nearby field.

"Hey, c'mon!" Archie Fairbanks had called to him. "Join us. It'll be fun, Randy. C'mon!"

He had smiled, trying to make the best of it.

"Can't," he said. "Got chores."

Archie wrinkled up his nose and said, "Maybe next time."

"Yeah, thanks . . . next time."

There weren't any "next times."

"They're a rough and profane group," his mother had told him. "You don't want to get involved with them, son."

"They don't seem so bad," he tried to point out to her.

"But you're a Protestant," she said. "That Archie is a Catholic. You can't have anything to do with that kind of boy. You need some real Christian companions, son."

His hands were hurting now, hurting badly, and he stopped slamming them against the hard ground but remained there, flat on his face between the two graves, sobbing out the anguish he was feeling.

Several minutes passed.

Maggie's waiting outside this place . . . and I've got a new life with her, with my beloved. I'm going to be free of you at last. I—

Those words tore him apart emotionally, ripping through his mind.

"I don't want to hate you any longer," he said aloud. "I don't want to leave you here, so cold, so alone, buried in my hatred."

A hand touched his shoulder. He looked up, startled.

Maggie.

"Please," he begged, "please, I didn't want you to see me like this. It's not right that you see me like this."

"Hate them or love them, Randy, but leave them here," she said. "Don't take them with you, because if you do they'll always control your life."

He got to his feet.

Randy was convinced that he should have been ashamed of that moment, ashamed that a woman had had to come to him and attempt to give him some semblance of strength, instead of the other way around. He was ashamed that he, a man, was too weak without her.

Yet there was something about the way she said what she did that took away that shame as though it had never existed.

. . . as though it had never existed.

He went over those few but crucial words in his mind. It was time, he knew, to get all the poison out, the shame and the bitterness and whatever else.

"I've wanted to come here and dig up their bodies and spit in what was left of their faces for what they did to me," Randy told her. "But, of course, I didn't, for I always came around to realizing how awful it was to think of doing anything like that.

"They died so helpless, Maggie. They wasted away until they weighed no more than seventy or eighty pounds. Two vibrant people had become mere skeletons with just some old skin stretched over the bones."

He hoped she was understanding him, hoped she sensed how deep into himself he was digging.

"How can I hate that?" he said. "I should pity them, Maggie. It would be good even if I felt nothing, if I could think of them without any emotion at all. But it just isn't possible."

He touched her cheek.

"You need to be proud of me," Randy remarked. "You need to feel that you can depend on me, that I—"

It was then that she smiled, this woman whose love he desperately needed but of which he had felt so unworthy.

She smiled with great warmth, her eyes sparkling.

"I do depend on you, my love," she acknowledged happily. "Without you, I might not have been able to go on, you know. I wouldn't have taken my own life, at least not by a knife or by poison or whatever. I couldn't have done that, of course but, I am sure, I would have retreated into a corner somewhere and just stayed there, permanently locking out the rest of the world.

"I would have died of that, dear, dear Randy. I would have died of all the loneliness, of a ghastly emptiness, of thinking only of the dead, of seeing my mother, my father, my sister in their coffins, their bodies so very cold, oh, how cold, drained of life. How could that be? How could I survive? How could I ever want to go on? How could I?"

She pointed toward the opposite end of the cemetery.

"Their bodies are buried in the church cemetery back in the city," she reminded him, "left behind like old baggage that is worn out, useless, no longer able to hold anything. But my parents themselves are no longer anywhere near Philadelphia.

"Nor is dear Roberta, my sister, my friend. They're gone, the three of them. It may be fifty years before we are reunited, but that is going to happen. The separation's only temporary—"

She stopped, that thought hitting her again with great force.

Half a century, maybe, before I see again the three loved ones who once were so much a part of my life. It will be so long, so long before . . . before—

"Hold me, Randy," she said. "Please hold me."

He put his arms around her.

They stayed like that for quite a while, pressed tightly against one another, each with the same pain.

And each needing one another, desperately needing one another.

"We become part of one another's lives, and we think, oh, how we fervently hope as human beings, that it will go on forever, these relationships we have," Maggie whispered. "And thus, we do absolutely nothing to prepare ourselves for being wrenched apart, except maybe involuntarily, dreaming nightmares over which we have no control. I remember that I had dreams, almost like premonitions. I found myself—"

"—going into a big house and hearing familiar voices but seeing no one," Randy said, "and smelling familiar odors, but there is nobody around and—"

Blessed assurance, Jesus is mine . . .

Where were those words coming from?

Not from the church before them, surely not an empty old church during the middle of a typical week.

But where—?

Maggie's eyes widened as she went on. "In the dream there is nobody around, and all I can do is just stand there, feeling quite trapped, it seems, the house wrapped around me like a very large coffin. And I start to—"

"—scream until I am awake," Randy added, his face filled with emotion. "And when I awaken there is blood on my pillow, and I realize that—"

They looked at one another and embraced again.

"—part of it hasn't been a dream," Maggie said, "and you really have been screaming. How wonderful, you say at that point, that most of it is only a dream."

"Until it really happens," Randy added, "which means that it is no longer a dream at all, and I have to face everything I dreaded."

"But not alone, neither of us has to face it alone again," Maggie told him, joy filling her in a wondrous rush. "In that fact there is some little bit of hope, and it is that hope which will sustain us, my love."

He didn't answer but continued holding her, enjoying her encompassing warmth as she pressed against his body.

They left in a short while.

But just before the gate swung shut behind them for the last time, Randy saw a little clump of flowers off to one side.

"I never gave them anything like that before now," he said, his voice cracking a bit. "I wasn't allowed to attend the funeral. I stayed away from

this place because they had rejected me in the end, and I wasn't about to show them any—"

"Take them the flowers, Randy," Maggie urged him. "Take them, my love."

She smiled warmly.

"It will be all right this time. No one will stop you."

He nodded, his cheeks quite wet by then.

"Yes, yes, it will. I see that," he agreed, wanting very much to believe that she was correct but scared that she might be wrong.

He reached down and picked a few blossoms, breaking each stem at its base, and turned back into the cemetery.

Part Three
The Westward Journey...

It is only in adventure that some people suc-ceed in knowing themselves—in finding themselves.

Andre Gide

From a home with more than 2,000 square feet of space and all the conveniences available at the time . . . to end up as she did was quite a shock to Maggie. She thought she had prepared herself for any possibility.

She had no doubt what she wanted to do with her life and no doubt about the man with whom she wanted to spend it. And yet the shock of what she was doing hit her a few miles after they had left Pennsylvania behind.

"Are you all right?" Randy asked, knowing her well enough to be able to tell when something was bothering her. He sensed something had changed her spirits in the days it took them to leave behind the state where she had been born and would probably never see again.

He slowed the horses then stopped them altogether; turning to her, he looked deep into her blue eyes.

"If you want to go back, I won't object," he told her without hesitation.

How easily I betray my feelings to this man, Maggie thought with a smile of appreciation. Here I am, trying to keep everything inside me so he'll never guess, and he knows anyway.

She shook her head, hoping he would drop the matter, but he didn't.

"I'm serious," he went on. "Your happiness is all that matters to me."

She reached out with two fingers and pressed them to his lips.

"There is nothing there for me now," she said. "Oh, I know some people, yes; I do know a great many people there. But the only one who matters to me now is you. My home today is anywhere you and I go from now on."

He hugged her tightly to him.

"I feel your heart beating against my chest, Maggie," he said.

"I feel yours, my love," she assured him.

"Let's not move for a little while. Let's just stay like this."

She had no interest in moving, either, for it seemed that her heart and his were literally beating together, during this single, glorious moment that, out of all that had ensued over their past and all that surely was in store for them, would be remembered. Later, she would treasure this brief moment.

After a bit, they broke apart. Maggie closed her eyes, for a few seconds.

"Saying good-bye?" he asked with great tenderness.

"Yes . . . a final good-bye."

"So did I."

And they went on from there . . .

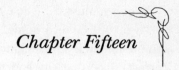

Chapter Fifteen

The two of them pushed through Ohio next and found the people more hospitable than could have been imagined, too much so, they discovered.

And where they least expected it—in Ohio—they encountered a white man and his two black slaves, who redefined their Yankee-bred thinking about an issue that would spark, in less than a decade, the devastating American Civil War.

The two black men were Josiah and William.

They were owned by James McAteer, a Scottish settler who had lived in the state since shortly after the War of 1812.

One of the wagon's wheels had become loose near the entrance to McAteer's property. Josiah had been in the front gate, applying fresh paint after finishing some repair on its hinges. Noticing them stopped on the road, he put down his paintbrush and walked over to Maggie and Randy.

"You all got trouble?" he asked. "Can I help?"

Still conditioned by what life had been like for them in Philadelphia, which meant no exposure to slavery except what they read in the local newspaper, they thanked the very large man and said his help would be appreciated.

With a wave of one arm, Randy indicated the house set back some distance from the gate, not a plantation-type residence certainly but still impressive with its brick front, two floors that seemed to suggest an interior with at least ten rooms, and a front lawn that was immaculately kept, dotted with rosebushes and other decorative plants.

"Your house is very fine," Randy told him.

Josiah laughed heartily.

"Not my house, Sir!" he exclaimed. "I do live there, though."

"Is it your family's home, then?" Randy asked, making an assumption that, in Philadelphia, probably would have proven quite correct, since that city had its share of wealthy individuals who would pass their holdings from generation to generation. Those such as Maggie's parents, however, while not blessed with endless financial reserves, nevertheless had done quite well, in part due to an enduring sense of frugality that occasionally frustrated both their daughters.

"No, Sir, it's not my family's," Josiah said succinctly.

"Oh . . ." Randy responded, deciding not to press the matter further.

Josiah helped him with the task of getting the wheel off the wagon so it could be repaired.

"Got a blacksmith's shop, kind of like that, you know, in a shed back of the house," he said rather proudly. "Why don't we take it there?"

Randy nodded as he inquired, "Can my wife, Maggie, come also?"

"Surely she can, Sir!" Josiah replied animatedly. "Surely your beautiful missus can come."

As the three of them were approaching the big house, another black man came running out from it.

"This is my son, William," Josiah said, introducing him proudly. "Some folks say we look like twin brothers. But it's not true. Ain't he just one big buck!"

Maggie and Randy were surprised by the use of the word *buck*. But not nearly as much as by what Josiah said next.

"I'm one proud boy!" Josiah remarked. "I wish, though, that his mother had lived to see how fine he turned out to be."

Their expressions must have spoken volumes, for Josiah and William nearly doubled up with laughter.

"You from back East, ain't you, Sir?" Josiah asked cheerfully after he had stopped laughing.

"We are," Randy acknowledged, looking and sounding more than a little bewildered.

"Well, out here, we don't care much about names and words, you know; we really don't. What I called myself just then don't always mean what you all must hear about where you come from. I call myself a darkie from time to time. But I don't appreciate *coon* or *nigger,* you know. The master ain't like that. He's a kind man."

The three adults chuckled as William ducked his head in embarrassment. Hearing the voice, another man, red-haired and bearded, appeared in the doorway, squinting slightly in the bright sunlight.

There could not have been a better moment for James McAteer to arrive on that little scene. He had heard the laughter all the way around the back of the house and decided to see what caused it.

"And this here's the master. Master James, these good people are the Stuarts," Josiah told him. "They come here all the way from Philadelphia, and their wagon wheel come loose. That's Mizz Maggie, and there's Mr. Randy."

McAteer was, if it could be imagined, even bigger than Josiah and William, and he had a winningly gregarious personality that put them all at ease.

And he was as observant as he was friendly.

"I think the three of us have stunned this couple," he said, enjoying the moment. "Will you get my whip, Josiah? I think that would fit their perceptions a little better than what we are doing right now."

"Whip, Sir?" Josiah repeated curiously, scratching the top of his head in puzzlement.

McAteer said nothing for a moment but smiled broadly.

Finally Josiah caught his meaning and started laughing again.

William, eager to enter the conversation, stepped forward and said, "We don't have no whip here. We never did have one. Master James has always been a good and kind man.

"Papa and I ain't perfect and, sometimes, he gots to punish us, but we knows we deserve it when he does that, and it's jus' fine with us. We need to be taught sometimes, we sure do."

Now it was Maggie and Randy's turn to laugh. And McAteer

and Josiah joined in heartily.

William looked curiously from one to the other, unaware of what he had said that made them react as they did.

Josiah put his hands on his son's shoulders.

"You were so serious!" he said. "And that was a real long speech you gave, son."

James McAteer seemed typical of the pre-Civil War spirit of the times.

In the 1840s and into the 1850s, with the emphasis in the United States on agriculture, including such products as cotton, farmers depended upon one another, particularly in times of drought or flooding or fire or even disease.

Whatever the catastrophe, neighbors helped neighbors. And most landowners treated the westward-heading pioneers the same as their neighbors.

After the wheel was fixed, McAteer invited Maggie and Randy to stay for dinner. Already tired of beef jerky and the other pre-served foods they had brought with them, they accepted eagerly, though they had one reason for hesitating.

"We did not pack any clothes for dining in such a beautiful home," Maggie acknowledged.

"That's not a problem," McAteer told them cheerfully. "You shall dress as you must, and the walls will say nary a word."

Maggie ended up putting on a colorful floral-print dress with a row of lace around the neck, which was not so bad after all, she decided. Randy, on the other hand, could find only a clean work shirt and trousers.

"We'll take him at his word," Maggie said, adjusting Randy's gal-luses. "At least we still have something clean to wear."

They had changed clothes in the back of the wagon, and when they climbed down and turned toward the McAteer house, they gasped at what they saw in the moonlit night.

The walkway to the front door was lined with large candles, each set on top of a thin wooden post stuck into the ground and enclosed with a glass chimney to protect it from the evening breezes.

Maggie and Randy were awed as they strode up that candlelit path, both by the thoughtful lighting and the scents of lilac and jasmine carried by gentle breezes.

When they reached the entrance, Randy knocked twice.

Josiah answered, opening the door for them and then gracefully stepping aside as they walked in.

"Those candles . . . you went to a great deal of trouble for us. That's so kind of you," Maggie said.

"The Bible says we're not to hide our light under a bushel," Josiah replied. "We ain't ever going to do that in this house."

McAteer was sitting at a long, dark, handmade table in the dining area. He stood as soon as they entered.

"I am honored to have you join us tonight," he said, smiling. "I am very fond of the way food is prepared in New Orleans and elsewhere throughout Louisiana. If you are not familiar with that kind of cooking, you are in for a special surprise tonight."

Neither of them had ever had the kind of meal that had been prepared that evening by these kind strangers.

Dinner began with *pain de mais,* which was Cajun-seasoned corn, as well as *pain de froment,* golden yeast rolls. Next came *salade de carotte, pomme, et raisin,* a delicious blend of raw carrots, apples, and raisins. The main course, McAteer explained, was *poisson frais roti avec une sauce rouge de viande de crabe,* in other words, baked fresh fish with red crab gravy.

The side dishes included *gombo fevi et tomates etouffes,* which was smothered okra and tomatoes, *cibleme douce avec muscade et vanille,* an unusual combination of sweet squash with nutmeg and vanilla, and *feves de black-eye avec bequine et tasso,* a hearty blend of black-eyed peas with bits of slab bacon and tasso along with chopped onions, green bell peppers, celery, garlic, and fiery cayenne peppers.

Maggie and Randy ate with such gusto that it must have appeared to McAteer that they had been starving for a very long time.

After all of that, they had a choice of three dishes, but McAteer persuaded them to try a little of each: *tit gateaux de creme de fromage et pacanes grillees,* which was cream-cheese-and-roasted-pecan cookies, *creme a la glaace de merise* (homemade cherry ice cream), and *tarts aux mures d'eronce fraiches a pate douce,* which turned out to be a delicious peach sweet-dough pie.

Apart from the food itself, the other revelation was that both Josiah and William were allowed to sit at the table and eat with them, though they had to get up now and then to serve the meal and clear the table.

"You seem somewhat taken aback," McAteer observed when Josiah and William had left the room to fetch more coffee and bring dessert.

Randy's face reddened.

"I am sorry my feelings were so obvious," he said, feeling quite awkward about the whole matter.

"I suppose I should not be surprised that you are so surprised," McAteer observed. "Philadelphia can hardly be called a bastion of enlightened thinking about the slave-master relationship."

Randy tried his best to let that remark pass but found his determination was falling short.

"What do you mean by 'enlightened,'?" he asked pointedly. "Is it only this need to understand why you can own other human beings? Does that reaffirm your own worth in a way that would not be possible otherwise?"

"It is not much different than your owning Maggie here!" McAteer retorted. "At least Josiah and William retain their own names. Maggie had to take yours as part of the union."

"But that's the way it's supposed to be," Randy replied inanely. "Besides, you can't say that I own—"

"And what those two men have here is not what is supposed to be, could that be what you are saying?" the other man interrupted.

William had walked back into the dining room just then while his father was still in the kitchen.

"May I speak, Sir?" he asked.

"You may certainly do that," McAteer told him.

William was smiling as he spoke.

"I had a friend named Micah," he said.

"Sit down, William," McAteer remarked, pointing to William's chair at the table.

William did so.

Any noise in the kitchen—pans banging, cabinet doors being shut, footsteps across the floor—had ceased.

"I once had a friend named Micah," William started again. And then he launched into a tale about a black man, a freed slave living back East.

Micah was poor, able to get odd jobs periodically, but he never seemed to earn enough money to feed himself or his family regularly or to house them anywhere but in a miserable, rotting shack.

"He was picked up for loi—loi—" William struggled with that one word.

Without warning, McAteer reached across the table and took the other man's right hand between his own.

"Loitering, William," he said slowly, "the word is loitering."

William smiled with no sense of awkwardness.

"My friend Micah was picked up for loitering," he continued, "but there were white people in the same place who were left alone and not arrested."

"Where was this?" Randy asked.

"I think in New Jersey, or maybe it was New York," William replied. "Micah, he . . . he was put in jail. While he was there, some folks broke into the little home he was living in with his wife and his children. All of them was killed!"

McAteer broke in.

"Even when he was alive, Micah lived a nightmare, my friend," he said, staring straight at Randy. "He and his family were hungry all the time."

He banged his fist down on the table.

"Things are far, far worse for black people back where you both came from than almost anywhere in the South. Yes, there are some poor souls, beaten by their owners, fed inadequately, and all that. But those are the exceptions. I know from my travels!"

"But they're still—" Randy started to tell him.

"Slaves?" McAteer exploded understandably. "That's what you

were going to say, isn't it? But I ask you this: Which is worse, freedom and starvation while watching your family slip away from you because you can't feed them, or so-called slavery with plenty of food in your stomach and a fine roof over your head?"

Josiah was now standing in the large doorway between the kitchen and the dining room.

McAteer noticed this and nodded for him to come in the rest of the way.

"Do you have something to say?" he asked.

"Yes, Master James," Josiah replied. "I wanted to tell this man that we wouldn't leave you even if we could do that. We don't know nothin' else, and if livin' free is like what those free black people like Micah have for themselves, then I jus' don't care to be free. Here, we're free to eat, to sleep, to play, to do whatever—"

"But in a shack somewhere out back, isn't that it?" Randy blurted out.

Josiah shook his head sadly.

"You got it wrong, Mister," he said. "My son and I have never lived in a shack. We've got a better place than that, and we eat good, real good—you can see that for yourself."

"Why don't you show him?" McAteer asked gently.

Both Josiah and William seemed excited about this prospect.

Maggie and Randy stood and followed the two men.

They turned into the vestibule and started up the winding staircase to the second floor, stopping at a pair of large double doors in the middle of the hallway.

"This is where Mr. McAteer sleeps, I suppose," Randy remarked. "Yes, that's all fine and good—"

Josiah shook his head again.

"No, Mister, this is where my son and I spend each and every night of our lives. We sure do," he said.

"But I can't believe—" Randy protested.

William swung open the doors.

The room was as finely furnished, as well kept up, as any room Maggie and Randy had ever seen: A very large four-poster bed with a cotton canopy over it. There were no rugs, as was typical in fine homes of those times, but the tongue-and-groove floor had been meticulously polished and was beautiful to see in its handcrafted elegance.

"We're responsible for it," William said proudly. "We polish it ourselves. Every few years, we take turns sanding it down, we do, and we put a nice fresh coat of lacquer on it and then keep it polished some more. Ain't no scratches that I can see. What about you, Papa?"

"None," Josiah replied, echoing his son's pride. "We need to be careful. This is property that Master James has entrusted to us, and neither of us would want to disappoint him."

"Because he would punish you?" Randy asked.

"The disappointment we'd feel is punishment enough," Josiah told him. "Sometimes, when we let the Lord down, He goes ahead and rebukes us, don't He? It's the same thing."

Maggie nodded.

"Well, it seems to me," Josiah continued, "that there is other times when He don't do anything of the kind. It seems, sure does, it seems that He's let us off that old hook and done nothin' to us, nothin' at all.

"But if we love the Lord, really love Him, that still small voice within us jus' keeps on after us, accusing and accusing and accusing us until we can't stand it no more, and we're driven to our knees and are askin' Him for forgiveness."

"You have to beg James McAteer for forgiveness?" Randy asked. "He makes you get on your knees?"

William stepped in this time.

"It ain't like that at all!" he said, some real anger showing in his expression and in the tone of his voice.

"We do it, not because he demands that we do it," he said. "We do it because, whatever it is we've done wrong, that jus' means we've let him down. Don't you see that? He don't threaten us with nothin'. We act the way we do because Master James has earned our love!"

Randy glanced about the room. In the freestanding closet, he could see a great many clean shirts and trousers.

"All yours?" he asked.

"Bought and paid for by Master James," Josiah replied.

On the wall were a number of sketches of people and places and animals such as horses and dogs.

"I drew them," William said, smiling. "Master James had someone make the frames so they could be hung up real nice like that."

There was a large bureau in the room as well as several chairs.

"So clean . . ." Maggie whispered.

"Not all black people are dirty," Josiah said good-naturedly.

"I didn't mean anything by that. I'm sorry," she apologized.

"No need to say anything else," he assured her. "We are slaves, and we are clean because we take pride in the way we live. We know free blacks who are livin' like pigs. We ain't never gonna be interested in being anything other than we are!"

"But you might be happy having your freedom," Randy tried to tell him.

Josiah held up his left arm, palm facing outward, a frown on his pitch-black forehead.

"Don't try to look at my boy and me as though you know what should make the two of us happy. We are happy because we have food to eat, clothes to wear, a big old bed to sleep in. We don't hate no one, and no one hates us.

"We have the Holy Ghost inside us. When we die in this world, we're gonna walk them golden streets with angels everywhere around us. What more is there? Mister, can you answer that for me?"

Randy walked up to Josiah, smiling, and hugged the man, then turned and did the same with William.

"You feel, then, that Mr. McAteer loves you as much as you love him?" he inquired.

"We do," Josiah said, "we surely do."

"I can see why," Randy acknowledged.

Chapter Sixteen

The next morning, Maggie and Randy said good-bye to James McAteer as well as to Josiah and William and continued on their journey toward the Mississippi, where the legend of Riversong cast its spell . . .

There was a point at which the lure of the Mississippi River seemed to wane, and they were tempted to put down roots before they ever reached its legendary shores.

Their plan had been to keep going for as long as they possibly could each day, then to sleep as much as they could at night. Then they would awaken each morning at first light and continue on toward Big River. Once they reached it, they both believed it might be possible to lessen the pace but not until then.

That had been the plan.

However, instead of forging westward day after day, Maggie and Randy found themselves stopping again and again, enticed by the natural hospitality of Christian families along the way.

After they had been given permission to unhitch the horses and camp on a farmer's property, they would invariably get into fellowship with the entire family, enjoying home-cooked meals again and again, singing hymns and folk songs together during the evenings, or just sharing conversation about their different lives and what the two of them might face during the weeks and months and years ahead.

Every so often they would stay inside a farmhouse instead of in the wagon, and Maggie had to admit it felt good to have a real roof over their heads rather than a simple canvas top.

Such times were pleasant, but they also drained some of Maggie and Randy's dedication to continue ahead.

It's so peaceful here; the people are so friendly and good, Randy thought at one point during a stay in western Ohio. *I wonder if we're doing the right thing by going any farther, to risk the dangers that surely will be awaiting us. Shouldn't we consider putting down some roots right here and raising a family nearer civilization?*

Then he would look at Maggie and want to talk with her about this notion but eventually think better of it and say nothing, knowing how determined she was to reach the western frontier.

Ironically, Maggie occasionally had the same idea in mind, but she did not want Randy to think her courage had deserted her. Along with it, she feared, would go his respect for her.

Eventually, though, the idea of stopping short of their original idea became so compelling to both of them that they did talk about it but decided that they still wanted to change everything in their lives, to make a complete break and not compromise their dream by staying in a region that was a little like what they had left and a little like what they were seeking.

With only that wagon as their home . . .

Ironically, as they traveled through Indiana and Illinois, their attitude toward the wagon changed drastically from simply considering it a somewhat ramshackle necessity for their travels to an altogether different view. In their new mind-set their feelings for the wagon bordered on affection; they started seeing the wagon as a home, a miniature version of what they had known back in Philadelphia.

A bedroom and a living room.

That was how they divided up the interior of the wagon, with their narrow bed against one side and a small bench on the other.

These two pieces left almost no room for anything else, and Maggie's ingenuity had been challenged as she had assumed the task of putting everything into place. Somehow she had managed to cram in a spinning wheel, two trunks, and a tiny bureau as well as a coal-oil lamp and a grandfather's clock.

In the process of deciding what to take, Maggie and Randy had vowed to be practical, bringing along only the most cherished small mementos of their lives in Philadelphia.

Only the bulky grandfather clock proved an exception; it had been handed down in Maggie's family for three generations, and neither of them felt that it would hurt to bring it along.

Tucked into one corner of the wagon, under one of the trunks, was a tiny wood-burning stove, which would prove the most essential item of all when they reached prairie country west of the Mississippi and started construction of their first frontier home.

With their whole world carried in that one creaking conveyance, they finally approached the Mississippi. Their sense of smell told them it was directly ahead long before they could see it.

Randy stopped the horses for a moment on a ridge overlooking the river bottom.

"There it is!" he declared.

To Maggie the scent was one of water and fish and mud and other mingled odors that spoke undeniably of Big River. And then something else entered her mind . . .

She suddenly remembered what Mama had told her long ago about the compelling force of Riversong.

A mystical call from invisible sirens.

Beckoning, tempting.

Drawing people to the banks of Big River.

And then destroying them in its treacherous waters.

Or if not there, then, later, Riversong somehow following after them, like marauding demons out to destroy . . .

"It is so . . . so . . . wide and strong and . . . deep," she said.

"Yes, it is all that," Randy agreed.

"It's what I've anticipated for so long, and yet . . . somehow, I don't feel ready for it. It's not what I expected—more ominous, somehow."

"There will be a great deal that you don't expect in the weeks and months to come," Randy told her. "I've seen it all before. I've tried to tell you as much as I could, but some details . . . oh, Maggie, we've cut anchor. We've got to face whatever is ahead, Dearest."

She stared at the far-off water, shimmering under the sun yet muddied as though stirred by a violent storm, then she looked up at Randy and smiled.

"The Lord enabled the Israelites to pass through the Red Sea," she reminded him, "so I suspect He'll help just the two of us now, even if He doesn't part the waters and allow us to go across on the riverbed itself!"

They camped nearly five days and nights at the river ford while Randy built a small raft, lashing together logs he cut from the nearby woods plus others from a pile that had been left by earlier travelers.

When the raft was completed, they used the horses to drag it into the water then rolled the wagon onto the raft. While Randy set the brake, chocked the wheels, and lashed the wagon securely to the little vessel, Maggie tacked a rubber sheet under and around the wagon's bed, hoping to keep her necessities dry. Inside the wagon, she had already tied down the bed, the bench, and the trunks as best she could. Only the grandfather clock was untethered. She had run out of rope and could only hope for the best.

Finally Randy eased the horses into the water, backed them into place in front of the raft, then looped long leather lines over their heads and around their necks, leaving nearly ten feet of distance between each horse and the raft. Satisfied, he stepped back, standing knee-deep in the muddy Mississippi, and said to Maggie, "Well, I guess we're ready."

She smiled brightly, hoping Randy couldn't see her nervousness, and settled pertly onto the raft, resting against one of the wagon wheels. Randy crawled onto the raft beside her and whistled to Joe and Tess.

"Head up, there, Joe! Gidd'up, Tess! Let's cross the Mississippi!"

The horses threw their heads and pawed at the water, sending droplets of water high into the air. They sensed danger—but also trusted their master. Slowly the long lines tightened as they lumbered into deeper water. And then they were all floating.

"Oh . . . Oh . . .we're . . . !" cried Maggie as she felt the water lift the raft and catch it in the current. Only the horses' heads were visible, and they weren't so much pulling the raft as they were swimming with it as it bobbed along in the quickening current.

"Look out! There's a log coming right at us!" Randy saw the tree trunk rolling rapidly through the water just as the raft reached the middle of the river. Suddenly a great wave of water washed over them as the log crashed against the raft, knocking the wagon loose from one of its tethers.

Inside the wagon bed, the old clock tore a hole in the canvas as it was rocked by the violent motion. It tumbled out of the tilted wagon, bounced on the edge of the raft, then slid into the swirling, menacing water. Assorted pots and dishes rattled through the hole and bumped onto the raft before following the clock into the river.

Involuntarily, Maggie reached out for the things falling out of the wagon, leaning over the water and sliding perilously close to the edge before Randy's strong arms grabbed her.

"O God, O God, O God, please save us!" she cried prayerfully.

They were at the mercy of the current now. Though the horses struggled mightily toward shore, the little raft's primary movement was downriver.

Suddenly an unseen force beneath them whirled the raft a-round, spinning it over the lines and jerking the horses backward. Snorting, their panic showed in their wide, terrified eyes and the frantic pawing of their hooves against the water's surface. Maggie thought then they would all perish. She was sure of it. And as if confirming her terror, another sudden surge of the vile, muddy water hit them, smashing against Maggie like a heavy rock and knocking her off the raft and into the mighty Mississippi.

For a moment, Randy froze. For him to leave the raft surely meant everything would be lost—the horses, the wagon, every-thing. But to lose Maggie was worse than losing everything, and she was not a swimmer.

He plunged into the water, fighting to swim across the current and catch her as she repeatedly rose and sank, terror distorting her face and stealing her voice.

She sputtered once as he grabbed her, but then he too started to sink, pulled down by her weight and the undertow.

Both Maggie and Randy could feel the life being torn from

them, sucked from their bodies by the overpowering force of the river.

Lord, I wanted to live with him for the rest of my days, she thought. *If it is Your will that we die together, then we also go into Your heavenly kingdom together, hand in hand. I can accept that if it be Your will, Lord.*

Maggie gave in to the pain that filled her oxygen-starved lungs, and the world went dark. That's what she would remember later, the darkness . . . and then the sound of shouting voices and a multitude of hands on her body, pulling her upward . . .

Randy regained consciousness before Maggie did.

But it was a slow process as he slipped in and out of the velvety darkness, once, twice, a third time.

Finally, it was over, and as his eyes opened painfully, Randy saw a man bending over him, a rather stately bearded man, exceptionally large of frame but not heavy in the same way as Morgan Bowder. He was wearing a wide-brimmed hat and the plain dark garb of someone from one of the religious groups that had settled among the farmlands of Pennsylvania.

"Rest for a bit, son," the man said. "You came mighty close to dying there in the Mississippi."

He smiled reassuringly.

"That river has claimed more lives than any of us could ever count. And it will surely get worse as the number of settlers increases."

The man inhaled, then exhaled portentously.

"It's an untamed river, that one, inhospitable and intemperate."

Riversong . . .

The beckoning of those invisible sirens.

Demons, whether real in this case or nothing more than the stuff of myth, demons that could bring to destruction any settlers not strong enough to resist . . .

Apparently in his half-conscious state Randy had been muttering about the curse, because his benefactor spoke of it right away.

"Riversong means nothing more than the fears of men and women," he said. "It taps into something dark within the human soul. More than a century ago, Riversong did not exist. But as lives were lost, it became a reality, passed from one settler to another, from one generation to the next."

"Maggie!" Randy blurted out. "Where—?"

"She's over with the womenfolk. They're waiting for us to join them."

"She's still unconscious?"

"Afraid so, but I think she'll be okay."

Randy struggled to his elbows.

"Who are you?" he asked.

"Name's Jeremiah Stockley," the man replied. "And yours?"

"Randy . . . Randy Stuart."

"Pleased to meet you, young fella," Stockley said jovially as he extended his thick, work-honed hand.

Randy reached out and shook it, but still feeling weak, he fell back against the thick goose-down comforter someone had placed him on a few hundred yards from shore.

"I've got to see Maggie," he gasped, desperation taking control of him. "Please, where is she?"

"Turn your head to the left, son," Stockley told him. "She's there and. . . . Look, she's beginning to stir."

"Praise—" Randy started to say then stopped.

"You were about to praise the Lord, weren't you?" Stockley commented. "You must be a Christian. You been to any of the meetings of that evangelist Charles Finney?"

Randy shook his head slowly.

"Your Maggie has?"

"I don't know . . ."

"He talks like that—'Praise the Lord! Praise the Lord!' Why did you stop yourself?"

"I'm not sure I believe. Maggie wants me to, but I'm just . . . not sure. Anyway . . . thanks, Mister. You . . . you saved our lives."

Stockley frowned.

"You were just given a second chance, son. You shouldn't thank us, my family and me. It's God who intervened in your life and your Maggie's."

A short while later, Randy was able to stand and walk over to Maggie.

Out of the corner of his eye, he could see what apparently were Stockley's own wagons and quite a gathering of men, women, and children watching him with curious, friendly looks on their faces.

Three women were kneeling around Maggie as she rested on a beautiful thick quilt.

Seeing her impossibly handsome husband approach, she smiled with relief that he seemed only shaken and was otherwise unharmed.

"We have some new friends," she said softly. "We owe these folk a great deal, Randy."

"Not us," one of the attending women pointed out.

"The Lord," Randy added for her, nodding and smiling in her direction.

"You are believers then!" another exclaimed happily.

"Yes . . ." Maggie said. Then she looked up at her husband. "Tell her, Randy."

"Sure, sure, me too," Randy Stuart remarked just a little too quickly, but no one seemed to notice.

After Maggie and Randy had regained more strength later in the day, Jeremiah Stockley took them to their own wagon, which he and the other men in the group had been able to salvage, along with the horses. They were stunned to see the wagon had not sustained much damage to its structure, except for the torn canvas top, which the women had already patched.

"But you might need that canvas for yourself later," Randy said, astonished at their willingness to share.

"Our supply was not depleted," Stockley told him. "Your need was by far the more immediate, friend."

"Only the things that were tied inside the wagon remained,"

Stockley said. "But we were able to retrieve some of the clothes we found floating in the water."

Inside the wagon, Maggie and Randy found unfamiliar shirts and dresses among the soggy pieces of their own.

"You have given us your own clothes!" Maggie exclaimed. "We cannot allow that. You will need every bit of them for yourselves."

"We planned for this," Stockley assured them.

"How do you mean?" Randy asked.

"We packed more than we could ever use. We view ourselves as following the Lord's command to make a new home west of the Mississippi and be His ministers along the way, helping fill the spiritual as well as the material needs of those we meet."

Maggie stood on her tiptoes, put her arms around Jeremiah Stockley's neck, and kissed him on the cheek.

"Thank you," she said. "Thank you so much."

Then she bent down, sighing, as she spotted a piece of the grandfather clock's wooden cabinet bobbing in the waves at the water's edge. She shivered a bit as she leaned down to retrieve the splintered board. "One of the last real links to my old life . . . "

She stood, feeling a bit forlorn for a moment. Tears welled up in her eyes as her mind filled with images of her family.

"Would you perhaps like to join our little wagon train?" asked Stockley. "It would be an honor to have you with us."

She glanced at Randy, and he at her.

The thought was an enticing one, to be sure.

Safety in numbers was an obvious justification, and the group's companionship seemed more than a little appealing.

But being with other people, even those as nice as this group, however fine it was in moments such as they were experiencing, nevertheless went against the grain of what they had been planning for themselves as a married couple for a very long time.

Having only one another as company and no one else with whom they were forced to share their privacy had been a special attraction, the basis for a bond they believed would strengthen their marriage.

"I think we should go on as we planned originally," Randy finally told the other man, reading Maggie's thoughts and knowing she agreed with him. "But it would be very nice indeed if we could spend the evening with you and then start on our separate way in the morning."

Stockley nodded, though obviously disappointed.

"I like you both," he said. "You make a very natural couple, a fine team. The Lord may have some real blessings in store for you."

His expression grew serious.

"But the way ahead will not be pleasant at times," he warned them. "What happened to you today is just a taste of what may lie ahead. I have many friends who have gone this route before. You may be tempted at some point just to give up and head back to familiar territory."

"We know the truth of what you are saying," Maggie told him, "but we are determined. Reaching California is not a dream we will allow to die!"

"Mrs. Stuart, you must never forget that our God could well have other plans for you," Stockley admonished. "The fact that you have come this far may not be a complete indication of His will in the matter."

Prior to returning to their wagon, Maggie and Randy had dinner with the Stockley clan, simple fare but tasty and nourishing, with a dessert of shoo-fly pie that everyone lingered over, sorry when the last piece had been eaten.

Before Randy went back with Maggie, Jeremiah Stockley called him aside, and the two sat for a few moments on two flat rocks at the shore's edge.

"You are struggling, are you not, my friend?" Stockley asked with a display of great sensitivity.

"Yes, Jeremiah, I am," Randy replied.

"What is your difficulty, if I may ask?"

"Maggie has been raised in her faith, has accepted it as natural and real. For my parents, it seemed only another convenient way to control me. They used guilt and God's judgment and heaven and hell and all the rest as weapons or rewards, depending upon how they wanted me to act at any given moment."

Stockley sighed as he pulled back his shoulders and looked up at the clear night sky.

"O, Lord," he said, "can there be forgiveness in You for those Christians who are twisting the Holy Scriptures to their own ends and causing hell on earth for so many?"

The two men were silent for a short while.

"Have you ever felt that your wife was trying to control you in the same way, son?" Stockley asked.

"Never!" Randy exclaimed, offended at the very notion. "She is the very opposite of what my parents were. She is kind, loving, patient."

"Then why have you not found it easier to take the dear Jesus into your life as your Savior, your Lord?"

"Because my life has been so dirty until now, so filled with sin that it might shock you if I related even a portion of my conduct since I left home as a young man."

"I am nearly fifty years old, friend. Little remains in this sin-cursed world that would surprise or shock me."

"But, Jeremiah, you have no idea of what I have done with or to the women I knew before I met Maggie."

"It matters little about the severity of sin, Randy. Christ's death was not conditional; the forgiveness He purchased for us did not stop at one particular sin as if some kind of spiritual brick wall had been thrown in its way."

Randy could not accept that.

"I appreciate your outlook, Jeremiah," he said as he stood and extended his hand for the final time.

Stockley stood as well and, ignoring the hand, reached out and hugged him instead.

Then, as Randy turned to go back to the wagon where Maggie was waiting, the older man said, "Randy?"

"Yes, Jeremiah?"

"Is it so much that you feel the Lord cannot forgive you, that your sins have been too much for His death, burial, and resurrection to cover? Or—"

"Yes, that is it," Randy replied, surprised at the other man's keen perception. "I suspect, in my heart of hearts, that there must be some point at which even divine forgiveness ends."

"—or, my new young friend, is it that this is far more a case of your not being able to forgive yourself?"

Randy had no answer.

Chapter Seventeen

Maggie Engebretsen Stuart stretched her thin old legs and then moved them back and forth, trying to get the circulation going faster through veins that had carried a great deal of blood over the decades she had lived and which now seemed on the verge of collapse, no longer aided by a vibrant heart but cursed by a tired one, a heart that was not capable of beating for very much longer.

Jeremiah Stockley . . .

How she had grown to love that man in so short a period of time!

He had reminded her a bit, in manner if not in physical appearance, of Morgan Bowder, always helping, never asking for much in return.

Maggie had regretted having to say good-bye to Jeremiah Stockley the next morning.

Stockley's offer to have them join the others had been so generous and did seem to offer some clear advantages.

But right or wrong, the two of them had said good-bye and continued their journey alone.

There were other mishaps as the days and weeks passed. One day the wagon's right back wheel came off, the sudden jolting plunge of the wagon bed jarring them badly. Yet the fact that Randy worked well with wood and other materials helped, and he was able to get them started again without a long delay.

At night, they often slept outside the wagon, covered by a large quilt Maggie's mother had made years before, lovingly sewing piece to piece then quilting the colorful top to the batting and backing over a period of several months.

Maggie imagined that she still smelled her mother's sweet scent as she touched the side of the quilt that was now hers. She could picture the woman sitting on the front porch of the family home, working on the quilt hour after hour in the evening twilight until it was finished.

"It will help you remember me," her mother had said with such deep love that it seemed almost palpable. "When you wrap it around yourself on a cold night and it chases away the cold, you can think of—"

Her mother's voice had broken at that point, and Maggie had bent down and kissed her gently on the forehead . . .

"I still have it, dearest Mama," she whispered as her hand touched the quilt that now covered her and Randy, keeping them warm against the gathering chill of that evening somewhere on the prairie. "It's been worn through in a few spots, but then it's had to survive a great deal. I'll never let it go, Mama. I will never let it be taken from me."

Maggie felt Randy's strong, broad back against hers and sighed as she thought of what had happened to them in the months that had followed their near-fatal encounter with the mighty Mississippi River.

We thought we could vanquish anything, she remembered all those decades later. *We thought even that river would not stop us. But it nearly did. And it wasn't the only obstacle we faced. Yet, for a while, we still felt invincible.*

Maggie felt a chill just then, and pulled the quilt higher over her shoulders, visions of the past few weeks dancing across her mind.

Randy and Maggie had come in contact with other pioneers and had had marvelous times of fellowship but there were also

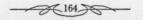

occasions when their food had nearly run out and Randy had been unable to find fresh game on his hunting forays.

That was perhaps one of the most difficult aspects of their new life to which she had to grow accustomed.

Seeing the bloody, freshly killed creatures.

Eating those animals that, back in Philadelphia, had been pets to her, such as rabbits and deer, took a great deal of getting used to, but when the alternative was dying in the middle of a deserted prairie she managed to overcome her squeamishness.

Randy skinned them, and Maggie did the cooking. That was their arrangement. But the first time this happened, Maggie thought she would not be able to keep her side of the agreement.

"I'll do it then," he told her, with no trace of irritation.

"But it's supposed to be *my* job," she retorted.

"I know that, but we've had to make some pretty substantial adjustments. Let me help you with this one."

They were standing beside the wagon, weeks after leaving the Mississippi behind. Dusk would come soon. Randy was hungry, and so was Maggie. Until then, if the hunting was poor they had been able to depend upon the dried and preserved food they had brought along with them or purchased at trading posts along the way. There had also been happy, gregarious meals they had been invited to share with other travelers or with landowners they met along the way.

But from now on, they realized, there would be few occasions when anyone else would do the cooking for them, and the food-stuffs they had brought with them were long gone.

That moment signified their solitude more than any other thing thus far.

The sounds of approaching night filled the air, owls and wolves and scampering creatures they could not see.

"What is the attraction of this place?" Maggie asked as her gaze wandered over the wide, endless prairie all around her. "Why did we succumb to its fascination?"

"New life," Randy replied, standing behind her and slipping his arms around her waist. He carefully kissed her behind each ear.

"Or death?" she muttered, feeling a little frightened.

They had seen a great deal of death, the graves of settlers lining the trail, cabins burned to the ground and, everywhere, traces of hostile Indians.

But always they themselves had been left alone. They'd been spared the blood-curdling war cries in the middle of the night, although they had heard them in the distance, and the sounds were as awful as any they would ever encounter.

"I know what you're saying," he said honestly, following her gaze into the star-sprinkled sky. "I feel what you're feeling."

"I don't think I have any regrets, at least not yet," Maggie mused.

"Then what's going on?"

She held her arms wide.

"All of this!" she exclaimed. "It's so immense. Back in Philadelphia, we dreamed the dreams of our passion. Now we're living the reality. Sometimes I feel cut off, Randy, cut off from everything that once made up the whole of my life."

She turned around so that she faced him.

"New dreams," he said. "Dreams that you and I create."

He smiled broadly.

"We do it together, Maggie. This is not an empty world out here. It is like a piece of clay just before a sculptor starts to work on it. It is ours to take and hold and make something out of it. There are countless thousands like us right now, coming out here. Some will stay in the middle of the country, either because they like it there or they're just too worn out to go on. Others will travel farther. Many are determined to make it all the way to California."

Randy paused. Then, lowering his voice even more, he added, "I think we belong in the last group, Maggie. We're stronger than others. Our dreams are bigger. We can't just bury them in the middle of a lonely prairie."

She could say no more, and kissed him then, with that act showing not only her love for him but also her part in the dreams that both would continue dreaming, no matter what . . .

It carried them far, that dream did.

It helped them survive hunger, thirst . . .

Then a lightning storm had destroyed the wagon and most of what had been left in it, and that included their clothes. They were left with only what they had been wearing at the time, and whenever they washed those clothes in a stream, they were left with almost nothing to cover themselves.

At first Maggie felt embarrassed, but it was much less a problem for Randy. Eventually she got used to living like she did because she had to do so. There was simply no other choice.

A few minutes later, they headed west.

Part Four
Life at Its Fullest

Faith is the substance of things hoped for,
the evidence of things not seen.

Hebrews 11:1

That time as they were traveling west of the Mississippi, when they had only the clothes on their backs, proved to be, ironically, one of the best times of their marriage, for they literally had only each other.

For Randy, it meant being able to show Maggie the kind of man he wanted always to be for her, strong, resourceful, able to hunt and provide food for the two of them, learning to live off the land.

For Maggie, living a life of raggedness and need was one last severed connection with her old life as she remembered helping her mother and her sister make scrumptious meals and sew new dresses.

She told Randy about this.

"It must be so much tougher for you," he acknowledged. "For me, this is proving to be kind of liberating, frankly."

Maggie looked at him.

"This is not such an ordeal for you then," she said.

"Some of it is, of course," he told her. "At the Mississippi . . . that was awful. And the lightning nearly wiping us out. But the rest . . . not so bad. I mean, here I am with my wonderful wife, whom I love more than life itself, and—"

He held her as tightly as he dared without hurting her . . .

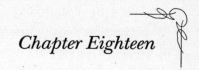

Chapter Eighteen

Eventually they were befriended yet again and invited to join a wagon train that was passing by. This time, having no wagon, no supplies—no choice—they accepted the invitation and were welcomed into that mobile Christian community with as much warmth as Jeremiah Stockley and his family had extended.

Eventually the wagon train stopped near a frontier town, and Maggie and Randy, having lost nearly everything they owned, again had no choice but to stay and get jobs to support themselves— Randy as a barn hand at the livery stable and Maggie as a cook in a restaurant.

It took a long time, three years in fact, before they were able to start building a cabin of their own, staying in the meantime in a small boarding house on the outskirts of the little frontier town.

But it all came together finally in the Stuarts' modest home that rose up from the prairie and, a few months later, in the birth of their child . . .

"Patrick?"

It was the name Randy had favored a long time, one he even had dreamed about over the years as they hoped Maggie would become pregnant.

Now that she was at last expecting a child, he was saying that name just for the pleasure of how it sounded.

"It's just right for him—if it's a him," Maggie agreed.

They had been talking in bed on a particularly cold night in mid-February when Randy had popped the question: "I was wondering about a name, Maggie. What do you think about giving our son the name Patrick?"

Afterward, he repeated it again, liking the very sound of it.

Both were enjoying this new game of finding a proper name for their baby.

"Yes, it's a fine name, Randy. That's for sure, but what if the baby just happens to be a wee little girl?" Maggie asked the obvious question. "Shouldn't we be prepared for that possibility, Darling?"

"A girl?" he said, toying momentarily with the thought. "Why in the world would we have a girl, Maggie? They're such silly, weak creatures."

Her eyes opened wide in pretended anger.

"So that's what you think of us?" she replied.

"Only kidding, Dear Heart."

"I was tempted to bite you real hard for saying something like that."

"Then I'll say it again!"

Maggie, her head on his chest, her fingers playing with the hairs in the center of it, mulled the name over in her mind. "Shouldn't we consider others?" she ventured. "Might Oliver be better? I've always wanted a child named Oliver. Or if it's a girl, then perhaps Olivia."

"You are kidding, aren't you?" he asked. "Well, I hope you're kidding. Oliver's a sissy name. It's terrible, Maggie."

She lifted her head and looked into his eyes.

"I am, Randy; truly I am," she said, smiling broadly.

"Do you like Patrick?"

"How can I tell? I haven't met him yet."

Randy chuckled at that one.

"Please be serious, Maggie," he added. "Do you really like Patrick? Or Patricia if it's a girl?"

"I do, I do," she assured him. "But, Randy, do you know what is really the most wonderful thing of all?"

"What is that, my love?" he asked.

"To realize that we're living life as the Lord intended. Nothing could be better than that, you and me here together, side by side, holding one another and trying to find a name for this miracle growing inside me, our blessed baby!"

They delivered the baby themselves.

Maggie had never been allowed to do this at the hospital, at least not entirely by herself, since that was considered the work of a man in those days, but she had assisted with many deliveries, and was able to help Randy do his part.

There were no complications.

Randy gently caught the infant as it emerged from the womb, wiped his wrinkled little face, and then wrapped him in a cotton blanket before holding him up so that Maggie could see him. And in that supremely beautiful moment, both of them felt as though nothing else mattered, certainly nothing in the world outside that isolated cabin on that bleak parcel of prairie.

"I can finally say good-bye, Maggie."

"To those ghosts of yours? At last?"

"To all of whatever happened before we met."

"Every bit of it, my love?"

"Every sordid bit. I feel like climbing a mountain and shouting to the world below that Randy Stuart has found what he's needed for a long, long time."

"Freedom?"

"That's it, Maggie: the freshest, sweetest freedom a man could ever want."

Randy had tried much earlier, of course, to attain that freedom from enslavement to his parents' memory by moving away, as far away as he could manage at that time, with the hope of putting it all behind him in a physical sense.

But ultimately he had failed because his emotions, his soul, were still back where it counted for him, back East in the same home in which they had become warped, and only the trip west, with Maggie, seemed to set him on the path to freedom. Now, with

the birth of his son, the escape from his troublesome past was complete.

"I was in two places at the same time," he said, "here in the West and back within the prison they had created for me."

As he spoke, he realized something else.

"Maggie?"

"Yes, my love?"

"I said that without bitterness, you know. It was like I was personally detached somehow and giving an objective report about someone else.

"That's wonderful!"

"It is, Maggie. It is!"

Happiness.

Maggie embraced it as someone who had been in a kind of emotional desert and was now being given precious water to save her life.

"Mama, Papa . . . "

She spoke often as though they could hear what she was saying.

"If only you could see your grandson now. You would adore this boy. You would want to hold him close to you and feel the greatest love."

This still happened in the rush of being a new mother. Later, though, Maggie would let go too. Instead of thinking so often of those she had lost she would concentrate on the family she had gained.

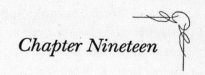
"Oh, my love, my love, how happy we were then," Maggie recalled out loud as her old, tired mind dealt with those images of the past.

Moments that had once seemed the stuff only of wishful thinking . . .

Days passed, days that seemed ideal, that seemed to be handed to them directly from God Himself.

Languid days of cuddling their son, enjoying the feel of their flesh against his, pink and soft and so new, and then against one another as well, without inhibition. Some days they hardly stepped outside the cabin at all, content to let all but the most essential chores slide for a while.

That home, that cabin . . .

It had become a protective and special place for them, and they had convinced themselves that, as long as they were able to ignore the world directly beyond the front door, they would be safe.

When Maggie dreamed at night, there was no longer a frantic rush of dark and melancholy visions of loneliness and pain.

Gone.

She could sleep without apprehension, for the old dreams, bordering on nightmares, had been replaced by scenes in a field of lilacs, their sweet scent filling the air, the bright overhead sun touching her cheeks with its warmth, the sound of laughter in her ears, a man's laughter and then a child's, filled with joy.

There were other scenes of different places, and some included Patrick but not Randy. In this dream she held her son up high, toward the heavens, proclaiming, "O Lord, the blessings You have bestowed! Thank You, precious Jesus!"

A few more dreams came along during certain nights. She saw herself alone with Randy in vividly sensual dreams that she was not embarrassed to have, because she could indulge them without shame.

Then Maggie would awaken either with Randy's strong arms holding her or his soft lips kissing her . . .

"It feels so fine to be so happy," Randy said one night, his eyes half-closed, his voice husky. "I don't think I have ever felt like this before. It's so complete. I have you. I have Patrick."

He smiled in a way that would have gotten her to do anything at anytime for any reason.

"Nothing else is of any consequence. I once doubted that any of this would ever happen to me, Maggie. I thought I'd never experience—"

She reached out, touched his lips, silenced him.

"Enjoy what the Lord has provided," she said simply.

They were sitting before the fireplace, enjoying the warmth. Maggie was nursing Patrick, who seemed as content as any baby could be.

"You're so beautiful," he said, wanting her more than ever. "So very beautiful."

Hearing that added to the blissfulness of the moment for her.

It was one more answer to a prayer of hers, prayer uttered when she was alone, sometimes as she washed their clothes in the wash-tub or while Randy was off hunting game to feed them or often just while she stood in the kitchen preparing a meal, and then at night, to herself, without Randy ever hearing. It was a quiet prayer, yes, but a prayer of great fervency. She had prayed this way, day after day, week after week, for all of the long journey westward because she had never lost sight of the damage that long-held guilt had done to the man for whom she would surely sacrifice her own life if that was what it took for him to live.

After their son had dozed off in her arms, a drop of milk glistening on the corner of his rosebud mouth, she put him in his cradle and patted his back until she was sure he was comfortably asleep. Then she settled down beside Randy, snuggling close.

If it had been apparent that he had tried to hide anything from her, that would have proved quite another matter, but he hadn't. Instead he had begun to share some of the dark secrets of his past, and she could usually deal with the subject honestly whenever it arose without feeling disturbed in any way.

"With most of the women," he admitted, "it was, well, just routine, occasionally not even that, a mechanical act and nothing more. I felt sorry for the women at the same time I hated myself for being part of their problem.

"They weren't interested in anything deeper than purely physical pleasure, Maggie.

"Trouble is, I was doing the same thing. I tried to feel more respectable by making them seem even worse than I was. Yet when I couldn't get what I needed from any one of them, I myself went from woman to woman, which simply mirrored what they were doing. I mean, how could I be so hypocritical and look at them with such contempt? How could I?"

"It was never any different, Randy?"

He hesitated, earnestly trying to decide how candid he should be to her under those circumstances.

"It could have been, maybe once or twice, but if the woman wasn't responsible for destroying the relationship between us each time, then it had to be my fault, didn't it? Either way, it ended up with no hope for either of us."

He smiled as he said, "Two things now . . . two requests."

"Fine," she replied. "What are they?"

"Let's change the subject—that's the first thing. Can we do that, Maggie?"

She nodded.

"What's the other, Randy?"

She would have done anything for him then, for at that moment she loved him so deeply and totally, that she imagined her love to be something quite physical that she could hold in her hands and offer to him without reservation.

So she was ready when it became apparent that the second

request was not one of words. He spoke not at all, but as his hands moved over her body and she felt her every nerve tingle, Maggie knew that her beloved Randy was telling her all that she needed to know.

Later, as the two of them were lying quietly together, Patrick started to cry, and Maggie got up and went to him.

"Is he all right?" Randy asked.

"Fine," Maggie said warmly. "He just needs a little attention; that's all."

"Can I help?"

"No, it won't take long, just a quick diaper change."

Randy closed his eyes briefly, marveling at just that little moment.

My son, he thought half-disbelievingly. *My son needs a little attention, and my wife is taking care of him!*

He repeated those words yet again, savoring each one, realizing what that earthy little moment actually signified, the greatest degree of fulfillment he had ever felt in his life, before which all others were meaningless.

He looked up to find her standing in front of him, holding the baby.

"Let me hold our son," Randy asked as gently, as tenderly, as he knew how, his face aglow.

Maggie sat down next to him and handed her husband, her lover, that soft, delicate little body.

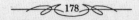

Part Five
The Darkness Deepens . . .

Abide with me, fast falls the even-tide;

The darkness deepens, Lord with me abide.

Henry F. Lyte and William H. Monk

Five more good years . . .

A blessed time, one that neither thought would end the way it did.

"We have so much to be grateful for," Maggie would say frequently over the course of those precious years. "Praise God!"

And Randy would look at her and smile, and she wouldn't even notice that he seldom echoed those two simple but powerful words.

Patrick proved to be a wonderful child, strong and healthy, as were his parents. As a baby, he had seldom kept them awake at night, his temperament pleasant, loving. As a little boy, he was astonishingly obedient . . .

"An angel," his mother would call him.

"But I don't have wings, Mama," he said when he was old enough to talk. "Are they going to grow later?"

"So much joy," Randy said again and again. "Life is perfect for us."

They had enlarged their little home out there on the western prairie where they had stopped while still claiming the dream of a permanent place in California. But as their happiness continued unabated and Patrick grew so quickly, California's lure faded more and more.

Truly, these were the sweetest years Maggie and Randy had ever known. Joy, it seemed, would stay with them an uncommon length of time.

Until a day that had seemed so calm at its beginning.

Just after sunup, Randy had set off with little Patrick, now nearly six, to pick up supplies in town while Maggie remained behind. She stood in front of the cabin and watched them ride off together on the graceful palomino until they disappeared in the late-autumn blend of golden browns that tinged the tall prairie grasses.

Chapter Twenty

Maggie stood for a moment just outside the doorway, her eyes scanning the rolling prairie stretching forever beneath the near-cloudless sky.

The air . . .

As always it was pure and sweet; she had never lost the joy of feeling it caressing her lungs.

"O God, thank You," she said. "There is so much here that I don't deserve, yet You have chosen to give me these blessings anyway."

She bowed her head a moment, a feeling of utter dependency gripping her, dependency that was humbling and made her realize how much she needed to be in prayerful communion then and always.

"Just a few years ago . . ." she started to say, and then she became momentarily lost in the memories of life in Philadelphia.

After a few minutes, she turned and reentered the cabin. As always, she had work to do.

By midmorning, low, billowing clouds had drifted across the sky, and in the distance she heard the loud, ominous crack of thunder.

I hope they get back soon, Lord, Maggie thought. *This storm may be a big one, and they should hurry on home.*

They didn't.

In the meantime, the storm had begun.

Another hour passed.

Then another.

Maggie opened the front door and walked out onto the porch.

The rain!

It was being driven by high winds, falling in sheets of gray that limited her vision to only a very short distance in front of her.

Nothing.

She went back inside, her clothes soaked by the mist that blew onto the porch. After changing, she tried to occupy herself with planning the evening meal. She set three places at the table and lifted the lid to stir the broth for the stew she had planned for supper. Then she sharpened the knife and began cutting the meat from a venison quarter for the stew.

Randy, Patrick!

She cut herself because, her mind far away from the venison in front of her, she had not been paying close attention to the task at hand. Mentally she was not there at all but outside, on the plains, searching.

Dusk came.

The storm had been a sudden one, but violent and devastating, for which there could be little preparation.

And from which there was little safety if you happened to be outside, in the midst of it.

"Stop it!" she said aloud. "Randy's been on the plains nearly six years now. He knows what to do. He won't—"

More time passed.

The food still cooking, Maggie sat down and opened her Bible, searching for passages of reassurance.

They became readily apparent, and she reacted to them intensely, as though for the first time.

Another hour went by.

She walked over to the window for the tenth time, almost afraid to pull the curtain aside and look out—and be disappointed again.

A figure in the distance, walking slowly.

No horse.

The horse was gone!

It might not be Randy. There is only one figure. It couldn't be Randy. He'd have Patrick with him. He'd have—

Maggie sighed with relief only to have her throat muscles tighten severely.

That man, whoever he is, seems . . . seems to be carrying something, something that . . . that looks a little like—

The thought froze in her mind.

Dear God, she prayed silently, panic grabbing her so tightly she could scarcely breathe. *Dear God, don't let it be him! Not Patrick!*

Randy always enjoyed being out on the plains with his son. On their way back from town, he sometimes pretended the trusty palomino needed a rest. Then he would head toward a pleasant grove of willows just under a rise and invite Patrick to rest a moment too so he could watch the little fellow scamper about in the tall prairie grasses or investigate a butterfly perched on one of the willows or . . .

"Papa, I love you," Patrick was saying with a bright smile as they sat together in the grass under the willows, not far from where the palomino grazed nonchalantly.

"And I love you too, son," he replied.

. . . and I love you too, son.

Patrick was half of his father's reason for living.

If I could really tell you how much you mean to me, Randy thought, *if only I had the proper words to say.*

The boy's attention was abruptly distracted by the slightest movement somewhere to his left.

A prairie dog had popped out of a hole in the ground and was sitting there seemingly studying him.

"Papa!" Patrick exclaimed.

"He likes you," Randy said, smiling.

The prairie dog didn't move a fraction of an inch, transfixed by the sight of this brown-haired little boy and the big man beside him.

Then, without warning, the nervous little animal disappeared back down into its burrow.

"Where's he goin', Papa?" Patrick said, downcast. "I thought he wanted to play with me."

"I guess he heard someone callin' him," Randy said with a mischievous smile. He reached out and patted his son reassuringly on the back, thinking it was time for them to head home too.

But just then the prairie dog came back, and this time he wasn't alone.

Now there were two others, one nearly the same size as himself, the other quite a bit smaller.

"He's back—and he brought his family to meet you, Patrick," his father remarked.

Patrick looked at him, an expression on his face that seemed to be saying, *How in the world do you know that's his family?*

"Like you and Mommy and me," Randy said, pointing at the little critters as though positively identifying each one.

Patrick's eyes widened. "Wow, Papa! He has a family too, just like me."

After a few minutes, the prairie dogs returned to their home.

"Ah, they've left again. I liked them," Patrick said rather sadly.

"Wait, look!"

One of the prairie dogs had returned to the surface. It scurried over to Patrick while looking warily at his father, something round and hard carried in its little jaws. The animal dropped something at the boy's feet and then hurried away.

Patrick picked it up, looking at it curiously.

"That's a nut, son," Randy commented. "The little guy probably found it somewhere last fall and hid it away in his burrow. Guess he wanted you to have it."

"Wow!" exclaimed Patrick. "Wait 'til I show Mama!"

"Yes, that's what we'll do: take it home to Mama. We'd better head on back right now. When we get home, you can show her your little friend's gift."

Patrick's eyes were sparkling in the most endearing way.

Randy leaned over and put his arms around the boy.

I love you and your mother, he thought. *I love you more than anything or anyone else in this world. I would die for you both.*

As he got to his feet, pulling Patrick up with him, he kissed his son, who did the same thing in return.

"I love you, Papa," that feisty young voice told him.

Randy playfully grabbed the boy, pulling him into a hug and then just holding Patrick another moment, this vibrant young character he had helped to create.

A slight wind was blowing in across the plains, a rather chill edge to it.

Storm brewing, Randy thought as he looked toward the sky and saw dark clouds drifting across it.

"It's turning cold, son," Randy said. "We've got to leave now."

Randy got on the horse first, then leaned over and gently pulled up his son.

Such small bones, he remarked to himself for probably the hundredth time since Patrick was born. *He's just a fragile little guy.*

As it turned out, they were still quite a distance from home—much farther than Randy would have liked.

Suddenly realizing this and regretting it, Randy looked nervously at the dark clouds that were rapidly taking over the sky.

"A storm is coming," he told his son. "We'd better hurry."

The boy was disappointed to have to leave, but he didn't complain.

They were still more than a mile away from the cabin when the thunder commenced.

In a short while, huge bolts of lightning ripped down from the sky.

"Look, Papa!" Patrick exclaimed, wide-eyed, full of wonder, and not at all scared. "Look at that, will ya!"

The sense of wonder that was a part of the little boy captivated his father as well.

Directly ahead of them was a lone tree standing like a sentinel in the middle of the prairie. It probably was more than a hundred years old, Randy guessed, vowing to remember the tree as a picnic spot for the three of them.

Hardly a second before that thought ended, lightning hit the tree, splitting it down the middle and igniting a spark that soon grew into a blaze.

The palomino reared, and both Randy and Patrick were thrown to the ground. The horse raced off into the distance.

Patrick landed hard against the trunk of the burning tree while Randy landed several feet away from it.

"Papa!"

Randy heard his son scream in sudden pain.

He tried to stand and rush to the boy's side, but something was stopping him . . . a whirlpool of darkness that was drawing him in. He suddenly had no strength and fell back, losing consciousness.

Chapter Twenty-one

Rain was falling, oh, how fast, and how much and for how long it came down upon that land!

Great soaking waves of it were being driven against him.

Randy was able to open his eyes only with great effort.

At first memory fled, and he had to reorient himself, had to get his senses under control and use them properly.

Then he started coughing, violently so. This made him dizzy, and he fell back against the ground again.

Muscles were aching all over his body.

He knew he had to move. Just remaining still meant a death sentence for him.

He tried to stand again but fell back the second time.

And then he remembered.

The thunder.

That lone tree struck by lightning.

Patrick falling!

He tried harder to get to his feet, the strain almost causing him to black out, but this time he succeeded though he was still wobbly.

Randy could see that the rain was coming down in a massive torrent. Visibility was limited to only a few feet in front of him.

He saw—

Ahead, just ahead, barely so, but it was there, glimpsed through the terrible storm.

A shape.

That tree!

The stark, smoldering outline of what was left of the tree!

Directly in front of him.

Groaning, Randy stumbled toward it, his heart beating so fast he seemed on the verge of an attack.

The horse! his mind screamed. *Where is the—?*

The palomino was nowhere around.

"Patrick!" Randy shouted, deep, cold fear gripping him. "Patrick, where are you, son? Tell me you hear my voice!"

To the right of the tree.

A small form, barely visible . . . so still.

He hurried to it, bent down, picked up Patrick, hugged his son.

"O God, O God! Don't let it be like this!" Randy screamed in desperate anguish. "Don't let Patrick be taken from Maggie, from me. We love the boy so very much. Please, I beg You, please don't —!"

Patrick moaned slightly as Randy stumbled.

He knew he had to get back to the cabin. The storm was becoming more fierce, and the temperature had dropped. Randy knew there was an increasing risk of pneumonia if they didn't get dry and warm soon.

But where? Which direction? Where do I head?

The horse!

It would head straight back to the cabin. If only he could find some hoofprints in the wet ground.

He searched frantically, realizing that the rain probably had washed away any tracks left behind.

No, it hasn't! There! In the mud!

Just enough had survived to show him the way.

Randy held his son close to him and began running, stumbling, walking, talking to the boy as he struggled forward. He wanted to give his son some focal point, some familiar sound to latch on to, like a life preserver.

"We will make it," he said.

He said a great deal else during that nightmare journey. He told his son how much he was loved, how much he was needed.

"I may not have told you that enough before," he admitted. "I may have meant it but not told you often enough, and I want you to know now. I need you, Patrick. I love you."

He spoke of moments they had had together, that first fishing trip, the time Patrick had warned him about a rattler, that—

"I promise," he muttered. "I promise you'll be all right, son. Please . . . please believe that. Please—"

Once he looked down at Patrick's young face, and thought he saw the eyelids open slightly, thought he saw a fleeting moment of recognition from the boy, and then it was gone.

So cold, Randy thought. *It's suddenly so cold out here, and I have nothing to wrap around him. I have nothing to—*

His own strength was dissipating.

He could hardly hold Patrick.

Finally he fell, his legs giving out, and the two of them tumbled to the ground, which was now quite muddy.

"O God, O God," he mumbled raggedly.

As they fell, Patrick had landed on his little arm, which was now bent backward at a strange angle.

Broken.

And you didn't cry out. You—!

Randy put his ear to his son's chest, frantically trying to detect a heartbeat.

None.

"No!" he screamed. "No, that's not so. It can't be so!"

He couldn't tell how much time had passed.

The ride into town had taken two hours, and they were less than halfway back when he had stopped at the willows. To walk the remaining mile or so, if walk was the correct word, certainly meant a much more extended period.

As Randy continued, his mind filled with mere fantasy, reality taking second place, scenes of him and Patrick together, not from the past and now being relived, rather what he had hoped for during the many months and years to come—Patrick becoming a healthy teenager, emerging as a physical copy of his father but without the pain Randy had experienced, without the emotional nightmares he had been toting around for so long.

"I'm . . . going . . . to save you from . . . all . . . that," he said fiercely, his voice now quite hoarse. "I'm going to give you . . . every bit of the self-respect I had never had . . . until your mother . . . until your mother entered my life. You won't be . . . crippled inside . . . the way . . . I was. You won't have to . . . look . . . at your . . . own reflection and . . . and . . . turn away in disgust."

Randy detected a murmur and stopped for a few seconds, trying to hear it again, above the wind, the rain.

"Hang on . . . Patrick," he said, his voice nearly gone. "It . . . can't . . . be much longer. . . . We just have to hang on and—"

A voice calling him!

Randy looked up, saw a solitary figure in the distance, walking slowly toward him through the rain.

"Help!" he screamed. "Please help us!"

It was an old man.

As the figure came closer, he saw the white hair, the short beard.

Alone!

The old man was walking alone and upright, as though no storm at all was raging around him, and he was being protected from it.

Now standing calmly before Patrick and Randy as though he had been waiting for them.

"My son's been hurt . . . very, very bad," Randy told him, panting. "Do you know, Sir, where we can get some help?"

"I do."

The voice was calm, baritoned, untroubled, as though what was being asked was not so special, so urgent.

"I beg you, show me, please!"

The old man smiled beneficently.

"You already know, Randy Stuart," he said, with no sign of distress.

"My name! You know me? How can that be?"

"Many things can be if you but let them."

Randy was annoyed. He wanted clarity." He wanted help. He could not tolerate game-playing.

"You speak in riddles. My son may be dying."

"That is correct. He is dying."

"I can't let that happen. I must do something."

"That is the trouble here," the old man said knowingly, a sad, tender expression on his weathered face. "You, Randy Stuart, can't do anything."

The lines in his forehead became more pronounced.

"Son, you have no control," the stranger told him, "no control over what is happening right now. Only—"

"God? Is that what you're saying? Why doesn't He step in and help us? Why does He seek the sacrifice of an innocent child?"

"Why are you unwilling to let that happen? Why are you trusting Him so little even now, Randy Stuart?"

The old man shrugged and started to walk off.

"Don't," Randy pleaded. "Don't leave us—please!"

The stranger turned and glanced back at him.

"Remember Abraham," he said, "as you hold your Isaac."

And then he disappeared into the fury of that storm.

Chapter Twenty-two

Randy could scarcely hold Patrick's little body any longer. His throat felt like a raw sore. But he had to keep talking, he thought, as much for himself as for his son's sake so that neither of them would die.

"Someday . . . I'll . . . teach you . . . to ride," he strained with the effort of speaking even those few simple words. "Some . . . day we will. Patrick, we'll go out . . . on the prairie together . . . me on the palomino and you . . . on . . . on—"

He started sobbing then but tried to go on.

"I'll see you strong again, your arm healed," Randy said, his voice gaining some strength amidst the pain. "I'll . . . see you catching a wild mustang not too long from now . . . and taming it, making it your own, son."

Light.

Ahead!

The faint outline of—

The cabin!

In only a few minutes he had made it to the front door and handed Maggie the near-lifeless body of their son before he collapsed at her feet.

Patrick was still breathing when Maggie wrapped him in a thick blanket and placed him by the fire.

He wasn't completely conscious but seemed enough aware of her presence to reach out for her hand and hold on to it so tightly that she had difficulty pulling free to fetch her supplies. She could hear him murmur slightly, apparently complaining.

She had helped Randy off with his clothes and wrapped another blanket around his shoulders. Then she had struggled to drag the old bed across the floor, closer to the fireplace. He fell into it, and she laid Patrick next to him.

Then she pulled a chair next to the bed and spoke soothingly to her son, stroking his soft, brown curls while reaching out and taking Randy's left hand with her right.

Just a little woman, she told herself. *That's what my papa used to call his dear Maggie. Just a little woman . . .*

It struck her how alone she was then, only Patrick and Randy with her.

She had been alone in that same sense for years now but was so involved in living life with the two of them that she had seldom thought, after those first few months, about life back in Philadelphia.

Crowds of people.

Even in those times, Philadelphia had bustled with activity. She used to think that a good portion of the citizens ate at the family's restaurant some time or other since it was busy seven days a week. And then the hospital itself, well before the epidemic, was continually admitting, treating, and releasing patients. It would not have been impossible to imagine that the Philadelphians who weren't at the restaurant managed to spend their time at the hospital.

Nearly 2,000 miles away . . .

She sighed as she recalled those days, realizing how much she had given up to be with Randy and how joyous it was to become the mother of his child, knowing that all the hordes of people for all the years she'd lived back East could not give her the fulfillment just two brunet-haired charmers had brought to her life.

And now they'll both die right before my eyes, and I'll wish that I could be joining the two of them, I'll want to—

Hours passed for Maggie like that.

Neither Patrick nor Randy gave any hopeful sign of reviving.

She could do just so much.

Having been a nurse proved helpful to her, but she still came face-to-face with the limitations she had felt again and again as she treated patients at the hospital and often found their condition worsening and eventually having some of them slip away until there was no life left in their ravaged bodies.

Only You, Lord, Maggie prayed again and again. *Only You can keep these dear ones from slipping away from me.*

During the night, the already chilly temperature had dropped even more, and the autumn rain quickly turned into an early blizzard, though the wind blew so hard that some time passed before a layer of snow took hold on the frozen ground.

Even so, that layer of snow over the prairie eventually deepened, the wind causing huge drifts everywhere.

By morning, Randy showed some signs of reviving.

A short while after that, he opened his bloodshot eyes and then turned slowly in her direction.

Though he could not speak at first, she could look at his eyes, the expression on his face, and feel a deep and tender connection between them, something that did not exist for her with anyone else, something that proved to her the necessity of marriage because she could not picture, even for a moment, how she could survive without someone, without Randy. She could not see at all how people could go through life in total loneliness, total isolation, if not by choice, then by circumstance.

How can those people survive? she wondered. *How can they avoid shriveling up inside and hoping that each morning will be the beginning of the last day of their lives?*

She ran her fingers through Patrick's soft brunette hair and started to reach over and do the same with Randy's, then stopped abruptly.

Patrick's eyes were now open as well, and they seemed to be looking up at her. There was a smile on his face.

"Thank God!" she exclaimed.

Just then she heard Randy groaning a bit and saw that he was

moistening his lips with his tongue and mumbling something about water.

There was no water inside, so she threw on a lamb's wool jacket, found a wide-mouthed jug, and went outside.

The blizzard had stopped, for the moment, anyway. And there was plenty of snow covering the ground.

Maggie scooped a couple of handfuls into the jug and went back inside, where she held it before the fire. Then she got a cup, and poured some of the water in it and sat down beside her husband, holding his head up slightly and bringing the cup to his lips.

Randy was yet barely conscious but enough so that he could tap her gently on the hand, and whisper something that sounded like "I love you with all my heart, dearest Maggie."

She looked again at Patrick. His eyes were still open.

Thank You, Lord, she breathed. Then she caught her breath and held it.

Patrick's lids didn't blink. His mouth hung open slightly; his chest gave no hint of moving.

She put a finger under his nostrils.

Then she stood and slid quietly under the covers beside her son, pulling his small body onto her and holding him in her arms as though by doing so, life would somehow pass from her into his dead, cold little body.

The blizzard had commenced again.

And now, in its third day, it showed no immediate signs of abating, its howling constant, seeming to urge anyone within its grasp simply to give up and die, for there was no excuse in fighting to survive.

Tons of snow were being slammed against the little cabin hour after hour, piling up in large drifts around it, which tended to insulate them inside because the heat from their fire did not dissipate as freely.

Yet, at the same time, that warmth meant that Patrick's little battered body couldn't remain inside.

There was no alternative to putting him directly outside the cabin before the storm ended and piling snow on top of his body as best they could.

"O Lord, O Lord! I can't do it," Maggie screamed.

"We've got to," Randy told her. "We can't just keep him inside. Maggie, there's no telling when the storm will end and the snow will melt enough so that we can get to the ground."

"I can't just . . . just leave him there. There'll be animals that . . . that smell his . . . his flesh, Randy. They'll try to—"

She brought her hand to her mouth, suddenly feeling ill. Randy hobbled over to her in time to catch her before she hit the floor of the cabin.

"We have to," Randy whispered, "we have to do this, Maggie."

She had felt faint. When she was able to stand, she leaned against her husband's still muscular body, gaining some strength from its very nearness.

"I don't know if I can do it," she whispered again, her tears soaking his shirt. "I don't know if . . . if I can just stand there, and . . . and release him into the—"

More words would not come. Randy, realizing this, spoke instead: "We'll do it together. We've done it all together, Maggie. I couldn't have survived without you back East. And you couldn't have done so well either, without your family. Together we are stronger, Maggie. Together we'll make it through this. We'll—"

He pulled away then, turning from her so that she would not see his face. Maggie reached out one hand, touched his shoulder.

"You don't have to pretend, Randy," she told him, her thoughts clearing abruptly.

"Yes, I do! I'm the man of this household. I—"

"Yes, you are, my love, but you're not some massive oak tree, big and strong and able to weather any storm. Maybe we've reached our limits here. We can't change that, but we can go on somehow, not as storybook legends of strength and endurance but as what we are, two human beings out here alone . . . and . . . and—"

Maggie Engebretsen Stuart felt that aloneness then more than ever before, looking about the cabin, hearing the blizzard howl outside, sensing the presence of that lifeless body, that sweet, sweet child's form lying shrouded in the bed just a few feet away . . .

An hour later, Maggie and Randy had struggled outside, the driving wind never stronger as it nearly flattened them against the cabin.

Both managed to dig away some snow, then they slowly, lovingly placed Patrick's body, tightly wrapped and tied in a sheet, in the excavation.

"His eyes!" Maggie had exclaimed as they had wound the sheets around his body. She realized she hadn't dealt with them properly.

The lids were still open, a smile remaining on his face.

She had reached down and gently tried to shut them.

"You can't," Randy had told her. "There's been too much dehydration. You'll tear the eyelids to pieces if you—"

She had backed away a bit, ashamed that she hadn't remembered something she knew well enough from her earlier years as a nurse.

Next, Maggie scooped up some more snow and, with her hands, patted it on top of the little shape, then some more, Randy doing the same by her side until there was a thick layer over the body.

Then Maggie stood up straight, looking about her as though disoriented momentarily by the wind-driven snow, the cabin in back of her, the truth of what she had just done forming a kaleidoscope of torment that confused her.

"I don't want to be here," she muttered. "I want to leave this awful place."

Maggie started to wander off, dazed, away from the cabin, and Randy stumbled after her, gently pulling her back and then inside the cabin.

"We're going to have to keep watch," he told her without emotion. "We'll need to take turns, especially after the wind dies down.

There are wolves, you know, and . . . and—"

Randy stopped for a second as he stood in the middle of their cabin. Tears were welling up in his eyes.

"You prayed so much for Patrick," he remarked, "and we both watched over him if he caught a cold or sprained his ankle or anything else. And now . . . and now . . . now—"

I can't act like this, can I? Randy thought. *I've got to be strong, to be the pillar in your life, Maggie.*

They held one another, both trembling because of what the two of them had been forced to do with their son's body.

They waited then, for the storm to lessen, for the animals in the night.

Eyes too small for the size of the head, small and red and—

The wolves came shortly after the wind died down a bit, their sense of smell developed through centuries of their kin hunting in that same region, getting to know every mile of it, their territorial instincts not muted for an instant.

The first pack came in the midst of Randy's initial watch, hardly visible as they were in the encompassing darkness, their gray pelts blending in with the snowy night. He had fallen asleep for a few minutes and opened his eyes at the sound of low snarling as one of the wolves felt challenged by another member of the pack.

Randy lifted the shotgun from its pegs on the wall, then opened the door and fired a shot into the group.

All of them looked up, startled, and ran.

Awakened by the noise, Maggie hurried to his side.

Don't look, he begged her. Please . . . don't look!"

But Maggie had already started to glance past the partially open heavy wood shutters that she had helped Randy build.

No wolves remained just then.

But at the spot where Patrick's body had been placed, she saw that the packed snow had been disturbed, and sickness suddenly gripped her stomach.

A hand.

A small, fragile-looking gray-toned hand, much like one on a marble statue, was sticking up stiffly through the snow.

"I'll go out and take care of it now," Randy muttered as he pulled on his coat again.

"What good will that do?" she said frantically. "They'll come back. They have Patrick's scent now and—"

"We'll keep shooting!" Randy snapped. "Until we run out of every last bit of ammunition we have, and then I'll take the ax, and I'll go out again and . . . and I'll smash them with it. I'll—"

He saw the hurt on her face.

"I'm sorry I spoke harshly. But there'll be more of their kind, you know," he told her, trying to justify himself in the midst of an apology. "In some way, among them, a signal goes out, and they—"

He knew that all too well, knew it from harsh past experience during his first frontier odyssey. One of the circus people, a senile old man, had wandered off from their camp and been set upon by a pack of wolves.

A search party had been quickly organized to hunt for him, Randy among its fourteen members. They had found him moments later, still alive, but being attacked, the wolves having surrounded the old one and already torn at him so severely that his would-be rescuers realized then and there that he could not survive.

They managed to scatter his attackers, but he died in considerable agony within two hours after being taken back to their camp, which immediately set off a period of sustained mourning that Randy would remember for a very long time. It was not only the duration of it that stuck with him but the sheer intensity of the feelings that were shown by the gypsies, emotional people for whom this tragedy proved devastating, affecting them continually during the months to follow.

I remember the sheer terror shown by that old man. And the dark, awful determination on the dark, unholy faces of those beasts, their red eyes—

He winced as the sight came back to him full-bore.

Once they had discovered a source of fresh meat . . .

He hoped Maggie wouldn't notice that he was fighting to keep himself from trembling visibly.

"—and the first pack bands together with at least one other, and then they attack as a much bigger group," Randy was telling her.

He was right.

A few hours later, after Randy had gone back outside and packed more snow on top of their son's body, nearly twenty wolves this time crept up to where Patrick was buried and started to dig ferociously at the snow.

Maggie's watch.

As with Randy, she had little strength or energy left, and she too had dozed off.

When she awoke, the wolves had completely uncovered Patrick's shrouded body and had even torn away the sheets that had bound him.

Maggie stood, uncomprehending for a few seconds after being wrenched from sleep by the fierce sounds arising from the wolves' activity. She screamed as she hurried to the front door and stepped outside.

The shotgun was heavy.

Unaccustomed to its use, Maggie aimed the long barrel unsteadily and fired.

The wolves were startled by the sound of the shot, but this time they did not run, probably because Maggie looked like the confused and rather frail figure she was right then, and somehow they had decided, in their instinctive way, that she posed no threat despite the weapon that made so much noise but did little else.

Maggie saw, for an instant, what she had managed to hit with the single rifle shot that had been fired.

None of the wolves.

Maggie screamed then as she turned away from what was left of Patrick's face, screamed as suddenly that scene became a literal nightmare with no chance of awakening from it. The wolves were now running at her, tearing at her clothes, the teeth of at least one of them piercing her arm. And then she caught an almost surreal glimpse of Randy, racing outside, a bright lantern in one hand and the ax in the other, his manner so berserk that even the wolves apparently decided he was not to be tangled with at that moment, and they retreated, but not before taking their spoils with them.

Chapter Twenty-three

Randy was outside again.

He had gone outside often after the blizzard ended and there was no more snow on the ground, the interior of the cabin suddenly suffocating to him.

Maggie stood in the doorway, watching him for several moments and saying nothing at first.

Lord, we've got to go on somehow, she thought. *We've got to get past this. O Lord, we can't allow ourselves to—*

Patrick's death had occurred nearly two months before.

For Maggie, the process of mourning had been devastating, but she was beginning to make the slow and anguished climb back.

Not Randy.

He remained mired as deeply in sorrow as during the hours immediately following that stark tragedy, scarcely talking to her, sometimes just sitting on the floor beside Patrick's bed. Sometimes she would come in from being outside and find him lying across the bed, sobbing and, once, beating his fists against the headboard.

Maggie tried, tried desperately to break into the inner part of him that was resisting her, mired as it was by memories of Patrick and those plans, those grand and beautiful plans they all had shared for the future. But she failed, and in doing so, in admitting that she could not do anything to help him through his pain, she felt as though more than Patrick had died that awful day.

There has to be a reason for all this, she begged. *Please, let me see what it is, Lord, and give me the wisdom to be a comfort to him.*

The irony of that occurred to her.

In those days, men were supposed to be the unfailing source of strength for their womenfolk.

But with Randy in his present state, that was different.

Now Maggie looked through the doorway and saw him sitting on the porch step. Quietly she stepped across the porch and put her hands on his shoulders.

He looked up at her. His cheeks were wet.

"It's so hard, Maggie," he said, "so very hard."

"God will see us through," she replied. "He will help us survive this, Randy."

His shoulders slumped.

"You know, I sit here and turn my eyes toward the sky, and I ask Him, 'Why has this happened?' I wait, Maggie. I really do wait, you know, thinking that I will hear something, that I will sense something, that I will get some clue, some glimmer of mercy—simple, kind mercy that I could expect from such a God as you describe.

"And yet there's no answer, Maggie, no matter how much I plead for one. I don't get a crumb of an answer back from God, not one!"

"We just have to have—" she started to say, realizing that she was falling into easy platitudes precisely when that should not have been the case at all.

Randy stood up abruptly.

"—faith? Ah, that's what you were going to say, isn't it? How handy that would be. Just have faith; that's all it takes, right? Then the rest will follow, like a river on its course. I'll be blessed, Maggie; isn't that it? I mean, I'll have the peace that passes all understanding, and all will be well with the world.

"But that's not happening, Maggie, and don't you dare try to tell me otherwise. I have no peace, Maggie dear, and I perfectly understand why! I would be lying to you and myself if I said otherwise."

Randy started back to the cabin, then abruptly stopped and whirled around.

"Patrick was my proof, Maggie. Don't you understand that? Can't you see? Patrick was my proof that . . . that—"

She walked up to him, stood directly in front of him.

"—that you're a man, Randy, that you can be a father better than your father, more loving, more sensitive," Maggie said, feeling emboldened, "someone who won't make his son an emotional cripple for the rest of his life?

"They robbed you of everything, your parents did, and you've been trying to put the pieces back together one at a time. Fathering Patrick was a big step, one of the most important steps you could ever imagine. I know that, Randy. With him alive, with our son laughing and playing around us and calling you 'Papa,' you felt much more complete as a man."

"Yes, yes, that's what I've been trying to say," Randy cried. "Now that Patrick's gone, now that he—"

"But the way you're reacting, it's as though he never existed. Don't you see that? His body is gone but—"

"But we don't even know where those devils took him!" Randy interrupted. "He became just another chunk of . . . of . . . Oh, Maggie, our son was nothing more than a quick meal for their stomachs!"

"I was there! They came after me too, Randy. I have some scars on my arm to prove it. I could have been their next meal too or have you forgotten all that?"

He started to turn away.

"No!" she demanded. "You *will* face this!"

"Oh, I intend to, Maggie. Yes, I do intend to do just that," Randy said, his voice now in a curious monotone.

He turned back toward the cabin, ignoring her as she stood there, not knowing what he meant and chilled by the dark expression on his face.

His dream that night did nothing to help, a dream that made Randy's life from then on all that much worse . . .

"Papa?"

"Yes, Patrick?"

"I love you."

"Son, I love you too. Your mother and I both do."

"Someday I want to let you take my little boy in your arms and hold him the way you hold me."

"That would be wonderful. Yes, I would really enjoy doing that, Patrick."

"Oh, Papa?"

"Yes?"

"I hope we both live a long time."

A teenaged Patrick Stuart stood at the same moment as his father, and they embraced, forgetting the makeshift fishing poles that rested on the shore of the large lake in front of them.

"Let's go now, Patrick," Randy Stuart said. *"Your mother said she was preparing a special meal for us today."*

"Okay, let's go, Papa. When Mama says it's going to be something special, well, you know she means it!" Patrick replied, his tall, hard-muscled body and brunet-haired good looks making him seem more like a younger brother than a son.

The two of them retrieved their poles as well as the fish they had managed to catch that warm and peaceful afternoon, got on their horses, and rode back to the cabin.

Maggie had seen them coming and was waiting at the front doorway.

Soon they were seated at the table where they had had virtually every meal for more than fifteen years. Two tall candles had been placed in the center.

Stuffed acorn squash, fresh venison with pumpkin-pear sauce, rice salad, cauliflower fritters . . . a memorable meal, by the best prairie standards. And it had all come from Randy and Patrick's successful hunting the day before—and from the small garden Maggie tended at the rear of the cabin.

Patrick smiled at his parents and said, *"Mama, I'd like to offer grace this time instead of you or Papa. Is that all right?"*

Maggie and Randy both smiled and nodded, then they all joined hands.

Tears were trickling down Patrick's cheek as he spoke:

"O Lord, dearest Jesus, thank You for Thy bounty, for Thy mercy, and for the deep and blessed love the three of us have for each other . . . Amen."

They raised their heads. Patrick wasn't alone with his tears.

Randy looked at his son and started to say, *"You bring the truest joy any—"*

Suddenly, he saw Patrick's eyes widen in apparent anguish, mouth opening and closing just once but no words escaping, and in the next instant, being pulled away from him, as though down a long and dark *tunnel, accompanied by the sound of a rushing wind, that young and healthy body spinning wildly, around and around.*

And then Randy awoke from that dream, wrenched from it by the echo of his own terrible screams.

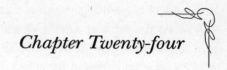

Chapter Twenty-four

Randy found the reality of losing Patrick to be more and more intolerable, time making his emotional wounds worse, not in any way healing them.

The tragedy was now obsessing him to the exclusion of virtually everything else in his life.

Now he was leaving the cabin for ever-longer periods of time.

When he returned, Maggie could smell whiskey on him, which she knew he was getting from a trading post a few miles away, and she noticed that he was often talking incoherently. Even more distressing, he was becoming abusive to her—when he wasn't ignoring her altogether.

Randy Stuart had died months before he actually closed his eyes for the last time, his heart ceasing to beat, his lungs no longer moving. The part of him that had captivated Maggie, the part that had been good and charming and kind, was carried off that night of the wolves.

That night of the wolves . . .

She could scarcely hear their distant call at night without bolting up in bed, covered with perspiration, reaching out for Randy only to find that he was not there, that he had either fallen into a drunken heap at the table or ridden off alone again across the prairie, leaving her to fend for herself.

There was food. Oh, yes, Randy always saw to that.

There was ample wood for the insatiable fire.

Randy left behind whatever was necessary for her body to survive on a purely physical level. But he took away with him what her emotions craved, Randy himself, his body next to Maggie's at night, his muscular arms wrapping around her, his lips touching her own, moments of blessed togetherness that could have forestalled any anguished thoughts about the death of their son, at least until morning chased away the brief respite of night's comfort

If Maggie had allowed herself to do so, she could have struck back harshly at Randy, struck back at him with words and even with her fists pummeling him. She greatly resented his utter selfishness in nursing his unseen but very real wounds without paying any heed to the heartache that had been inflicted upon her as well. By going away, he made life worse for her while doing nothing to make it better for himself.

"If you would just let the Lord—" she started to say to him at innumerable moments during the weeks before his final disappearance.

Randy's expression would freeze the rest of the words in her throat. Then he would turn and stalk from the cabin, into the gathering dusk.

Always Maggie waited on the porch until she realized it was of no use to do so, until she saw the low shapes moving in the darkness, prowling shapes, and once, the quick flash of moonlight on white, snarling fangs.

If you would just let the Lord take over . . .

But Randy seemed incapable of doing that.

Maggie herself experienced difficulty whenever she glanced at that spot from which Patrick's body had been dragged by the wolves, wondering how she could simply place any such burden at the feet of Jesus and then walk away from it.

How can You expect that of me, Jesus?

Maggie could hear no answer, no answer at all for a very long time.

Then came the evening when Randy left and did not return.

Since he had gone away before for long stretches, Maggie chose at first not to become immediately concerned when the sun rose and still, he wasn't back.

By the second evening, though, she knew this time was different.

She stood outside on the porch, paying no attention to the chill breeze that had blown over the prairie from the far-off mountains.

Lord, let me see him in the distance, Maggie prayed. *Let me see my beloved. Let me run to him and put my arms around him and tell him as many times as necessary that we'll survive together because You gave us to one another and nothing can break us apart if we stand firm. Help us stand together, Lord, knowing Your angels are all around us.*

But no one came.

Not Randy.

Nor any of the other settlers.

Even the wolves seemed to be in hiding that night.

Maggie realized that in the morning she would have to climb on the back of the horse and do the best she could to find him.

The very thought chilled her.

Will I find my beloved in the arms of one of those disreputable women in town? Or will I find him—?

Maggie went back into the cabin, blew out the lamp, and climbed into bed. She slept very little that night, and when she did she saw the images again, ghostly, awful images of Patrick, of Randy reaching out to her, begging her to join them . . .

Randy had taught her to saddle and ride a horse, so she knew what to do, how to sit astride instead of sidesaddle, how to get the animal to obey her. But she still wasn't relaxed enough for riding to have become second nature to her, whereas for Randy it had been every bit that.

She had asked him more than once how he took so naturally to it, placing no importance on the fact that Randy never answered her directly, usually replying that it was by instinct or whatever. Whenever he spoke in this manner, he avoided looking directly into her eyes so that she knew he was hiding something, but something, in that context, that seemed of little consequence. So she had always let it pass and just accepted this talent of his, which she doubted she would ever share.

Now, setting out alone across the empty prairie, she struggled to remember everything he had tried to instill in her.

I pray, dear, dear Randy, that it isn't for nought and that I can help you in whatever way you need me now.

In truth, she knew he did not need her at all. She felt that as surely as though it had been written on a sheet of paper and thrust in front of her.

She tried to remember which way Randy had ridden off on the palomino two days before.

Where, Lord? she prayed desperately. *Take command of this horse and point us where we should go.*

Maggie's little sorrel mare seemed to want to go north, her head turning in that direction, moist air coming out of her wide nostrils in rapid little puffs of white in the chill dryness of the morning. While Maggie sat in the saddle and tried to see the last image of Randy and the palomino, disappearing over the horizon, the mare pawed the dirt, eager to get started. Maggie loosened the reins and clucked softly, and the horse headed north, toward the mountains. That was where she let God take her.

The Kiowa-Sioux had been settled in that plains region of the American West for hundreds of years, one of a host of offshoots of the Sioux nation that included Lakotas, the Western Sioux, and various subtribes such as the Hunkpapas, Miniconjous, Oglalas, Oohenonpahs, Sans Arcs, and Sihasapas.

Randy had educated Maggie in such details before they left on their journey, as well as during it, pointing out to her along the way interesting aspects of the Indian way of life.

"To the north of us, the Blackfoot, Crow, and Northern Cheyenne tribes are dominant," he had told her late one afternoon as they were resting after a long day on the trail. "A little farther south, there are the Arapahos and the Southern Cheyenne along with the Pawnees. Below us, south of the Red River, are the Comanches and the Apaches."

Maggie had shivered at the repetition of those names since the only times she had heard any of them was through the wildest tales of ghastly massacres by rampaging bands of enraged braves.

"It's not often like that in real life, as the dime novels would have us believe," he told her. "Braves from different tribes mostly attack one another. To some of the tribes, acts of war are rites of manhood.

"They have been raised to show as little fear as possible, and one way of demonstrating that is to ride courageously and rather exuberantly into battle. Actually taking the life of an enemy is almost anticlimactic. The bravado leading up to that act is the more important thing to them."

The two of them had been sitting on the ground as they talked, leaning against one of the huge wheels of their wagon as they rested the horses awhile.

"How do you know all this?" Maggie asked.

He looked away, in the distance, as he said, "Call it a hobby. Call it a secret passion of mine. I find them fascinating."

"You find savages fascinating?"

"They're more than that, Maggie."

"They worship strange gods."

"They know no better."

"But that doesn't excuse them from God's plan of redemption."

Randy fell into silence for a moment before leaning his head against the rough spokes. He was about to speak again when, abruptly, the ground seemed to be shaking under them.

"An earthquake?" Maggie asked as she jumped to her feet, not knowing what to do.

"No," he said. "Buffalo!"

He was pointing north as he spoke. Maggie glanced in that direction.

A brownish-black wave had appeared in the distance, solid, it seemed, until it was closer. Then they could see what it was, thousands of buffalo moving as though a single unit across the prairie half a mile west of them, running, turning together. Spooked by some unseen threat.

"If they were much closer," Randy observed, "we'd be in very serious trouble. Nothing can stand in their path. Everything would be smashed by the time those beasts made their way past here!"

After the herd had gone by, he smiled appreciatively.

"The Indians use every morsel of every buffalo they kill," he said. "It's amazing how much use they get out of a single carcass."

"The hides and the meat," Maggie remarked. "Tell me, what else is there, Randy?"

"A great deal. You have no idea how ingenious they are. The buffalo's bladder is used to make sinew pouches and medicine bags; they're even used as food containers and other things. The hooves are either cut into hard pieces and strung to become rattles for their babies or ground into a fine black powder they mix with water to form a very effective glue.

"Buffalo bones are transformed into everything you could imagine, from knives, arrowheads, shovels, and hoes to paint brushes, gaming dice, splints, and sled runners. The horns become cups, spoons, ladles, fire-carriers, and even parts of the more elaborate Indian headdresses."

He looked at her, his eyes wide with excitement.

"And that's not all," he added. "Truly nothing goes to waste, Maggie. The winters are too severe on the plains. What they catch now, during the spring and summer months, must last a very long time. The buffalo herds are their survival, Maggie, their survival!"

"So we're going to be cutting up buffalo then?" she had asked, genuinely concerned that this was the case.

"Yes, Maggie," he replied, "both of us just may have to do that."

She had always known that going west would mean giving up the daily meat deliveries to her door in Philadelphia by a traveling butcher who both slaughtered and cut up the carcasses of cattle, hogs, and various fowl for entire neighborhoods.

But actually trapping or killing some kind of animal herself and then cutting it up, cooking it—and eating it. Well, that was something altogether different. It had taken Maggie quite awhile to become so accustomed to this repugnant process that she could actually eat the fresh meat she had prepared.

Randy had caught animals throughout their journey thus far, but mainly little ones such as rabbits, squirrels, or various fowl, and the whole process was reduced to something grisly, yes, but with the virtue of being quick, a few slices with a big knife and it was over, and Randy did it all himself.

But not a buffalo!

They were simply too big. But it was obviously a task that she herself would have to help with, the sickening images coming to mind and causing a familiar queasiness in her stomach.

"We could learn a great deal from the Indians," Randy was saying, his words cutting into her thoughts.

But Maggie wasn't about to give their kind any credit, and this registered in an expression of repugnance that wrinkled up her face.

"Where is that Christian spirit you've talked about so often?" he asked pointedly as he saw her reaction.

Randy had caught her with that one, firing an arrow into the center of her hypocrisy.

"Or is Christian redemption only for white folks and perhaps an occasional black or two?" he prodded, a little too hard.

Maggie slapped him before she realized what she was doing, instantly regretting her action and expecting him to get to his feet and stalk off. But he did not do that.

That wasn't his reaction at all, and she loved him all the more for it.

"Forgive me for that," he said instead, quite earnestly. "We can't expect to deal with everything the future will hold, now, in a single instant. I shouldn't have said anything."

She was the one to jump to her feet, not in anger at him but at herself.

"I slapped you because you were right," she said, "and I couldn't stand that. I couldn't stand to see the truth flashed before me like that."

She walked off a few yards, then stood still.

"No one is rejected by God because of the color of his skin," she said. "How could I allow myself to think any other way?"

"You did so because generations before you did, Maggie," Randy remarked as he walked over to her and put his hands on her shoulders, his nose nuzzling her long soft hair.

That episode on the trail had been a moment of cleansing for Maggie, a moment that she had thought would last a lifetime . . .

Until she began the search for Randy and found him nearly dead, stretched so tightly his arms had been disjointed, his hands and feet tied to stakes hammered into the hard, rocky ground.

Chapter Twenty-five

Maggie had heard the moaning first.

She had followed the direction of the sound until she saw Randy a few hundred feet ahead. His clothes were in a haphazard pile beside him.

She saw that he had been cut over virtually every part of his body.

And she could see vultures hovering overhead.

Slipping out of the saddle, she hurried to Randy's side. "He's still breathing!" she said aloud, as though to convince herself he was alive.

"My love, my love!" Maggie sobbed.

He started to gag, his insides wracked by dry heaves.

"Maggie . . . I'm . . . dying," Randy murmured. "I . . . I . . . Don't look at me like this, please! . . . please . . . don't—"

"I won't let you die!" she insisted with great desperation as she struggled to free his hands from the leather cords that held him. "We have too much life left to live together. I shall get you back to our home and soothe your wounds with ointment and keep you warm by our fire!"

His eyes started to close again.

"No!" she said hysterically. "No, Randy, you will not leave me like this. I'm taking your hand in mine, and I want you to hold on to me. You are not to let go, my love. Let me be your strength. Hold on to me now!"

Maggie could feel his fingers, above the leather cords that bound him, gripping hers, and she started to breathe a sigh of relief.

He smiled for barely an instant.

"Good-bye, Maggie . . . good-bye forever . . ."

"Not now!" she protested. "No! And not forever!"

Those eyes closed, that mouth shut, that familiar head topped by brunette hair fell to one side and was still.

Maggie Engebretsen Stuart became quite hysterical, putting her arms around him and pulling herself to him, holding her beloved tightly, so very tightly.

It was only a minute or two later, perhaps longer; she could not be sure. She could not be sure of anything just then, whether she wanted to go on living or rest her body next to Randy's and die and thus so much more gracefully, so much more calmly, than he had, but die nevertheless and go on to be with him in eternity, without the awful, awful loneliness and despair certain to be with her through the rest of a life that lasted even an instant beyond that terrible moment . . .

A voice.

Gentle.

A voice not within her, though she was in such a state that she could have been deceived in precisely that way.

A real voice.

Not a figment of her mind.

And a hand.

Resting with utter tenderness on her shoulder.

She looked up, the dirt and dust on her face streaked with tears.

An old man.

An old Indian.

"Do you need help?" he asked kindly.

Maggie pushed away from Randy in her anger and jumped to her feet to assault the old man, hitting at him with her fists. But despite his great age, he showed sufficient strength to grab her wrists and shake her until that spasm of rage passed and she collapsed into those old arms and sobbed out her feelings.

"Why?" she said. "Why this man? Can you tell me that? Why this good man? What could have made your people do this to him, to me? We never hurt any of you. We stayed by ourselves and left you alone. Why did this happen? For the love of God, I need to know why!"

"There was a reason, a reason you cannot know now," he told her. "The answer will come later. Now, let me help you take his body to where you live."

Maggie had no choice.

She knew there was no way she could manage to do it by herself.

The two of them wrapped Randy's body in her pack blanket and lifted it onto the old man's mule, where he tied it expertly to the animal's back with the leather cords that had bound Randy to the stakes.

Then he helped Maggie onto her own horse and took the reins of both animals, leading them in a southeasterly direction.

"You know where we . . . live?" she asked.

"I know," he replied simply. "All of my people are aware of you, and we know who has done this to your husband."

She was too weak and distraught, too dazed by the shock of what had happened, to ask him for an explanation.

The two of them, Maggie and the old Indian, were silent for the rest of the way.

Toward dusk, they arrived back at the cabin . . . the cabin she and Randy had built together.

The old man offered to help Maggie with the burial, but she would not let him.

"Find me the ones who did this, and then I will thank you," she said defiantly.

"And what will you do with them?" he asked her.

"I shall cut their eyes out and then their tongues, and then I shall—" she said, trying to continue.

"You do not have it in you even to talk or to think like that," the Indian pointed out. "But for those who took the life of your husband, there was no other way—spilled blood for spilled blood."

"Randy never did anything to harm your kind!" she declared, contempt creeping into her voice.

"You do not know the truth. The truth you have not heard

guided their actions. If you were an Indian and you had trapped such a man as your husband, you might have done what they did."

"Randy could have done nothing to justify his torture, his gruesome death."

He looked at her sadly, shaking his head with despair.

"Don't treat me that way!" Maggie screamed. "I do not need your heathen pity. I need justice."

"They held off for a very long while, you know," the old man went on. "They had no desire to leave a child without a father. They tried to be as fair as they could manage, these people did."

Maggie shouted at him again, "But it was all right to leave me without a husband!"

"They thought the child innocent. They would not have harmed him. They would protect him."

"Was I not innocent also? How could they pretend to protect either one of us by slaughtering the man we loved?"

Maggie ordered him away after that, wanting no part of his help.

She would bury Randy by herself, no matter how difficult it was or how long it took.

Maggie's fingers were bloody by the time she had piled the last rock on top of Randy's grave. She had buried him in the willow grove where he and Patrick had stopped to rest that stormy day . . .

Just a short while ago, she thought, *you and I had finished building our home, and we were so tired yet happy and looking forward to—*

Pain.

All over her body.

She looked at her bruised, battered hands.

Two of her fingernails were blackened, cracked when the rocks fell on them. And dirt had gotten into the many cuts that marred her skin, making both hands throb.

Maggie was totally drained.

Merely standing was an act that required a debilitating amount of effort. Then her surroundings started to spin, and she fell to her

knees, banging one of them on the rocks covering the grave.

O God, I don't know what to do!

Maggie was utterly alone, more than 2,000 miles away from what once had been home.

But home wasn't there anymore, either!

Home was not just a place, not just familiar surroundings and habit patterns.

People.

And those who had mattered the most to her—all of them—were gone.

No one left.

She was the only one.

A chill gripped Maggie's body quite apart from the encroaching cold of that prairie evening, and she could feel herself slipping more and more into an abyss, a dark place of dead emotions and suffocating despair. All normal thoughts, coherent thoughts, thoughts essential if she were to survive, now were being crowded out by those that were quite irrational.

A sense of panic was beginning to take over as she glanced about herself . . . the flat prairie around her, in the distance the mountains. All around her was nothing but that dreadful sameness, as though everyone else on the planet had disappeared. She had survived, but it was with the maddening certainty that her life had been destroyed, that she was alive but wanted to be dead.

It had become a place of death.

Like the image the desert had become to Maggie.

She remembered the stories other travelers had told her of the skeletons of animals they had seen, the rocks piled over makeshift graves.

Countless numbers of settlers never made it, succumbing to the heat, to the poisonous snakes, or perhaps to the unfriendly Indian warriors eager to have yet another white kill to brag about to the rest of their tribe.

Her hand had gone reflexively to her head as she thought of the scalp-taking ceremonies she had heard about even while still in Philadelphia.

"But we made it!" she shouted to the nothingness around her.

"We're more than halfway to California. We—"

She reached out toward the pile of stones next to her, resting her now-throbbing hand on a smooth, round rock she had placed on top of the pile, tears slipping over her lids and trickling down her cheeks.

If I just sit like this and if I do nothing, nothing at all, I will surely die out here in the middle of nowhere . . .

She desperately wanted to call out, to scream, but she knew there would be only mocking silence in response.

I must stand. I must try to get back to the cabin.

Her teeth were chattering—from the chill, from despair. While she had been preparing the grave, she hadn't noticed the rather sudden plunge in temperature, but now the chill air couldn't be ignored any longer.

A storm.

She hadn't noticed the clouds gathering earlier either, focused on gathering the energy to dig that awful hole and thankful that the ground wasn't frozen. Eventually she had stopped, having dug all she could dig. Then she had eased his body into the grave, filled it back up with dirt, and covered it with stones because she had been too weak to make the grave deep enough.

Deep enough . . .

The implications were ghastly.

Despite the chill, for a brief spell she dozed off there beside the grave and had a quick, nasty dream, a dream in which she returned to the site the next evening and found pieces of Randy's body scattered about. Some coyotes were there; as soon as they saw her, they scampered off, carrying—

That image jolted her awake, screaming.

"O God, no!"

After that, Maggie determined to stay awake as long as she could, fearing what other terrible visions sleep would bring.

She had to get back in the cabin. Immediately.

At least that much common sense was able to penetrate her brain and take hold of it.

Maggie finally stood, cold, nauseous, her arms aching.

She put one foot in front of the other, then again, then again, until she reached the little mare, hobbled nearby.

Oh, Randy, she thought. *How can I just abandon this land we came to together? How can I just turn my back on it? Perhaps if I stay long enough, I will die here too, and when someone comes along, surely they will bury me next to you. I would like that, Randy . . . to have my body next to yours again.*

The wind was quite loud, a sound much like that of a sad chorus, like some dirge once distant now as close as—Something touched her cheek.

Snow! Even this late in the season!

"We've got to get back," she said aloud, then sobbed as she realized there was no longer any "we" but just herself.

The mare knew the way home. Maggie looked back once at that pile of stones, then headed into the building storm.

Soon the snow was falling at a much faster rate.

She stopped for a moment, trying to get her bearings.

Where? Oh, where? I'm sure it was—

She was no longer sure at all.

She should have been able to find the cabin. She knew the area so well.

Yes! Ahead!

Something flickering in the darkness.

Light!

She stopped abruptly, her heart pounding fiercely.

Too much light!

A short while later, she found the source, visible even from the distance that remained ahead of her.

The cabin was ablaze. Someone had set it on fire.

She stood a hundred feet away.

All gone. There's nothing left. Why do they hate us so?

But she knew the answer to that question as soon as she had uttered it.

We're the intruders. We're the ones who have ripped their land from them. Whatever they do is in self-defense.

She tried to pretend that what Randy had told her would help, would keep her from being consumed by hate.

It didn't.

She started shrieking to the emptiness around her.

"Others have robbed you! Others have raided your villages, raped your womenfolk, murdered your sleeping babies. But not this one, not my Randy! Not me! Why us? We have done nothing against you."

Panic was nibbling at the edges of her awareness, panic that grew in a great rushing surge.

She had no place to go!

And she could feel the cold reaching deeper into her body, taking hold of her bones, grabbing her lungs and—

She turned the mare away from the blaze, as difficult as it was to tear herself from that compelling sight.

Her strength was gone, and she fell forward in the saddle, feeling the snow's coldness against her body, thinking how comforting it seemed, numbing her moment by moment, until there was little sensation of any kind except the rocking gait of the mare beneath her, carrying her into oblivion . . .

Maggie Engebretsen Stuart knew she was close to death, knew she had fallen into a kind of temporary cocoon of the most extreme cold she had ever known, cold that soon became a strangely comforting shield for her. Every part of her body was numb, but not her emotions. Her mind soared even as the darkness enveloped her, darkness that soon gave way to something else altogether, a world of recollection, of moments torn from the past and served up to her as though current. She saw again the moments with her sister Roberta as the two teenagers discussed men, Roberta eager to start dating and Maggie somewhat bored by the whole matter. And she recalled other vignettes, some of them with her parents—quiet times they all had spent together, times of peace and joy. She saw Randy, riding beside her on the wagon seat. And Patrick, nursing at her breast. And underlying all the scenes was the knowledge that it all had been taken for granted, lived for the moment but never treasured. Until they were gone and could not be retrieved, lost forever . . .

Randy . . .

Images of Randy came to her repeatedly in that strange state of frozen isolation of mind from body. Randy appeared to her as before, living and happy and so virile, Randy as she had desperately wanted him to be, victorious over the despair and melancholy that had caught hold of him.

But Randy wasn't at the very center of what she saw and felt there, alone, in the blizzard-driven cold.

No, not Randy, not her beloved.

The most persistent image was of her mother.

"Oh, Mama!" Maggie's mind cried out. "It's so cold here. You mustn't stay. You will become quite ill, dear one."

Her mother smiled sweetly.

"I tried to help you whenever I could," she said, "I really did, you know. But the Lord had something else in mind."

Maggie knew that was true, and she told her mother so, holding close to her the privilege of that strange and beautiful moment.

"You never let my tears dry by themselves, Mama. You wiped my tears away. And then you held me and sang of the love of Christ."

Her mother's head was bowed in apparent sorrow, those familiar, strong shoulders of hers slumping.

"Don't cry, dear, dear Mama. Please don't—"

Nevertheless, her mother was sobbing, her frail body shaking with the effort of it.

"I took care of you, Maggie. I stayed with you throughout the night when you had a fever. But now—"

A loud sigh.

Maggie heard it as though this sound had been amplified a hundred times in volume.

"I must leave, Maggie. I cannot stay. I must leave you alone. I must leave you here to find your own way, my sweet, sweet child."

In her mind, Maggie wanted to run to her mother, to hug her

one last time. But she had no legs, no hands, nothing that would move, and for all she knew, her heart itself had stopped beating.

When her mother lifted her head, it was a different face Maggie saw this time, a face with a glow about it.

And beside her was a figure of transcendent iridescence.

"I have to go, my dearest Maggie. Whatever happens now, know one thing, my sweet child, know it above all else over the years to come . . . know that your father and I are truly happy, that Jesus —"

Tears choked off the rest of her words save a final few.

". . . and that we will never stop loving you."

And then it was over, that strange moment, and Maggie heard only, as though from a very great distance, the fierce howling of the storm rampaging across that desolate prairie around her . . . somewhere west of the Mississippi.

Chapter Twenty-six

Warm.

Maggie Engebretsen Stuart's hands felt quite warm and faintly greasy.

But she could barely move them; something was wrapped around each one, restraining especially the fingers.

"Be still," the male voice said. "You are safe enough. There is no need to worry, Ma'am."

Soothing. That voice was soothing.

She obeyed.

Heat.

On her face.

Instinctively she tried to touch her cheeks, her forehead.

"Don't . . ." she was told.

That same voice. Strong. But also kind.

"Where am I?" Maggie managed to form the words.

"In my home."

She tried to open her eyes, but the lids wouldn't move very far. As with her hands, something had been—

How good that heat felt!

She stretched out her frame, sighing as her body soaked it up, tiny rivers of heat coursing along frozen muscles.

"I have to tell you something," the voice said, even softer than before, peace in it.

"Who are you?" she asked, frustrated that she could not see and anxious to know what was happening.

"I found you outside, miles from here. You were completely covered by the snow except for one hand. You must have been trying to push the snow away. Your hand was reaching straight up. That was what I saw."

"The mare? Did you find my horse?"

"Didn't see a horse, Ma'am. She must have run off . . . or . . ."

Maggie remembered now. Remembered it all.

The man had been attracted by the flames and headed toward them.

"I thought maybe someone could be rescued," the man told her. "But nobody was inside."

Maggie sighed.

"Everything we had was there," she said. "It's all gone now. Clothes. Furniture. Food. My books . . ."

"No, Ma'am," the voice assured her. "Something is left. You were given a single remnant."

"What was left? What did you find?"

"Your Bible. It's safe."

"How could that be?"

"I guess the flames must have produced an explosion at first. The Bible must have been blown clear. It's a bit singed and tattered, and there are some water marks from melted snow. But mostly it's fine."

Her heart was suddenly beating faster.

"You have it here, now?" she asked.

"I do."

"Could you bring it to me?"

She heard the man leave the room. A few seconds passed. The time seemed to drag on. She briefly had difficulty swallowing.

I am still alive, she told herself. *How could I still be alive after what happened, how could I—?*

"Would you place my hand on it, Sir?" Maggie asked when she heard him come back into the room.

She could feel her left hand being moved gently.

"There," the voice said soothingly. "Your hand is resting on the cover. God is with you."

She fell asleep then, more pleased than she could have imagined about such a simple matter. But her Bible had survived, and that was worth rejoicing over. Indeed it was.

Real pain suddenly. Before this surge of it there had been only a persistent throbbing.

Worse now. Much worse.

"Ma'am?"

The man again, speaking to her. His voice sounded more concerned this time, anxious.

"Yes?"

"Your right hand?"

The one that was hurting the most, such pain that she could hardly endure it, pain that—

"I—" the voice started to say.

"Yes," she prodded uncertainly. "Tell me what you must. Nothing could be worse than what I have experienced already."

"Your hand may—may have to—to—be—"

No!

Maggie could guess what the stranger was trying to say.

"You can't do that!" she begged him. "You aren't a doctor, are you? How could you even think of doing it?"

"No, I am not a doctor, as you say, but I have done that kind of thing before, to save a life. And you're a nurse, aren't you?"

"Yes, but how did you know?"

"When you were unconscious, you mumbled about a lot of things."

"Oh . . ."

Darkness came again. As she was slipping back into it, she had only one thought. *My hand!*

She surrendered to nothingness. But not before that voice had told her it wasn't only her hand that had been affected by the frostbite.

O Lord, don't let me awaken. Please take me now. O God, please take me now!

Maggie was in shock when she finally regained full consciousness and saw her benefactor.

Kind and gentle and eager to help her.

An Indian!

Maggie found herself in the expert but surprising care of an Indian named White Feather.

Tall.

She had not envisioned any Indians being so tall. This one seemed to be a bit over six feet in height.

That face!

Nearly as handsome as Randy's.

Clean-shaven, she noted, not realizing that all Indians were that way since most had never developed any facial hair.

He seems civilized enough, and yet— Terrified.

That she was!

Despite the man's kindness toward her, she was still terrified about what might be his intentions.

All those wild tales about Indians, especially the more brutal ones!

When their Philadelphia friends had learned of what she and Randy were going to do, they had tried to warn Maggie, loading her mind with gruesome stories of scalpings and rape and other brutalities.

Yet this was not all.

No hesitancy existed in those days about calling Indians what most actually were: "heathen savages."

For they were true heathens, indeed, worshiping strange gods and goddesses that were the antithesis of anything Christian. The various tribes were universally under a spirit of darkness, as missionaries assigned to them quickly found out. Pantheism was dominant, with the sun and the earth and other material things being idolized.

While unbridled portraits of barbaric Indians acting almost like cavemen were obviously stupid and grossly inaccurate, the later attempts to make them seem like exploited saints clearly went too far in the opposite direction.

In reality, the truth was somewhere in the middle between those extremes.

But, religiously, even the worst of the tales had an undeniably strong basis in truth, for these people, whatever the tribe, were without Christ, and they were eternally doomed if they did not ultimately accept Him as Savior and Lord.

Whatever the "politically correct" attitudes later that would label as repugnant the missionaries' efforts to convert the Indians and "cram the white man's religion down their throats," it was in fact Christianity that was their hope, their only hope, and not their pathetic paganism.

Maggie had done some research while still living in Philadelphia, and she saw the depths to which all the tribes, to one degree or another, had sunk into the most unholy worship that was nothing more than occultic deception and in many instances, led to demonic possession.

Flint Boy.

She learned about this god of some of the Indian tribes, for example. This god had a misshapen form and was capable of great deceit; he was also a mean and vengeful god who sent into the world a host of monstrous apparitions to bedevil anyone who earned his displeasure.

Then there was the ghastly Deer Woman, a goddess special to the Cherokee and Choctaw tribes. Her mission was to bewitch men and women and either cause them to die or become prostitutes!

Long Man.

The Indians also had a god of rivers, Long Man, and another one of stones and rocks who was called Changer because he had the ability to change into any of these forms. And there was also Crystal Woman.

Sorcery was a primary aspect of religion for every tribe, with goddesses in charge of casting spells and spelling out rites of worship. These included Pikiawish Woman and Qiyo Kepe and innumerable others.

Maggie understood what hatred the Indian tribes had for the white intruders, but she had wondered which came first: the savagery of the Sioux or the dictatorial and equal savagery of white settlers who thought nothing of appropriating the land of tribes who had lived on it for centuries.

Still, knowing what had happened to Randy, she was stunned when she awoke to find White Feather taking care of her.

But that apprehension quickly changed.

She saw clearly that White Feather would not harm her, that he was interested only in bringing her back to health and strength. To find an Indian with the goal of restoration rather than killing seemed a miracle.

And gradually, as he likewise felt more comfortable around her, he began to tell Maggie about his own life.

White Feather had been living alone since his wife, who had had the beautiful name of Brook That Sings, died more than two years before, the victim of an attack by a grizzly bear.

There was no doubt how much he had loved her.

And it was this love that spawned a bond of affection and respect between this Indian man and the white woman from Philadelphia, because she had known that kind of love too. And both of them knew what it was like to have someone who was loved so deeply suddenly be ripped from their lives. They both had felt that pain, and their mutual understanding undeniably made them closer to one another.

In a remarkably short time, White Feather became, in Maggie Engebretsen Stuart's eyes, someone very much like herself; they were both suffering a loss that would affect them until the end of their days.

Chapter Twenty-seven

Maggie's body healed well, even her hands.

This came about, she would contend, partly because of White Feather's mixtures of medicinal herbs and ordinary mud, sometimes with a bit of buffalo dung worked into them. Yes, these proved helpful. While she didn't relish the thought of such smelly concoctions being spread over large areas of her body, its effect seemed every bit an answer to prayer.

Actually, it amazed them both that Maggie was even alive.

"But there is more to it than that," she would say.

"More?" he would reply. "What do you mean?"

He had given her an opening, and she did not let it slip away.

"Faith . . ." she said softly, still feeling exceptionally weakened by what had happened.

White Feather was respectfully silent, waiting for his friend to finish.

She told him about the faith that had been part of her since she was a child.

"Healing is present today!" she declared. "But it's not the kind the faith healers use to trick gullible people into paying good money for an act that is no more than a sideshow."

She talked on and on, eager to chatter away, for this seemed to relieve her stress.

For a long while, White Feather did not agree or disagree with her. He merely listened.

He seemed nearly as "clinical" in his approach as the doctors and nurses with whom she had worked back East, managing to remain utterly detached even when he was called upon to rub his rather sensuous-feeling ointment over Maggie's frost-burned body.

One look at her hands would convince anyone she could not do this herself.

That an Indian was doing it to her made Maggie recoil, but he was gentle, and she relaxed, though it did embarrass her that he was seeing her as only Randy had.

Maggie asked White Feather, in a discrete way, whether he had "known" other women since Brook That Sings died.

"No," he told her simply.

"Not one?" she persisted.

"She was my love for a lifetime. Her body no longer resides in this house, but that does not end the bond between us."

Minutes before, White Feather had surprised her by confessing his Christian beliefs to her.

His conversion had come about when he had traveled east of the Mississippi, and along the way had happened to attend a revival meeting in a tent where he had heard the preacher named Charles Finney.

"He's wonderful," Maggie exclaimed. "I am so glad you were able to find someone like that man."

"As a result, I felt it necessary to give up some of the old ways and separate myself from my people because so much of what they believed was antagonistic to my new faith. We are not antagonistic toward one another now, but we will never be as close as we had been."

"Until the whole tribe is converted!" she exclaimed.

"That would be a miracle, a hoped-for one, but I do not count on it. I do not even think about it with great seriousness."

Maggie liked White Feather.

Having nowhere else to go, she stayed with him. And eventually she came to think of him as not just an Indian but as a kind and interesting man, and this helped build the rapport between them.

She was with him when he did what he had been wanting to do for two years: track down and kill the grizzly that had taken the life of his beloved Brook That Sings.

When they arrived at the forested mountainside where he had spotted the grizzly, a dozen miles away from where they both now lived, he insisted that she stay high up on a very steady branch of a large tree.

"But you can't be sure that this is the same one," Maggie pointed out. "I mean, how could you know, White Feather?"

"You are correct," he admitted. "But it does not matter. If Brook That Sings can see me now, she will know that I am doing it for her, whether or not the grizzly is the very same one. My act is undiminished if it is not."

"But why didn't you do it earlier? Surely there have been other such bears in this region. Why wait until this moment?"

"Because if the grizzly wins and I die, someone needed to be here, to take care of my body. I want to be buried next to Brook That Sings. But until now, I could not bear the presence of another human being."

"But I am a woman."

"You buried your husband. Would you not do so for a friend?"

Maggie smiled but with no real joy. The mere thought of going through that sorrowful act again reopened the floodgates of grief she thought had finally been closed.

"It would be difficult to lose you," she said. "You saved my life. How can I face the possibility that you might soon lose your own?"

White Feather hesitated before answering, not wanting to trample on Maggie's still-fragile feelings.

"I respect the way you are feeling, but you must respect the way I feel as well. You must realize that my feelings in this case run far deeper than your own. Please do not think that as harsh, as indifferent, as it sounds. You have your life. Now let me have the one desire that has sustained my life for the last two years."

"Is there nothing I can do? I know how to shoot."

"Have you ever killed anything larger than a deer?"

"Not even a rabbit," Maggie replied resignedly.

"Your husband killed all the game?"

"Yes . . ."

"Then you could do little if I were to fail."

Maggie could argue no longer, so she allowed White Feather to help her up into the tree he had chosen, then watched as he stood behind another tree in the clearing, armed with a heavy old musket.

In an hour or so the grizzly he had been tracking for days appeared on the opposite side of the clearing, emerging from the surrounding forest like a hairy, snarling version of Goliath.

White Feather shot the animal once but not between the eyes, as he had intended. The bear staggered but did not go down. Calmly, White Feather reloaded the old musket and was about to fire again when the bear charged him before he could pull the trigger.

It slapped White Feather to one side with a single swipe of its giant paw, and he landed just below the branch where Maggie was sitting.

The grizzly charged over to him and grabbed his head between its paws, then started to lift him from the ground.

Without thinking, Maggie jumped onto the fierce animal's broad, furry back, swinging wildly with a hunting knife White Feather had given her just in case of anything unforeseen happening.

Roaring madly, the bear dropped White Feather and stood up, trying to reach behind its head and pull her off.

She clung to the bear's hide as it bounced and twisted beneath her. Then she leaned forward and hooked her arms around its neck, clasping the knife with both hands and plunging it into the animal's chest right below the neck.

The bear swung its head backward, reeling in pain, and Maggie lost her grip on the heavy fur, tumbling to the ground. Enraged and confused, the grizzly nevertheless spotted Maggie as she tried to get to her feet but tripped and fell.

It advanced toward her, sending out a roar that would have terrified even the most experienced hunter, let alone a former nurse from Philadelphia!

Suddenly, a dozen arrows were shot through the air, several of them penetrating the grizzly. Still the great beast did not fall but continued to stand upright, flailing its massive paws.

Maggie saw White Feather reach again for the musket, aim it

carefully and, this time, hit the grizzly between the eyes. Finally the huge bear stumbled and fell, hitting the ground with astonishing force.

Maggie hurried over to White Feather.

"Your people . . . weren't they the ones who shot the arrows?" she asked, glancing from side to side but seeing no one in the thick forest around them.

"Yes," White Feather said, smiling weakly. "We owe them so much."

"And yet, still, they do not show themselves!"

"They have done this one thing. It does not mean I ever will be allowed back into their lives, at least not as before."

"What brought them here?"

"We are very close to their village. They have scouts all over this area. We were fortunate that they were able to act so quickly."

"So many men saved our lives and, yet, we cannot even thank them," Maggie remarked sadly.

"There may be a time," White Feather said knowingly. "As you know, God does not do things by accident."

He was right.

She knew that.

For now, Maggie had to be concerned about only one thing— getting White Feather back to his house and treating his wounds.

Maggie tended White Feather's cuts and bruises with great expertise, using knowledge gained from nursing.

Weeks passed, the two of them becoming closer but with no romantic involvement. Both had been through the greatest loves of their lives, and it would take a long time before either would want to reach out and fall in love again.

But something else developed between Maggie and the handsome Indian.

A friendship of extraordinary depth.

And then one day, not wanting to have any secrets or lies

between them, White Feather came to Maggie and tried to tell her why her beloved Randy had been killed.

Despite their close relationship, she was unwilling to listen, and White Feather realized he would have to show her.

Trapper's Cove.
An isolated place in the Rockies.

An obscure trading post where trappers took their pelts and bargained for sales. There were regular commercial places for this sort of thing in the larger settlements, but in Trapper's Cove, all the activity was clandestine because it involved game poached from Indian land. This was the black market of that era.

Not all the trappers survived their forays into Indian land.

Some were caught by the Sioux and tortured mercilessly before they were finally killed. Some were given a chance to "run the arrow," a kind of game practiced by warriors who gave their prisoners the length of an arrow's travel as a head start before they were followed.

Few would ever escape.

But the trappers who avoided contact with the Sioux came to Trapper's Cove well loaded with the dead bodies of helpless animals. In those days there was justification for killing the creatures because the furs were a source of genuinely needed clothing to protect against the ravaging winters that howled across frontier lands.

And yet many of the men seemed to enjoy the slaughter, seemed to get as much fun out of it as anything having to do with monetary gain or physical need.

"Skinning them is what I love," more than one had been known to admit. "There's something satisfying about it. I can't explain why. But it's there. Maybe it's the total control I have over an animal's life, and also what happens to its body. That's power!"

Trapper's Cove.
A shameful place.

Where rabbit, bear, buffalo, and other animal skins were bargained over after the carcasses had been wastefully discarded wherever the animals had been brought down. The weapons of choice were traps or rifles, but sometimes even arrows were used in a manner learned from friendly Indians and then turned around and used as a means of stealing from them.

"It is a tragedy when any tribe believes that attacking innocent white settlers is all they can do to protect their land," White Feather told her as they approached the cove, Maggie with her arms around his waist as she sat behind him on the horse. "But the emotions they feel are understandable. *Their* families are being attacked; *their* families are being driven from land that has been theirs for a thousand years. And you know what some white soldiers are using as justification for their heartless actions?"

Maggie shook her head.

"That Indians are just heathens," he said, "that they are savages, and it's all right to kill or maim them or steal from them because, after all, God condemns their pagan worship."

Suddenly, Maggie felt ill, remembering her own words along those lines as they were coming westward. She was coming to realize just a small part of what went on under the specious cover of Christianity.

"I don't believe I can go in there," she said.

"I think you should, Maggie. I think you should see why your husband was treated the way he was."

"Does that mean I'll excuse what they did?"

"That's foolish, and you know it. Of course you won't. But it might help to see why a few braves lashed out in such utter rage."

"All right, White Feather," she replied, "all right. I'll go in."

In her mind she added, *Lord, protect me, please. Guard my steps.*

Trapper's Cove was surrounded by snowcapped mountains that formed a natural barrier to the outside world. The only way in was over a treacherously narrow pass that snaked between the towering peaks.

Even so, the outpost was surrounded by a high stockade fence, like a fort. Maggie and White Feather were stopped at the gate and checked for weapons by several large, bearded men wearing sidearms and holding rifles. One of them questioned White Feather.

"I've seen you here before, haven't I?" he asked.

"Yes."

"You're Indian, and you've stolen from your own kind?"

"To eat. To survive."

The man grunted as though it were no concern of his and allowed them to ride past.

A short distance farther on, they got off the horse, and White Feather tied the reins to a timber railing that had been set up for that purpose.

All around them, voices formed a cacophonous backdrop that made it difficult for Maggie and White Feather to hear one another.

"It's always like this, day and night," he said directly into her ear.

"But don't the tribes know about it?" she asked.

"They do, but this place is a fortress. It is better armed than most cavalry outposts I have seen. And there is only that one entrance. You didn't see them, but guards were posted all along the way in. No attacking force could survive by riding in in a single column—and that's the only way you can come in. They would be picked off too easily."

Along the dirty roadway, booths were set up, skins hanging from each one.

"It's like a slaughterhouse," she said.

"Not *like* a slaughterhouse, Maggie," White Feather replied ironically. "It *is* a slaughterhouse. And not just for animals."

She stopped walking and looked at him.

"What do you mean, White Feather?" Maggie asked nervously.

"You'll see," he said as he pointed toward the left.

Flat up against the mountain, in a little alcove of its own, was another booth, similar to the others but with one important difference: no animal skins in evidence.

Only tufts of long, black hair hung from the small hooks.

Scalps!

N-o-o! Maggie's mind screamed, somehow knowing instantly what was being sold. *It can't be. Such as this . . . it can't be!*

White Feather saw her expression.

"Yes," he said, "that's what they are."

"But what does this have to do with Randy—" she started to say, then stopped, the truth again rearing up before her.

"Maggie," he said, "your Randy specialized in scalps during his earlier westward journey. He came out with the circus but then realized he could have more money—and maybe more excitement and adventure—as a scalp trader. He killed unwary and even peaceful Indians, took their scalps, and then traded them here in Trapper's Cove. At first, due to his inexperience, he was almost killed several times, but later, he became very good at what he did. Other men grew to envy him."

White Feather turned toward the short, nervous-looking man who was selling the scalps.

"How's business, Joe?" he asked easily, as though he wasn't bothered at all by being so close to the scalps of his own people.

"Good, pretty good. It took awhile to make up the loss, though, years in fact. Not everybody can do what Stuart did."

"Stuart? You mean Randy Stuart?"

The man nodded vigorously.

It was Maggie's turn to ask a question.

"The loss?" she said. "What do you mean by the loss?"

White Feather was aware of what the other man meant but wanted Maggie to hear the answer.

"Yes, when Randy Stuart left, well, we lost out for a long, long time. It's dangerous work, White Feather. You know that. Your people can fight like . . . well, like Indians when they're cornered. Randy kept guys like me going because he brought in such a steady supply."

The seedy little man looked at Maggie approvingly, then back again at White Feather.

"Got anything for me today?" he asked half-seriously, not concerned about bad taste. "I am low on certain things. I know how you feel about anything other than animal skins, but I can always hope, can't I? Heh-heh.

"I think you're a different sort of Indian, you surely are . . . hanging out with white women and all . . ."

He cast another lurid look toward Maggie.

"If you ever change your mind and need the dough, I'll buy whatever you can round up. I mean, ain't there still some tribes you and your braves wouldn't mind raiding and—"

He saw White Feather's eyes widen in anger.

"Just kidding," he quickly added. "You're only into animal skins. I know that. But not that Stuart! He got whatever was in demand."

. . . *whatever was in demand.*

Those words were all it took for Maggie.

She lunged for the man, hitting him, clawing at him.

He fell backward, tipping over part of his booth, and spilling out some of the previously hidden contents.

It wasn't only Indian *scalps* sold in that little alcove.

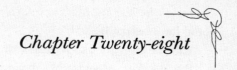

Chapter Twenty-eight

Erupting like that was hardly typical for Maggie.

But the overload she experienced at Trapper's Cove was far too massive at that moment.

In that horrid place she had seen what she could never have imagined having to face, and she was told that Randy used to engage—actually to thrive—in the same ugly and inhumane commerce.

Now back inside White Feather's familiar home, Maggie was still shocked and furious about what she had witnessed, but White Feather seemed to be taking it all in stride.

"That was quite a scene you caused back there," he told her, recalling the brouhaha Maggie had started with her attack on the scalp trader. "No telling what they would have done to us if that nasty Joe character hadn't stood up for you, rubbing his black eye and telling everyone what an honor it was to have Randy Stuart's widow among them."

White Feather chuckled as he said those last few words, hoping to make her feel a bit better.

She closed her eyes, her forehead pounding.

"Those were . . . were pieces of—!" Maggie exclaimed, stuttering, hardly able to talk.

She could not bring herself to say aloud what was still so traumatically fresh in her mind.

"How could anyone do that?" she asked disbelievingly. "How could they treat human beings like cattle or some other beast?"

"Randy did just that, Maggie," White Feather reminded her as gently as possible.

"I can't believe it," Maggie retorted. "I knew him too well. He would have been appalled."

White Feather shook his head sadly.

"But it's true, Maggie. Not believing it won't change reality. Randy had another side of him, one he was successful in hiding from you and so many others, but ultimately, he paid the price for it."

She was still unconvinced.

"But he was too gentle, too kind."

"Gentle? Kind? Would a kind, gentle man speak so harshly to his wife . . . and leave her on the prairie alone, unprotected, while he roamed around the land in a drunken stupor, indulging himself in self-pity?"

"It was the alcohol that drove him to do such things."

White Feather hated having to assault Maggie with such hard talk so soon after what she had encountered at Trapper's Cove. He looked at her face, pale and drawn, and what he wanted instead was to reach out to her, stroke her soft cheek with his fingertips, then take her in his arms and somehow give her some of his own strength to handle such matters.

The urge almost overwhelmed him. He reached out and touched her cheek with the fingers of his left hand.

"Maggie, Maggie, when your husband returned to Philadelphia, it was to escape a phantom."

There was always that dark portion of Randy Stuart's tormented soul, Maggie had to admit to herself, though not out loud, that secret "door" she would invariably come up against and be powerless to unlock.

It had been sealed off permanently, never to be opened to others . . . but often visited by Randy himself as the darkness occasionally threatened to engulf him.

"Darkness," she mumbled.

"Yes, Maggie, what about darkness?"

"It was always there, a sense of doom, I think. Even when he was happiest, it didn't completely retreat. It seemed to hover just out of reach."

"Like a storm threatening to unleash itself."

"Exactly!"

She looked up at White Feather, her expression changing.

"I think I know," she said.

"Do you really? Tell me, dear Maggie," he said.

"You were right when you said that Randy was trying to leave the phantom behind," she continued, her voice low. "He returned home to . . . to . . ."

White Feather bowed his head.

"Lord, give my friend the understanding that can come only from Thee," he said with great feeling.

He looked up. Maggie was sobbing.

"He was trying to change," she managed to say. "He was trying to shed everything that had haunted him, not just what he did here but also the childhood that had affected him so devastatingly . . . and . . . and start over."

"But when he went back East he left behind some of those whose loved ones he had killed," White Feather said reluctantly. "They haven't changed their feelings about him, Maggie. They remember every time they cry themselves to sleep at night."

Maggie sat up, looking from side to side.

"God, help me!" she cried out. "Randy really is gone and . . . and . . . oh, please, God, help me!"

White Feather was quiet a moment as Maggie struggled to get control of her emotions.

"Why do you think he took such a chance?" Maggie asked later as they sat together outside. "Why did he come back out here with me, back to the frontier?"

They were sitting near a small fire that blazed in front of them, not for cooking but to ward off the early-evening chill. Coyotes were crying quite near in the half-darkness.

"We cannot know for sure," White Feather replied. "But my guess is that he felt cleansed, invigorated. He thought simply taking a different route would be the answer, without realizing that some of my kind are basically nomads, moving about the land, especially as white civilization spreads westward."

The hope Randy must have had!

That talk about a fresh start . . .

White Feather closed his eyes for a moment.

"But the greatest reason was how much he must have loved you, Maggie," he said. "That love overcame his reluctance, his fear, his—"

"—reason," Maggie interrupted. "He knew how much I wanted to go and . . . and my sweet Randy—"

She couldn't finish that sentence, for the words were being trapped inside her by a rush of emotion.

"Only you mattered, Maggie," White Feather said. "He wanted nothing for himself, I suppose. He was totally devoted to making you happy."

The two sat in silence, the flames reflected on their faces in the deepening darkness of the wide prairie sky.

"He had such plans," she finally said, her tone wistful and melancholy as the images rose up. "We both did."

"So it could be said of those he killed," White Feather reminded her as gently as he could. "They were no different from your Randy Stuart, except in those days he had no family depending upon him. The braves whose scalps he took had another story altogether."

. . . Their loved ones remember every time they cry themselves to sleep at night.

The fire felt good, reassuring. Both of them reached out their hands closer to the brightly dancing flames.

"They must have known he was married," she continued. "How could they deliberately cause me the same pain their families went through?"

"Maybe it is true, after all, that savages don't think straight all the time," White Feather said irritably.

"I didn't mean anything by that," she protested.

He turned away from the fire, his big eyes looking directly into her own.

"Forgive me," he said. "I fight condescension so often that I sometimes see it where it doesn't exist."

Maggie chewed on her lower lip.

"Say what you want," he remarked. "I can take whatever you tell me."

"Am I so obvious?"

"You are."

"All right, then: If Randy had taken the scalp of a member of your own family, how would you have reacted?"

"I might have tracked him down," White Feather replied, "and done the same thing to him. I must tell you that."

"Even though you are now a Christian? Even though someone innocent would have suffered as well?"

"I am a Christian, yes, but I've been one for only a few years. I have been an Indian for much longer. My sin nature is no different from any other man's."

She appreciated his honesty.

"Maggie?" he asked.

"Yes?"

"I know enough of the Sioux mind to tell you something I didn't feel comfortable saying before now."

She paused, wondering what he had on his mind.

"I think they will try to apologize," he said.

"Apologize?" she said, astonished. "How could they ever suppose that I want an apology? How could they even think that, White Feather? What I want is justice!"

"Apology is only a word, Maggie. I assure you that their feelings go much, much deeper than that."

"Well, now, that's something to be thankful for, isn't it?"

She jumped to her feet, suddenly finding such conversation intolerable.

As he watched her go inside and slam the door behind her, White Feather's expression was one of infinite sadness.

Maggie awoke the next morning to the sound of sobs.

At first she had no idea who was sobbing so fitfully, perhaps a stranger who had wandered into the area.

"White Feather, are you hurt?" she called out immediately, but there was no answer.

Maggie pulled on her coat and walked to the front door, following the sobbing sounds. She opened it slowly, unprepared for what she saw.

In front of the cabin, the remains of a once handsome and vibrant stallion was sprawled on its side a few feet away.

Its throat had been cut.

Its blood had merged with the dirt to form a circle of red mud beneath its head.

White Feather was kneeling next to the carcass, his sobs so intense that Maggie thought he would become ill.

She walked over to him and knelt beside him.

"What is this?" she asked tenderly. "Who has done this terrible thing?"

"The braves who attacked your husband," he told her.

"Is this what . . . what you were saying last night?"

"Yes," he said, "oh, yes. But it's not just a horse, Maggie. It's the favorite stallion of one of the braves. It's the horse he rode for a very long time. It was an animal that had become his best friend!"

"And it was sacrificed?"

"That is what it amounts to, I'm afraid. This animal was sacrificed to obtain your forgiveness, and if not forgiveness, then understanding. It is an Indian form of the Hebrew blood rituals or—"

"—the death of Christ at Calvary."

White Feather's expression was solemn.

"Maggie," he started to say, cupping her cheeks in his hands.

"Yes?" she said, not certain at all what he might be telling her.

"Each brave will do this," he said.

"Each one will bring—?"

He nodded.

"How many?" she asked. "How many braves, White Feather?"

"I have no way of knowing. It might have been the ritual of . . . of—"

"Tell me!"

"It might have been the ritual of an entire tribe."

Suddenly she was shivering.

"You have to stop them!" she said, nearly screaming the words.

"Will you forgive them, Maggie?"

"White Feather, how can I ever forgive the butchering of my husband, the *murder* of my husband?"

"I am not saying your forgiveness will absolve those braves of any guilt. They committed a crime, and we all know that."

"Then what—?"

"Forgiveness, Maggie. Simple forgiveness."

"It is too much to ask, White Feather."

"Then it is too much to ask of the Heavenly Father that He forgive us!"

"I've not hurt another human being the way they hurt Randy."

"But our sins nailed Christ to that cross. Your sins, Maggie, and mine. You and I caused—"

"Please, no . . . no theology. Please, not now!"

Maggie's face showed an ill-concealed expression of disgust that White Feather noticed immediately.

"Don't you mean no theology should be coming from a reconstituted savage, Maggie? Isn't that it?"

Color drained from her cheeks.

She averted her eyes from him.

White Feather's shoulders slumped.

"So little does change," he whispered, "so little ever changes."

He turned then and, walking with slow, quiet, deliberate steps, he returned to the cabin and went inside.

"No, White Feather, I . . . I didn't—!" she called after him.

She hurried after him.

Inside, Maggie found White Feather packing some clothing in a faded and threadbare carpetbag.

"Where are you going?" she asked.

"Away," he told her.

"But I'll be alone here!"

"Isn't it better to be alone than to live with a stinking savage?"

"I never said that!" she protested.

"Not in words exactly," he said, "but the expression on your face spoke a great deal."

He turned and brushed past her.

"When will you be back?" Maggie asked, becoming panicky as she thought that he might not return and she would be completely alone again.

His answer was curt.

"Perhaps never," he said sternly.

White Feather strode outside, toward the corral.

She hurried after him.

"No, please, White Feather," Maggie begged. "Don't do this!"

He seemed to pay no attention. He walked resolutely across the yard, opened the corral gate and whistled to his horse, bridled it, saddled it, then lifted his foot into the stirrup.

"Don't go!" she said. "Don't leave me here."

In that instant she realized the utter selfishness of what she had said, words that showed fear over what might happen to her and nothing about what White Feather was undergoing.

"White Feather!" Maggie shouted.

He was gone from sight in less than a minute, a thick trail of dust obscuring his form and that of the horse he had tamed years before.

White Feather spent the time away from his cabin, away from Maggie, in the mountains an eight-hour ride away.

Mountains he had played in as a boy, with other Indian children . . .

He had returned to them before when he was troubled, separating himself from any distractions. Often, his people broke off from their tribe to go away to some distant place and die, particularly the ones who no longer wanted to burden others with caring for them. But each time White Feather broke away, it was an occasion not to embrace death but to sort out the pieces of his life and put them back in the right order.

Days passed.

Being alone was not an unpleasant ordeal for him. He had

grown accustomed to it over the years.

Now his anger made it seem that he had no other choice but isolation.

The white woman loathes me, Lord, he prayed as he sat beside a mountain stream watching silver-scaled fish swim lazily in its clear, cool water. *They all hate me. They hate any Indian they see. They see only the skin. They think only of the stories of atrocities my people have committed. Rather than deal with us, rather than talk with us, they hide behind their hatred and thrust it out before them like a battle shield!*

He found that his eyes were filling with tears.

Maggie sees in me a reminder of those who took her beloved husband from her. She tried to bury that hatred for a while, tried to pretend the loathing wasn't there, but she failed. Lord, she failed, and now we both are alone.

White Feather hadn't eaten since he had come to the mountains. Though hunger was present in him, something else was more pervasive, more compelling.

Guilt.

The woman retreats behind her anger, her hatred, he told himself. *And I do the same behind my offended racial heritage. I ask: What is the difference between the two of us? We both refuse to face what is true. . . . We refuse to face the reality of what is.*

He was trembling.

In his mind were visions of his tribe's village, the squaws at their daily tasks, the braves returning home with deer and other game, sweet little children running about, filling the air with the sounds of their laughter.

White Feather realized something then. He realized that he had been living on the fringes of the white world for a number of years even though he had been repeatedly rejected. Still, there had been moments at least of tolerance, of kindness. Once a fur trader had invited him to share dinner . . . at the man's home, three white children gathering around him, not in loathing, of course, but in wonder, for though they had been on the frontier all their lives, they had not had an Indian in their home before, and they started overwhelming him with questions. He tried to answer them as well as he could . . . then, afterward, as he was about to leave, he received a handshake, a smile, a package of food to take with him.

White Feather's heart hungered for such moments, which, though sparse, had occurred enough over the years to make him feel as strong a bond among some of the whites as with virtually any member of his tribe.

As a result, he had found himself being drawn more and more toward the white world rather than his own. At first, though he knew this was happening, he refused to probe the reasons. He refused to submit it to examination, for he secretly felt that it would soon pass and he would side as completely as ever with his own people rather than those who had invaded their world and were inexorably taking it away, ripping it from them, mile by mile.

I have not been to see my mother and father for five years, he admitted to himself. *I haven't even thought very much about them in all that time. Has it been, Lord, only because I am too busy, too wrapped up in what I must do to survive or—*

The rest of that thought hit him with the force of a fist aimed at his stomach.

—or because I choose not to think of them, to remind myself that they are Indians, that they will remain Indians for the rest of their lives, and that, somehow, I have moved on and cannot look back, because if I do, I will realize that—?

White Feather threw his head back and bellowed out his pain in words flung at the impassive mountains, a repeating echo coming back to him like endless accusing tormentors.

—I am ashamed of them, of what they are, ashamed of my family, my people, ashamed of my Indian heritage!

White Feather knew he could remain there no longer, and though hungry, he could not eat until he had returned to his cabin, to the white woman, to explain to her what he had just now faced about himself, hoping that she would not turn her back on him the way he had done to her only days before.

Maggie Engebretsen Stuart didn't.

Chapter Twenty-nine

For the next several decades, Maggie stayed on the prairie at the foothills of the Rockies.

She and White Feather remained close friends throughout part of that period, though no romantic involvement ever developed between them. Undoubtedly folks who knew them thought that would happen in time, but they were wrong.

He taught her a great deal about survival skills.

"If anything happens to me, there is much you will need to know," he said with the special blend of dignity and warmth that was typical of him.

Maize, beans, and squash were diet staples.

"The Indians call them the three sisters," White Feather told her. "That's very appropriate, since they're nearly always grown together."

"Why is that so?" Maggie asked.

"The maize takes certain elements out of the soil while the beans and the squash somehow put them back in."

Maize was used in a wide variety of ways: Gruel, essentially a beverage drunk at breakfast, was made with a small amount of maize added to boiling water; when boiled down to a paste it could also be rolled into balls and dropped into simmering broth to make dumplings. Hominy was prepared from maize kernels soaked for a few days in water, along with ashes from burning juniper, maize cobs, saltbush, or bean vines.

Blueberries were included with the diet whenever possible, along with raspberries and other berries such as salmon berries, thimbleberries, cloudberries, and other kinds. There were other edible berries as well: all of them distinctly apple-like to the taste.

Wild cherries and plums were among the additional fruits that could be raised or were already growing nearby, as well as at least two varieties of grapes, currants, gooseberries, rose hips, mulberries, and hackberries.

Maggie was astonished at all of the things White Feather taught her about the ways to use "the three sisters" and other native foods. And when White Feather taught her to identify all the native greens, berries, roots, and nuts that were edible, she marveled that she and Randy had never realized the plenitude of foods that had been everywhere around them.

"Maggie, all that you have learned up until now is only the beginning," White Feather promised her.

Vegetables were even more prevalent, ranging from mountain sorrel leaves to bistort, knotweed, and wild rhubarb. Other vegetables included canaigre, seep weed, pigweed, miner's lettuce, mustards, saltbush, chenopodium, beeweed, clover, monkeyflower.

He took her into a mountainside forest and waved his arms around at the greenery surrounding the two of them.

"This is like a garden," he proclaimed.

"Berries and nuts, you mean?" she asked.

"And much more—greens and roots to simmer for teas, and game too, if you can snare it. When nothing else is available," White Feather added, "you can depend upon what is growing in this forest."

There was much more that White Feather demonstrated to Maggie, but nothing was more important than the use of Indian medicines, which she always assumed were primitive and nearly useless.

"Willow, poplar, and wintergreen trees contain a sap that is helpful in many ways," White Feather told her.

"Give me some examples," she asked of him, trying not to let her skepticism seem condescending or mean.

He told her which sap helped reduce fever and pain. And he taught her that a similar result could be obtained from pipsissewa, spirea, and black, yellow, and cherry birch. In addition, he showed her which tree's sap was valuable in stopping severe coughs.

Balsam, fir, pine, and cedar break loose congestion of the nose and cleanse wounds, he said. Oak, raspberry, sumac, dogwood, and alumroot stop bleeding.

Maggie was forced to admit that she was impressed after hearing about all these remedies, and she was able to make use of them repeatedly as the years of her long and eventful life passed.

In addition to plants as a food source, Maggie learned more about wildlife that could be killed and eaten.

Randy had concentrated on deer and rabbits, but White Feather demonstrated many more possibilities.

Squirrels were one example, which included tree as well as ground squirrels. Rifles or bows and arrows, as opposed to traps, were used to get them. But with porcupines, clubbing proved the best way since they didn't move nearly as fast as other prey. White Feather also showed her how to use their quills as decorations on leatherwork after the meat was baked or boiled.

Prairie dogs could become a source of meat also. These frisky little rodents usually lived in colonies of burrows that sometimes contained up to a thousand prairie dogs—or more!

Remembering the poignant story Randy had told her of Patrick's encounter with the little prairie dog on his last day on earth, Maggie vowed never to harm one of the little animals. But she loved watching them with White Feather. She would never forget the first time the two of them peered over a rocky ledge and saw on the ground below the largest group of prairie dogs ever assembled in that spot or any other.

Thousands.

They busily swarmed in and out of their burrows, carrying in their mouths leaves and blades of grass and a variety of insects, including grasshoppers, stuffed in their cheeks or partially protruding from their mouths.

"They will stay for a season or two," White Feather told her, "and then they move on. Ranchers and horse breeders hate prairie dogs. Their burrows are like traps set for humans and horses, with many sprained ankles or broken legs resulting."

He turned to Maggie.

"But they could help us survive a long, harsh winter," he said.

She loathed the notion of eating them but understood that a choice between life or death was the critical one that had to be made and, ultimately, she was able to endure the task of having the little creatures for dinner, though she never became used to it and never enjoyed the taste of their tough meat.

Even with such varied sources of food during the years they spent together on the prairie, Maggie and White Feather periodically faced what all settlers did.

Scarcity.

The deer population would thin, especially with greater numbers of pioneers heading west. Rabbits were sometimes too hard to snare. Even the prairie dogs seemed to desert that region in favor of another, sparing Maggie the need to kill them.

At times like this, the two of them had to resort to eating other kinds of food.

Insects.

Grasshoppers were especially plentiful.

White Feather and some of his Indian friends caught them by digging a hole about ten feet wide and four feet deep in the tall prairie grasses.

Then they formed a wide circle around the hole and walked toward the pit, forcing the grasshoppers into it by beating the ground with sagebrush branches.

Later, White Feather strung them on thin green sticks and roasted them over an open fire.

Those that weren't eaten that first night were divided up among everyone.

"We have enough for a month!" proclaimed White Feather proudly after one memorable insect feast.

"Delightful," Maggie told him, less than enthusiastic about eating the bugs for a month.

He had seen her face turn white at the prospect.

"Sorry," he quickly added. "That isn't all we'll have to eat."

Maggie brightened up at that, smiling with relief.

"Some days it will be the hoppers," he said, grinning mischievously. "Other times we can have ants, lizards, and snakes. I have eaten like this for years. You get used to it!"

Maggie lost her smile.

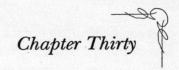

Chapter Thirty

More and more settlers moved onto the plains.

And Maggie became a teacher to the children as well as a nurse to many families.

She was so good in both capacities that she built up quite a reputation. Eventually she had enough money coming her way, along with supplies that were bartered for her services, so that she could live pretty well, at least according to the standards of the times.

Most of the new arrivals had come from east of the Mississippi as she and Randy had done, so they were divided into two camps regarding Indians: Either they had none of the prejudices that those already in the West harbored because of their unpleasant— and sometimes brutal—experiences with marauding tribes, or they held exaggerated fears fed by dime novels that portrayed all Indians as maniacal savages hunting for the scalps of any white settlers they could find.

The first group accepted the relationship between Maggie and White Feather as refreshing and encouraging while the other group utterly abhorred it, never giving up on the notion that the two of them must be engaging in sexual relations. After all, they were convinced, what else could be expected with the two of them living together?

"He is a heathen!" one woman named Cassie Weemer screamed at her one afternoon. "Nothing more needs to be said."

"My friend is not a heathen," Maggie retorted as the two of them stood outside the larger home she had helped White Feather build in town. "He has accepted Jesus Christ as his Savior and Lord!"

The woman, overweight, with a round, melon-like face, snorted with an exaggerated display of contempt.

"Christ would never accept his kind," she jerked her head toward the house as she spat out the words with conviction that seemed unchangeable. "Christ said the way to salvation is narrow. It's too narrow for savages such as him!"

"How do you know?" Maggie asked.

Cassie Weemer seemed more than a little self-satisfied.

"The Lord gave me a word on this matter!" she declared.

"A word to hate another human being because of the color of his skin?" Maggie asked, staring at her.

Cassie's jaws were firmly shut.

"Why is it that when people like you are confronted with the truth, you suddenly have nothing at all to say?" Maggie asked.

She glowered at Maggie, then turned away and started to walk toward the open, flatbed wagon in which she had been riding minutes earlier.

"I will pray for you tonight, Cassie Weemer," Maggie called after her. "That is what God surely wants me to do."

Cassie spun around as fast as her bulk would allow.

"How can you talk like you do?" she hollered defiantly. "I mean, Indians *murdered* your husband!"

"Not *this* Indian," Maggie retorted. "Do you hate all white men if one of them breaks in and robs you? Or cheats you? Or—?"

"They worship strange gods, gods of the rivers," the other woman interrupted, "and gods of the moon and stars, and they have blasphemous ceremonies that are unspeakable to real Christians."

Maggie had to acknowledge that Cassie had made a valid point with that statement, and she nodded accordingly.

"I know about all of that," she said, "and I agree with you. But why won't you accept the fact that the redemptive power of Christ's death, burial, and resurrection can change any man, even a once-godless Indian?"

Maggie's manner softened as she stepped closer to Cassie Weemer.

"It's been wonderful to have such a man as my friend," she went on. "He was a Christian before I met him, and I have been privileged to see any remnant of the old ways fade from him just as the morning sun banishes the darkness."

"I have never met this White Feather, and I shall not endeavor to do so," Cassie told her contemptuously.

"Too late," Maggie said, pointing over the woman's shoulder to the approaching man.

"I'm leaving now!"

"Won't you give him a chance?"

"No!" Cassie yelled with such venom that Maggie was taken aback.

"You have no god but hate," she said. "I pity you. Hate has displaced the Lord on the throne of your life."

Cassie started to climb up into the wagon and grab the reins of the two horses. But White Feather was just ahead of her on his stallion.

She hesitated as he approached.

Maggie saw what was happening.

"That's White Feather, you know," she said. "Does he look anything like a dirty savage? Examine him well, Cassie Weemer, and then tell me, if you can do so, what you think of this savage."

White Feather had stopped in front of the house now and dismounted. He walked up to Maggie and asked, "Is this one of our new neighbors?"

She nodded, giving no hint of what had just transpired between her and the other woman.

"She sure is," Maggie replied mischievously. "Let me introduce you to Cassie Weemer."

White Feather reached up toward Cassie, offering his hand.

"Pleased to meet you, Ma'am," he said pleasantly. "Would you join us for a bite to eat?"

Despite undoubtedly her best intentions not to react favorably, Cassie could not help herself. Her eyes widened as she studied White Feather.

"Please, share some simple fare with us," Maggie added, seeing an opportunity that would have seemed utterly absurd to contemplate only a minute or two earlier.

"Have to go . . ." Cassie mumbled.

White Feather placed one of his big hands on her own.

"You won't be putting us out in any way," he assured her. "We cannot promise you any kind of grand feast, of course, but at least it won't be caterpillars and bugs."

Cassie frowned at that.

"I don't think I could survive eating any of them," she replied. "It must be downright awful."

"Oh, it is," Maggie agreed. "But I had to ask myself, is it worse to starve to death? We've chosen life, no matter what the diet that makes necessary."

"I . . . can . . . stay, I guess," Cassie replied slowly, "but not for very long."

Genuinely pleased, White Feather smiled and extended both hands to help her down from the wagon.

"Praise God," he said. "Praise God!"

She looked at him, noticing the authentic joy on his face.

"Why should it please you so much that a stranger enters your home for a little while?" she asked, deeply puzzled.

"Because not everyone is so friendly," he told her, turning toward Maggie as she erupted in a brief coughing fit. "I think it results from the fact that I am an Indian. So many still hold to the old prejudices. Your being here right now is a breath of fresh air."

Cassie Weemer stayed nearly until dusk that day, this heavyset woman who had harbored so much hate in her.

"I . . . I don't want to leave," she admitted.

"We could rig up another bed," White Feather suggested. "Neither of us would mind if you stayed."

Cassie smiled as she spoke. "Thank you, no. I'd best be getting on home. I . . . I don't know what to say. You're not like I thought you would be."

"All of us human beings are savages when compared to what God wanted for all of humanity at the beginning," he remarked. "Adam and Eve threw that away, and we have been suffering ever since.

"Not a single man, not a single woman is anything but a savage, if we're truthful enough about ourselves and the relationship between us and the Lord. It is just a matter of degree from one person to another."

Cassie turned after getting back into the wagon and looked down at Maggie and White Feather.

"Why haven't you gotten married, the two of you?" she asked bluntly.

"Each of us is married to the memory of someone else," Maggie answered. "That may never change."

"I pray . . ." Cassie started to say.

They waited patiently until the words came for her.

"—that you, dear friends, will find great happiness," she added, "even more than you seem to enjoy right now."

White Feather then jumped up onto the wagon's sideboard and kissed Cassie gently on the cheek.

"Good-bye," she said, blushing. "I truthfully thank God that He brought you and me together."

And so did they.

Part Six
New Blessings, Fresh Anguish...

Blessed be children, at their most innocent,

who bring for a time something of the innocence of

heaven.

Anonymous

White Feather eventually married another Indian, a beautiful woman named Shining Sun.

There were two ceremonies—one according to Indian tradition in the village where White Feather was born, a second conducted by an old white preacher in a frontier town a few miles away.

Maggie, White Feather, and Shining Sun lived to be quite old, and all three remained close friends.

Then, unexpectedly, Shining Sun fell victim to a stroke and died a few days later, leaving White Feather, in his old age, again feeling alone and depressed until Maggie moved back in with him. They continued to keep their relationship platonic.

And so Maggie Engebretsen Stuart contented herself with another truth: Her Heavenly Father had answered the prayer she had sent heavenward so long ago in Philadelphia —not as she had wanted Him to, but the answer seemed clear. She had made it as far west as she was going to go.

Her yearning for California was forgotten for years as her second career —as a schoolteacher in the frontier town —became a source of great joy and fulfillment for her.

She had opened a school for Spanish and Mexican children as well as for Indians.

And she was so good at teaching that white families, learning of her skills and of her accomplished students, invited her to be a private tutor to their children after her regular school day ended.

Nor was knowledge of Maggie Engebretsen Stuart's remarkable skill confined to just that single state.

She became a phenomenon . . .

Her fame as a renowned teacher spanned decades that were among the most pivotal in the history of the United States. And still, in her old age, she continued to teach.

Then as she grew older and her hair turned gray and then white, a strange thing happened to Maggie.

The dream returned. And once more, Maggie longed to see California.

White Feather convinced Maggie to go.

One month later, the two long-time friends parted as Maggie slowly climbed the steps onto the train.

Only in heaven would they be reunited . . .

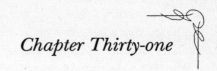

Chapter Thirty-one

Maggie Stuart stood in the pure white sand, the tiny grains warm and soft between her toes, and stared out at the foam-crested turquoise waves. She felt so strange to be standing where she had dreamed of being for well more than half a century, decade after decade of adventure and love, despair and longing, friendship and accomplishment.

Even stranger, she thought through a mental layer of mourning that had somehow managed to hang on through all that had happened to her, *to be standing here like this without Randy right next to me.*

That sunset!

It was beyond anything she could have imagined, shimmering off the billowing waves that slipped against the shore.

I wonder, Lord, if heaven is going to be anything like this, Maggie asked prayerfully. *If it is, Randy and I may do nothing for the first thousand years but look at the sun to which You have given such glory.*

She felt very old but somehow invigorated, an ancient woman who had spent what felt like a lifetime on the wild prairie of a frontier that had held her back from fulfilling her dream to reach the promised land of California. At times it had even seemed like some kind of sinister plot had been at work to destroy her altogether.

The things we imagine as age dims our good sense! she chuckled to herself as she pulled a shawl more tightly around her.

On the train west, she had met the Alessandro family from Virginia.

Wonderful folks, Maggie told herself. *I was honored to get to know them, Father in heaven.*

The Alessandros had settled in the northwestern part of the San Fernando Valley, which ran parallel to the rugged Santa

Monica mountain range. Maggie had also been headed there, having heard that a need existed in the valley for experienced teachers. The Alessandros had quickly helped her become involved with a school for Mexican-American children, where the officials had been concerned initially about Maggie's age and the fact that she was so obviously a product of an Eastern family devoid of ethnicity.

But she convinced them, convinced them quite solidly, of her abiding love for children, whatever their race or nationality happened to be, convinced them that she considered each child a wonderful opportunity from Almighty God to send a human being into the world as stable, as loving, as honest, and as pure as possible.

Very quickly, the officials' initial skepticism was replaced by great admiration for Maggie.

None doubted her sincerity, and all felt inspired by her outlook.

She was hired first as a counselor, and then later various teaching duties were added as the school's leaders realized the extent of Maggie's energy and abilities despite her advanced age.

I am a mother of sorts to two score and ten young lives, she thought, picturing her students as the sunset faded and full, nighttime darkness began to take over.

Patrick.

Wherever there were children, she still saw her precious Patrick among them, as though waiting for his own turn at some playground game or classroom drill.

When she gave a child advice, she was giving it to him.

When she listened to a child's problems, she was listening to his own and wanting to do everything she could to ease the boy's or girl's burden.

People wonder how I can be so good with the little ones. They think it is because God has given me a special gift, and they are right about this, for that is the biggest part of what I do, having it all come directly from the Lord and used to mold young minds, for His honor and glory.

She bit her lower lip, memories such as those that were surfacing always bringing tears with them, even though decades had passed since her son was taken from her. Thinking of him, she suddenly realized that Patrick, if he had lived, might now be silver-haired himself. Still, she pictured him as a young lad, for that was what inspired her to be such a talented teacher.

The gift of teaching, of counseling, is from You, Lord, loaned to me for a brief, while I'm in this world. But what I do with it is my gift back to Patrick—sweet, sweet Patrick.

Thinking of the boy, Maggie also recalled how completely their son's death had proved to be the catalyst to Randy's deterioration.

I thought there was hope, Lord, but there really wasn't, I suppose. Any feeling that Randy would pull through was just wishful thinking on my part. I wanted him to survive, to be with me forever, and for me that was the only reality I would accept, so when he didn't, when he—

She bowed her head, sobs ripping through her body.

Abruptly she felt a hand touch her waist.

Maggie turned and saw a dark-haired, dark-skinned little boy named Miquel looking up at her —one of her students, the son of a family who often befriended Maggie.

"Is you ready?" he asked.

"Are, Miquel," she corrected him.

His forehead wrinkled into a frown.

"Are?" he repeated the word, puzzled.

"Yes, child, you should say, 'Are you ready?' It should not be, 'Is you ready?' You understand that now, don't you?"

A smile spread across the boy's face.

"Are you?" he repeated.

She nodded, took his hand, and they walked together back to the carriage parked on a dirt road paralleling the beach where Miquel's father, Abel, was waiting for them in the carriage.

"You can stay longer if you like," he said, his voice only slightly accented. "Don't let my son's impatience stop you."

"It's fine," Maggie replied. "There will be other sunsets."

"And memories, si?" Abel added.

"Yes, they're —" she started to say, then smiled with some appreciation. "How did you know?"

"Your face, the way you were walking, the way you are sitting right now . . . this tells me much, Teacher."

She reached out and touched his cheek.

Abel was a widower . . . If only he were older or I were younger, she mused *before quickly dismissing the thought and settling down as much as possible on the padded seat for the ride home through the foothills that rose on both sides of the trail.*

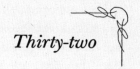

Thirty-two

Maggie had been able to continue working with "her" children through the turn of the century. She had seen a great many of them grow up and raise families, and she even went on to teach quite a number of *their* children.

And she had been able to see something else.

Prejudice.

Maggie came face-to-face with prejudice again and again, prejudice that meant danger, especially for Mexican Americans. Living in the southern half of California were a host of descendants and friends of the defenders of the Alamo, where a handful of Texans had bravely died while defending the little San Antonio mission against a brutal attack by Mexican General Santa Anna.

During the nearly seventy years that had passed since then, several of those descendants—or simply their admirers—had migrated westward, bringing with them the passion their families had passed down about the slaughter of their beloved heroes who had died for the cause of freedom. As the years passed, some of that angry resentment might have cooled a bit, but it hadn't disappeared, rooted as it was in hatred and patriotism.

"Their kind killed Davy Crockett!" one of them, Samuel Albertson, angrily exclaimed as he sat next to Maggie in the backyard of his elaborate log home built at the very edge of the Santa Monica Mountains, just two miles inland from the ocean. She had known him for years. She had asked the wealthy rancher and lumbermill owner for money for the school and for scholarship money for her students. Begrudingly and with long and loud protests, he had given her what she had wanted. And in the process they had somehow become friends.

He had been sipping from a tall glass of strong iced tea flavored with a mint leaf, the only way he liked that beverage. The recollection that Crockett had died at the Alamo suddenly made him slam down the glass on top of a round, highly polished table between his chair and the one in which Maggie was sitting.

Albertson, in his mid-fifties, was a very large man, muscular, not fat, a man who easily could be envisioned chopping down trees to build his own home and requiring little assistance to do so.

"And Jim Bowie!" he added passionately, his thick eyebrows twitching as he became so inflamed that Maggie worried about him physically. "Crockett and Bowie—two of the finest men this country has ever produced, murdered by a horde of stinking Mexicans!"

Maggie knew she had to respond carefully.

This man was influential in that region of California, and running afoul of him would not be wise.

"Their deaths eventually bought victory for all Texans," Maggie said as firmly as her aging voice would allow.

"How can you say that?" Albertson asked, his eyes narrowing as he turned and examined her closely. "They lost! The fort was overrun. Only the wife of an officer, her baby, and a Mexican nurse and, yes, a young black boy survived the bloody massacre. What in the world can be called victorious about that?"

"But, Mr. Albertson," she replied, meeting his gaze, "if it had not been for the delay caused by those at the Alamo—"

"Delay?" he interrupted. "What are you talking about?"

"I am old," she continued, angered, forgetting any need to treat him with extra care, "and I am weaker today than I was a year ago, and, yes, it could be said that I am very unimportant in the scheme of your world.

"But do you act as the gentleman you like to think you have become when you interrupt ever so rudely someone who is as burdened as I am with my obvious number of years on this earth?"

Albertson's face flushed red.

Maggie could tell he was struggling to hold back his temper— then, abruptly, his shoulders slumped, and he fell back in his chair.

"I happen to be one of Davy's cousins," he told her. "I met him, once, when I was very young. While I know he's been accused of being a braggart and a liar from time to time, I've thought of him only with affection and with the greatest admiration."

He leaned forward, reached out, took her hand, and added, "Please forgive me, dear lady. My passions run deep on this subject."

She nodded.

"I understand," she said. "Let me tell you just how much I understand. Will you allow me this?"

He smiled as he assured her, "It seems that remarkable women can get anything they want from me."

He did not elaborate. And he needn't have, for Maggie got the message, and it was her turn to be red-faced.

"My husband died a terrible death at the hands of heathen Indians," she said as she started the long story so sharply etched in her mind. "How easy it would have been for me to surrender myself to hating all of them."

Maggie paused briefly, every moment from that time coming back to her with a wrenching vividness.

"Go on, Mrs. Stuart," he said, with a voice suddenly kind.

And that she did.

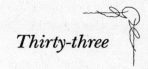

Thirty-three

When Maggie had finished, Samuel Albertson's bloodshot eyes were filling with some very rare tears.

"To lose someone you love under such circumstances may be the greatest tragedy any of us will ever face," he said after a few moments. "I did not know Davy Crockett well, of course, but look at how I react. Yet you—"

He stood and walked a few feet away from Maggie, his back to her.

She tried to stand but was momentarily too weak.

"I want to come to you, Samuel," she spoke with regret, "but I cannot just now. Please forgive me."

He spun around, now facing her.

"Forgive you?" he replied, astonished that she would think this was necessary. "You, dear lady, have done nothing! It is this crude bear that you see before you who needs heavy doses of forgiveness."

He walked over to Maggie, knelt on one knee in front of her, and reached up to take her thin little hands in his own huge ones.

"People much bigger than you seem afraid to stand up to me," he told her. "They look at my size. They are aware of my power, my influence in this region. I can physically squash anyone who displeases me."

He chuckled a bit.

"And I can do the very same thing politically as well as economically and socially. But to you, that means little. Why is this so, Maggie Stuart?"

She leaned forward slightly as he was still holding her hands and whispered, "If Jesus be for me, who can stand against me?"

Albertson pulled back from her but stayed on the ground, saying nothing this time, his eyes closed.

Maggie waited patiently, knowing he was struggling.

He opened his eyes finally and said, "This is all I have, dear friend. I have power, certainly. I can break bones. I can break lives. I control the sheriff and the town council and some key businesses. But—but—"

He jumped up, threw his head back, and screamed, "I am so empty!"

Maggie looked up at him and said, "I want to stand now, Samuel. Will you please help me do that?"

He reached out and with one hand brought her gently to her feet.

"You are three times my weight," she said, chuckling a bit.

"I have pain," he admitted.

"And not in your body, isn't that so?"

"It is so. I have been in pain longer than I can remember. But you seem to be at peace despite your memories."

She smiled warmly.

"I remember the joy I had with Randy," Maggie remarked warmly. "I remember the birth of our son, Patrick, on a lonely prairie in the middle of a wild land that threatened almost daily to destroy us even then.

"I wonder from time to time, if it would have been better not to have known Randy, not to have given birth to that wonderful child. . . . Would it have been better for me to have remained back in Philadelphia?"

Her eyes narrowed as she looked at him.

"And yet, I must admit, what did I have there?" Maggie went on. "They all died, my mother, my father, my sister, so many of my friends. There was nothing left for me in that place. Randy Stuart gave me the fulfillment I needed. He took me from despair and taught me so much about life."

"But you had to bury him. You had to leave him behind."

"In the flesh. Yes, I did leave his body in that grave. But I see Randy in my mind anyway, continually, after all this time. I feel him in my heart just as though he is with me now; I somehow feel that I am talking to him and to no one else."

"And you honestly believe that the two of you will be reunited, don't you?" Albertson observed.

"Oh, yes!" she declared. "I do believe that. I do expect to close my eyes to this life when the Lord calls me home, to leave this aged and suffering body, and to be taken past the gates of heaven to find my beloved husband and my beloved son awaiting me together on a street of gold, surrounded by—"

Albertson's expression brightened.

"Angels?" he offered. "There will be angels with them, won't that be it?"

"You believe!" she exclaimed.

"I've heard about such matters. That's not the same as believing."

Suddenly Maggie felt herself becoming very, very weak, her body limp, no strength whatever left in it.

Albertson saw this and grabbed her before she fell. He carried her back inside his house and ordered his Mexican servants to be ready for any emergency. Then he sent a messenger to find the only doctor in that entire region.

Chapter Thirty-four

Dying.

"That sure seemed to be what was happening," the old woman said, *going over more memories as the precious remaining moments fled . . .*

Maggie had no difficulty believing she was dying at last, after some false starts over the years.

Pain.

It assaulted her head, her chest, her legs.

She was in a near-coma, vaguely aware of movement around her, of sounds, her eyes half-open periodically so that she was able to perceive shapes, dim and indistinct, but feeling as though she was drifting away from the flesh-and-blood world all this represented.

"I'm ready, Lord," she said, supposing that no one could hear her, supposing that she was mumbling incoherently, only the Holy Spirit and herself aware of what her words actually were. "I've been more than ninety years in this world. And I'm weary, Lord. There is pain in the morning and throughout the day, pain somewhere in my body hour after hour. I sleep at night, but I dream of only one moment over and over and over again: Being with Thee, seeing Randy and Patrick again, ending this separation that has lasted so very long."

Moaning came from deep inside her body.

"Let it be soon, Jesus," she continued. "I'm so tired. Any purpose I've had has run its course. I'm ready, Jesus, I'm—"

She heard someone crying. Two large hands folded around one of hers. And there were words not her own.

"Someone's here to see you, Maggie," the voice told her. "He wants to say something to you. Is that all right?"

Another voice entered her hearing—a very young voice, a voice that stuttered and cracked and was interrupted by sobbing sounds, a voice that told her how much she was loved and needed and would be missed.

But she could feel her soul being drawn upward, could feel a light on her face, could see a familiar form.

Patrick! Dear Patrick! I'm coming, son . . .

And yet something was holding her back, something that didn't counteract the will of God in bringing her to Him, for that could never be, but she felt somehow as though she was being given a kind of choice, a chance to be with her loved ones or a chance to —That young voice.

It continued speaking to her.

Miquel! Little Miquel!

"I love you so much, Teacher," he said. "I'll miss you for the rest of my life. You made me not want to hate no more. You teach people not to hate me."

O, Lord, I don't want to hear those words. I don't want anything but what I've wanted for so long, to be with—

Another voice.

It had spoken earlier, but now she recognized it fully.

Samuel Albertson's.

Why is he saying these things? Maggie asked herself. *My husband, my son, are waiting. Why is he talking like—?*

"It's not only the kids, Maggie," he was saying. "I still talk hard. I still talk mean. I'm a vulgar man, a hateful man. And I call a child like this a darkie-blood Mex or whatever other nastiness I can come up with. But my heart's not in it anymore, Maggie. Since I met you, dear, dear lady, my heart's not in a lot of things that I used to embrace with mind, body, and soul, not realizing how very wrong they were."

"What . . . what are you trying to tell me? Are you coming to—?"

"Jesus, Maggie," he continued. "I want to accept Jesus into my wretched life as my Savior and my Lord."

Someone else can be Your instrument, Lord! Someone else can take over now from me. Surely that's true. O Lord, Lord, I planted the seed. Must I do more than that? Must I wait yet longer for Randy, for Patrick?

Yes . . .

That word came to her just as surely as it had been spoken in the loudest, the clearest, strongest possible voice.

But Lord—!

No argument would be heeded. No debate would be possible.

She knew that this was so, and she submitted to the will of her Almighty Father, as always before, when it pleased her and when it did not.

The light faded, the pain that had vanished now returned, familiar as ever, and her eyelids fluttered weakly, slowly opening.

Samuel Albertson was kneeling beside her bed. Next to him was Miquel. Both were holding the same Bible.

"He's ready," the little one told her. "I helped him. I really helped him! But I need you to do the rest!"

Maggie smiled, the despair gone.

Miraculously gone.

Maggie had had a stroke.

It was not her first.

Each one robbed her of a bit more mobility, a bit more strength. There might be others before she died. The next would bring her that much closer to death. Eventually, the final stroke would take her heavenward.

"I pray that I'm not paralyzed in the end," she said as she sat up in bed a week later, Samuel Albertson on a chair next to her. "I . . . I don't want to just sit and stare and not be able to . . . to do anything at all!"

"I know what that must mean," he told her sympathetically. "My Emily died that way. How I loved that woman, Maggie; how I loved her!"

"And how I loved that man," she added.

"Randy Stuart?"

"Poor, sweet, crazed Randy."

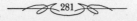

"So many years later, you still feel so strongly!"

"More strongly, Samuel, much more strongly. Every moment I spend away from him I anticipate more passionately being back with him. My heart aches to hear him say my name, and not just in old memories of him."

"Emily and I had no children," Albertson remarked. "When she died, I changed because I was alone; I had no one. There was nothing alive that was left from what we had. Photographs, yes, and surely plenty of memories and other things, a shawl that she had knitted for herself, some jewelry she treasured, but only that sort, only material things, so cold now, so lifeless."

He bowed his head.

"I guess you could say that I was always a rough one, but after Emily was buried, I became downright nasty, almost . . . evil."

He shivered as he said that word.

"I didn't think much about evil when Emily was alive," he went on. "She was everything good and fine, and she had the sweetest temperament."

"A Christian?"

"Oh, yes, redeemed through and through."

He chuckled to himself.

"I guess there's no other way," he admitted sheepishly.

"That's right," Maggie assured him. "All the way with Jesus or not at all is what I have thought most of my life."

Albertson was now staring straight at Maggie, and she was beginning to feel uncomfortable.

"Is there something wrong?" she asked.

He shook his head in a wistful manner.

"No, not wrong," he replied. "I was just looking at you and thinking how much like you my beautiful Emily would have been if she had lived."

She looked at her bony, wrinkled, vein-lined hands.

"With these hands I dug my beloved's grave with an old shovel and gathered rocks to pile on top of it," she commented as she held them up before her. "Now, it seems, I can hardly lift a teaspoon with them."

Albertson leaned forward, putting his large arms around her ancient and withered frame, the gesture so gentle it might have been a feather brushing her skin.

"I will take care of you, dear friend," he said earnestly. "When you aren't able to feed yourself, I will do it for you, or I will have one of my people do it. Or maybe we'll take turns."

"No, no!" she protested. "I . . . I couldn't allow that."

"You couldn't allow love, Maggie?" he said as he leaned back from her. "You're not really saying that, are you?"

"Love?" Maggie repeated, a bit befuddled.

"Yes, dear, that's what I said. I love you!"

She broke into tears.

"I love you as a friend, a teacher, the woman who led me to Christ, as someone who is so much like Emily. I love you in all these ways, and I guess there are more if I would think about it."

It was Maggie's turn to reach out and embrace him.

"I could not have a better friend," she remarked. "I could not be blessed more by my precious Lord."

"Except to have Randy here, I know," he suggested with more than a little insight. "I can't be what he was. I'm not capable of that. But I can be all that I am trying to become because of you."

He shrugged his shoulders.

"That's all I can offer, Maggie. You will have everything I can provide. There is nothing I would ever refuse you, believe me, dear, dear lady."

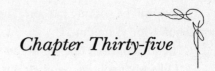

Chapter Thirty-five

Months passed.

Months filled with the greatest possible uncertainty over whether Maggie would pull through.

Her health did stabilize eventually, as well as could be expected at that age, but no longer was she able to make the five-mile journey each day from the home that had been provided for her by many thoughtful, caring local parents to the schoolhouse where she had been teaching.

In fact, she had not left Samuel Albertson's home since he had brought her there. But that presented no problem as far as he was concerned.

A very large house.

That it was, with expansive walkways made of colorful Spanish tiles and enough room for Maggie. Room enough for . . .

When Albertson came to her with his suggestion she was standing in the garden, tending to some flowers she had "adopted."

"Maggie, dear, I have an idea," he said, his manner one of anticipation over her reaction to what he would tell her.

"What is it?" she asked, turning slowly, a grimace on her face the only outward sign that she was having a little difficulty.

"Why don't I have a second schoolhouse built, this one right on my property here?" Albertson remarked proudly.

She was genuinely stunned.

"But that will cost too much," she objected.

"Cost?" he said, approaching the word as though it had been spoken in another language. "No, that's not the important thing to consider, my dear. This area is growing, as you know. Many more children will be coming in soon. The old schoolhouse hasn't been adequate for some time."

The idea pleased Maggie as she thought about it.

"I like what you say, Samuel. But —"

She hated to tell him what she knew she must in time.

"But . . . it's me," Maggie went on. "It's not your idea, which is a fine one. Children surely must have a solid chance early on in life. Those first seven years are the most crucial if they are to be well-adjusted later."

"So what's wrong? I know something is, Maggie."

"It's not just the physical buildings; it's the teachers, Samuel. Everyone has to be trained unless, by some miracle of the Lord's, they come out here, already armed with the very best credentials."

"But you could help us there," he reminded her. "You could instruct the students as well as their future teachers."

"Samuel —?" she started to say.

"What is it, dear friend?"

"I'm soon going to be a hundred years old. I don't know how much longer I will tarry before my Lord takes me home."

"Maggie?" he said, brushing the ends of his fingers gently across an old, deeply lined but still rather rosy cheek.

She was looking at him expectantly.

"You might have a year, you might have a decade, dearest one," he observed. "Whatever the time left, I . . . I won't see any of it with you. Right now, my main concern is to make sure that you have everything you need to be happy, my dear, and that these kids are taken care of after . . . after I've left."

He turned aside then as she pondered what he had said, her old mind not grasping his words instantly.

. . . I won't see any of it with you.

"Samuel," she asked finally, "Samuel, what are you saying? Please, come out with it, dear man!"

When he faced her again, tears were covering his cheeks.

"You're crying," Maggie said. "Are you ill—?"

The truth hit her then, and she struggled to remain standing.

He outweighed her by 200 pounds and stood nearly a foot

taller, but he could do nothing then, except lean over in a moment of rare emotional frailty and let her embrace him, admitting by this that suddenly he had no strength at all.

"What is it?" she asked. "What is wrong?"

"Years of logging. Yes, I did make a great deal of money, Maggie, but my lungs are shot. They're failing on me. It's come from all the sawdust I've inhaled, from the tiny splinters that have lodged inside.

"And it's not only my lungs. Some of that stuff's gotten right into my bloodstream, you know, and done its damage there as well. Maggie, what I'm trying to say is that I . . . I have only six months or less to live!"

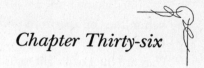

Chapter Thirty-six

The new, quite grand schoolhouse was completed exactly one week before Samuel Albertson died.

It was truly a handsome structure, more like a southern plantation house than a place of learning. Two stories tall, it was able to serve students from a wide area who came to it on horseback or in wagons and even by canoe on a river a short distance away.

The dedication drew political, social, and religious figures from a hundred miles in every direction. By that time, Albertson was not well enough to attend, confined twenty-four hours a day to his bed. Maggie Stuart was asked to take his place, and she agreed.

"I am here to speak for Samuel Albertson," she said, her thin, old voice somehow gaining strength and volume as the seconds passed. "As you can see, I am very old. Samuel is just fifty-six. Yet he will precede me, it seems, into our Father's heavenly kingdom.

"I have asked him, when he gets there, to say hello for me to my beloved husband, Randy, and to our son, Patrick. Samuel came to the Lord late in life. But he doesn't love Jesus any less than I who have known the Savior for most of my life."

She stopped a moment to sip from a glass of water on the oak podium against which she had to lean for support.

"All of life can be preparation for heaven, you know. And the proper education in the proper environment is preparation for life. Once education cuts its ties with Almighty God, from whom all good and decent knowledge comes, then we as parents will have every reason to fear for the future. During the most important years of a young person's life, school is second only to the home as the greatest influence on a young mind, heart, and soul."

She smiled as she turned slightly and looked at the children sitting behind her on the front porch of the whitewashed colonial-style building.

"They are the Lord's gift to us," she went on. "What we do with this enormous responsibility of ours as parents and teachers will show just how much we are looking to Jesus Christ for guidance, remembering that it is because of Him that they were brought into this world, these young boys and girls, that the miracle of their existence is a blessing from heaven itself and is beyond compare.

"I pray that Samuel Albertson's legacy is generation upon generation of the finest doctors, the most brilliant scientists, the wisest philosophers, the most inspiring teachers . . . the kindest and most decent Spirit-led men and women this nation has ever seen."

When Maggie had finished, she was helped down from the podium by Miquel and Abel Alessandro.

A moment later, little Miquel was hoisted up by his father and spoke to the group gathered in front.

"I pray that we help Mrs. Stuart . . . I pray that we help her whenever she needs us," he said haltingly. "She's always there when we need her!"

Nervous, he cleared his throat and added quickly, "May Jesus take Mr. Albertson by the hand soon so that he don't have no more pain."

He was so thin now, having lost more than a hundred pounds. His eyes were bloodshot, and his breathing came in irregular gasps.

"Oh, Samuel," Maggie said as she grasped his bony hand with her own. "Nearly fifty years separate us in age."

"A . . . long time . . . never knowing . . . you," he said with pain behind every word. "I know Emily would have . . . loved you."

His white-coated tongue licked pale lips.

Maggie raised Samuel's head as much as she was able and sent

some cool water down his throat.

"So good . . . dear . . . Maggie, dear . . . friend . . . so . . . very . . . good," this once robust and often profane man told her, his voice now little more than a strained whisper. "Water is such . . . a blessing . . . so simple. I took it . . . for granted. But now . . . tastes . . . wonderful."

"We all are guilty of that," she replied. "We smell flowers and pass them by. We see the moon and pay no heed. We touch one another and—and—"

She brought her hand to her mouth.

Yes, Lord, I've done that with Randy, with sweet Patrick. I've put my arms around both of them, thinking that nothing would ever be able to part us. There were times when I didn't thank You for them, when—

Suddenly, words of a hymn brought her out of her reverie.

"I'd rather have Jesus than silver or gold," Samuel Albertson was singing in a firm and clear voice.

Maggie, sitting in a chair next to his bed, was startled by the change in his voice. Hearing the robust singing, Miquel, Abel, and other members of the household staff gathered in the doorway.

He turned his head with effort toward them.

"I love you all," he said.

"Suddenly I feel so strong," he told Maggie. "I feel so happy, dear friend."

He closed his eyes for a second or two. When he opened them, there seemed to be a sparkle coming from deep within.

"Peace is like a river, you know," he went on. "You step into it, and it surrounds you with its cool, clear water."

He was looking at her with a smile.

"You are beautiful, my friend," he added. "You are very beautiful. I can imagine you now as you will be when the two of us will sing together with the angels."

"Samuel," she said, "what do you see? Can you tell me?"

"It's wonderful, Maggie," he replied joyfully. "The streets are gold, my dear, bright, shiny, the sun sparkling off them. I see angels, Maggie. They are like the finest cut crystal, filled with colors, iridescent. People I knew and loved are there, transformed.

My dearest Emily, my beloved . . . she's calling me, Maggie, and my name is being echoed by a multitude. They've all gathered together, and I am being taken. I am being lifted up, Maggie!"

Samuel pulled away from her for a moment, holding both hands out in front of him, palms upward.

"I've been forgiven everything . . . Maggie . . . everything. The meanness, the anger, the ruthlessness—oh, even the guilt is gone! I feel so free, Maggie, so blessedly free for the first time, so—"

His hands dropped back on the bed.

But still he lingered. Now his voice became a scratchy whisper again, so low she could hardly hear. He was saying something that she could not quite make out. So she bent over, next to his mouth, listening to words that brought tears without delay.

"A . . . man, Maggie . . . a . . . tall . . . handsome man . . . ," he was saying as his voice slipped away. "He . . . he just wants me to tell you that he's . . . waiting . . . that he'll—"

"Randy!" she gasped.

"Your son . . . Patrick . . . It's Patrick . . . grown strong and oh, Maggie, you'll be so proud of him . . . He . . . Patrick loves you so . . . very . . . much."

Abruptly, Samuel Albertson raised his head off the pillow and shouted, "Praise God! Praise Your holy name, Lord Jesus."

In an instant he had fallen back like an old, limp rag doll.

Maggie knew then that her dearest friend, her benefactor, was gone, truly gone.

Samuel Albertson had asked to be buried next to his wife, Emily, in an isolated section of his huge estate. The grave site was under a centuries-old weeping willow. Pink and yellow and scarlet rosebushes formed a natural fence around the north, east, and south sides of that spot, their sweet scent carried by gentle breezes that blew in from the Pacific Ocean.

The funeral services attracted 200 men, women, and children. Some of Samuel's former enemies, men he had bested as business competitors, not a few of them driven into bankruptcy as a result, gave memorable eulogies and tributes. Since his conversion to Jesus Christ, Samuel had made arrangements to pay back to all of them any of the money they had lost, and in several instances had set them up in new businesses, giving them complete ownership even though it was his money responsible for getting them back on their feet.

"I was astonished," said a tall, slender man in his mid-forties as he stood in front of the mourners. "I never expected Samuel Albertson, of all men, to do what he did. It required some relearning on my part to switch from building homes to making clothes, but at least Sam gave me that choice. He never forced one or the other upon me.

"If the truth be known, I was getting tired of the exhausting physical struggle of the building business. I rejoice over what I'm doing now. And that's all because of this one man—"

He cut himself off as tears started to flow.

"I am so sorry," he said finally. "But I . . . I hated him so much. He took away everything I had worked for because he had more money, more business smarts, more of everything I coveted. Early on, I . . . I would have shot the man dead if someone had handed me a gun and said, 'Go to it. He deserves to die.'

"It feels so strange, but I love him now. I don't know how to cope with that. From hate to love is a long and strange road. But it couldn't be otherwise for me, because I saw the change in him."

He tried to continue without breaking down again but failed. The crowd was patient with him, many of them feeling exactly as he did.

"I saw into Sam's heart, into his very soul, so clearly," he continued. "He actually fell on his knees before me and asked for my forgiveness, because, he said, he had been taught what true forgiveness was all about."

The man had been standing on a hastily erected plywood platform. Before him was Samuel Albertson's open coffin.

"I want to say something before God and every one of you . . . that if redemption can change this, my enemy, into my friend, then I need what Sam was given, or my life will be worth nothing henceforth."

He raised one hand above his head and said with clarity, "Lord Jesus, while this multitude and the hosts of heaven are my witnesses, I turn to Your Son as my Savior and my Lord and claim the redemption promised in the Bible, Your Holy Word."

He looked at the members of Samuel's family sitting on the front row—an aunt and an uncle, several cousins, two nephews, and Maggie Stuart.

He focused on Maggie and smiled. "Samuel told me that you were the Lord's instrument in leading him to salvation. I pray that you are given a few more years, dear Maggie Stuart, so that there will be other men like Sam that you can turn gentle and loving before you pass into the kingdom."

At that the air was filled with the joyous sound of people breaking out into sustained and deserved applause.

Chapter Thirty-seven

Unlike those other times when she had lost people close to her, Maggie Engebretsen Stuart did not suffer torrents of anguish after Samuel's death.

She was curiously at peace.

"I wonder why I feel this way," she would ask a visitor with whom she felt at ease. "Samuel meant such a great deal to me. Am I becoming cold, indifferent, just not caring anymore?"

But one other possibility seemed far more likely as she thought about it.

"When my mother and my father and my sister died, I knew they had gone to heaven because they knew Christ as Savior and Lord," she went on. "But a reunion between us seemed so far off."

She smiled as a memory of Randy surfaced.

"When my beloved Randy died, it was the same. How could I endure thirty or forty years or more without him while waiting to enter through the gates of heaven and see him standing nearby, ready to take me into his arms again and knowing that nothing would separate us ever again?"

The smile became broader, lighting up her face.

"Now, with Samuel, there isn't going to be such a long period at all. A month, a year, perhaps two. I can't say, but not long."

She looked up at the sky.

"And with him will be Papa and Mama and dear Roberta and Randy and my little Patrick and . . . and —"

No one who was with her during such moments was embarrassed by the tears that always came after she had expressed, in her growing senility, precisely the same thoughts to whoever would listen.

After Samuel's burial and a gathering of friends, relatives, and business associates at the Albertson residence, Maggie found herself exhausted and nearly alone. The entire household staff had remained on duty, but they too were ready for bed after a very long day.

A maid named Rosita Alvarez asked Maggie if she needed any help.

"I don't think so," she said and started to turn away, then she stopped and asked, "Would it be all right if I went into Mr. Albertson's den? I just want to sit there and look at his things and remember—"

Tears were starting again.

"That is all the way at the other end of the house," the maid reminded her. "Don't you want me to go with you?"

"You're so tired, Rosita. I can't ask you to do that."

"I loved him too," she replied. "I don't mind."

As they walked slowly through the house, Maggie realized that the devotion of someone such as this woman was extraordinary. After all, Samuel's strong emotions in regard to Mexican Americans were hardly kept hidden from anyone. Outsiders guessed that the only reason he hired them was because he didn't have to pay them very much, and the only reason they worked for him, so the suspicions went, was because times were tough and any paying job was welcome.

"You look exhausted," Maggie said as they neared the den. "You really don't have to stay with me."

"How will you make it back to your room?" Rosita asked. "I may be thin and bony, not some robust senorita in her prime, but I am much stronger than you might think—and forty years younger than you are."

It was apparently a point of honor with her, and Maggie decided not to order the woman away.

They reached the den.

Rosita had a key and opened the door, letting Maggie go in first.

It was paneled in dark wood, probably cherry, and the walls

were taken up with dozens of plaques, photographs, and framed citations of one sort or another plus some letters from important persons, including two presidents of the United States.

"The sum total of a man's lifetime," Rosita remarked with some despair. "How little it matters now, isn't that so?"

"Yes, Rosita, it is so. If Samuel had not come to Jesus, this is all that would have been left," Maggie replied. "Yet we must admit that, in worldly terms, he did live a full life."

Maggie walked slowly over to a large oak desk that was facing the doorway and sat down in front of it.

The center drawer wasn't locked.

Maggie glanced at Rosita, then opened it, a little nervous about getting so close to whatever she might find, the den reflecting, presumably, Samuel Albertson's real personality.

"It feels like we're inside his brain here, doesn't it, Senora Maggie?" Rosita commented warily. "It feels strange, you know. Until a few months ago, he never let any of us see what he was like behind that tough, hard, mean mask."

Neither Maggie nor Rosita could speak for several minutes. Maggie busied herself by glancing at other items in the drawer.

She found an envelope addressed to her.

"Rosita," Maggie asked, her hand shaking, "would you kindly come over and stand beside me, please?"

Rosita did just that.

"What's wrong, Senora?" she asked.

Maggie handed the envelope to her.

"Would you open it, please?" she asked, her voice even weaker than usual. "And would you mind reading it to me?"

"It would be my privilege," Rosita replied.

She accepted the envelope, which, unlike some of the others, was sealed. Carefully she took out the letter, smoothed out the creases, and began to read.

"Dearest Maggie," she said, "I would never have thought that I would be writing to you in this manner. Even now, when there is so little time, I cannot face you directly, my sister in Christ. Ah, the wonder of those words! I wasn't 'in Christ' or in anything good at all, even before Emily died. How much pain I visited upon her! She went to heaven never knowing . . ."

Rosita had to stop for a moment.

Maggie reached up and gently clasped Rosita's free hand until she could talk again.

"She went to heaven never knowing whether or not I would ever join her for eternity," Rosita continued. "She died in my arms, you know. She died just after saying something I will never forget. My blessed, beautiful Emily begged me to join her in her faith, her redeeming, Christ-centered faith. She said, 'I could not bear being in heaven without you by my side. I would rather have hell, Sam, for that is what heaven would be like if you were not there with me.' Her voice was so strong, Maggie, as though she was suddenly recovering and there had been a miracle. Then her body became limp, sagging in my arms, and I know now that an angel had taken sweet, sweet Emily by the hand and lifted her to glory without end.

"I was so bitter afterward, not willing to accept any of the truth of what had happened to her soul. I became the monster everyone said I was. I was never very far from being one anyway. Saying good-bye to Emily simply tipped me over. I had no regard for anyone.

"Until you came along, dear friend—oh, dear, dear one. You were so old, so wise, so kind, so unimpressed by the physical trappings of this world of mine. I saw in you sweet Emily as she would have become had she lived.

"It was almost as though she had come back to me. And I knew I couldn't treat you the way I treated everyone else. Feelings of courtesy, of respect, Maggie, yes, of compassion and joy and love returned.

"I owe that to you, my blessed sister. I owe my destiny itself to you, turning me from hell to the gates of heaven and beyond. I owe to you the assurance that, as I die to this world, I will live to the next, I will drift from pain and loneliness and the longing for Emily that I carry with me day after day.

"Soon I will be caught up to heaven as angels sing their welcome and as my beloved takes my hand and leads me to the precious throne. There I will stand before my Lord, and He will smile at me with the reality of forgiveness that His shed blood purchased.

"I cannot give you very much in return, Maggie, for it is all of this world, and yet you have given me time without end, eternity itself. But you will need care, and you will need money to live, and these I can turn over to you.

"Waiting for you now is a house, Maggie. It is built on a promontory overlooking the Pacific Ocean. A fund has been set up to make sure it is properly tended to and that you will never be hungry, that you will always have heat and clothes and food and whatever you need.

"I built something for you, Maggie, the last thing I will ever construct with my own hands in this life. I built a rocking chair, my dear one. You can sit on it and watch the sunset and feed the squirrels.

"Good-bye, Maggie Stuart. Shed no tears for this man. I am rejoicing now. I am at peace. I await the fulfillment of the holy promise of Almighty God, for I shall soon enter the place He has prepared for me.

"Good-bye, Maggie, but only for a while, as you well know. Remember that and cherish the promise as I do, my blessed, blessed sister."

Rosita handed the sheets of paper to Maggie, who sat quietly, grasping them in her hand, leaning her head back against the chair, her eyes closed.

In the background, she could hear Rosita start to sing, so sweetly, so very sweetly, "Abide with me, fast falls the evening tide."

She held Rosita's hand a little more tightly.

"His favorite hymn," Rosita told her. "Is it all right if I continue?"

"Yes, of course," Maggie replied. "Let's sing it together."

They sang all five stanzas.

And they stayed in that room long afterward, looking at other letters as well as various personal effects, and when they emerged and Rosita shut and locked the door behind them, it was very late.

The next morning, Miquel and Abel Alessandro drove Maggie

to the home that would be her last one.

A bright day.

No clouds showed in the sky; the ocean was calm, the sun sparkling off its rippled surface.

Maggie stood on the front porch, breathed in the salt-scented air, and then sat on one of the two rockers Samuel Albertson had made for her.

She had several more years of life left.

And she would live them at peace, with children coming to her periodically to listen to her stories and to bring her treats for the squirrels who apparently adopted Maggie as their human mother.

Adults were her visitors also. It seemed impossible that she could bore anybody.

Until Maggie's voice gave out and she could speak no more, she sent everyone away with tears, with laughter, with songs of praise for the Savior for whose heavenly presence she soon would enter.

Part Seven
Wiping Away the Tears

The hope of heaven amidst our troubles is like wind and sails to the soul.

Samuel Rutherford

Chapter Thirty-eight

The years passed by . . .

How many people had she outlived? How many hands had she held just before death made them limp? How many times had she kissed the cold foreheads of bodies at funerals?

But not for much longer.

Maggie knew that this was the case. Each year seemed to bring a new ailment. Each year brought greater weakness.

She became nearly blind and ultimately had to confine herself to her home, which she could navigate easily even without all her sight, knowing every turn and corner as she did.

But losing her eyesight meant Maggie could no longer read to a new generation of children. She could only hold the young ones in her lap and tell them such stories as she had memorized and sing a few happy songs to them as they listened with appreciation.

Eventually, the pace of visitors slackened because she just could not concentrate well any longer, and she would fall back into senile ramblings that would sometimes frighten the little ones.

And then, one night, that last night, she knew everything was coming to an end, everything that was earthly and mortal . . .

"And He shall wipe away every tear from their eyes, and there shall no longer be any death; there shall no longer be any mourning, or crying, or pain . . ."

Those words from the open pages of the Bible resting on Maggie Stuart's lap swept over her, and she repeated them several times, the Bible itself unnecessary at that point since her eyes had deteriorated to the point that she could no longer read. No matter. She had memorized the most beautiful verses decades earlier, and she simply loved to hold it as she always had. And now the verses came back to her easily as she sat on the wide porch of her home, resting in the rocking chair, watching the sunset, and talking to her Savior.

". . . There shall no longer be any mourning," she said, savoring each word as she closed the Bible and hugged it close to her.

If Maggie were truly honest as she looked back over the years, she would have to admit that she had been in mourning, in one way or another, since she had lost Randy, since she had stood by his grave, thrown her head back, and begged God to take her. *Please, Lord, take me now, for life without Randy can never be life at all, not for me!* she had cried.

So many years had passed since then. Decades.

And she was still alive, yet even now she could think only of Randy, no one else, none of the hundreds of men, women, and children she had met since then. Sometimes Randy's memory crowded out thoughts of even God Himself.

That truth made her heart pound faster.

Can it be so, Lord? she asked the Master. *Can it be that I came to love poor Randy more than You?*

No answer came, perhaps because it was already inside her, and the reality of it forced her to weep.

I wanted him beyond wanting You. I wanted to hold his body in my arms more than I wanted to stand before Your throne in worship.

She gasped, her mind flooded with thoughts just born, thoughts that she had been successful in burying or at least had managed to ignore until now. But finally, old and tired, she could not fight that battle any longer, her defenses as weary as she was.

Is that why You took him from me, Lord?

Maggie brought her hand to her mouth, trying to stifle sobs that threatened to rip through her body.

O, Lord, how foolish I was! she prayed. *All I had to do was totally trust You for the strength to wait.*

Years ago, getting on her knees in repentance wasn't an extraordinary act. She would simply do so and take the act for granted.

No longer.

Maggie Stuart's bones hurt. A headache had begun to throb at her temple.

Too much, she told herself. *Too much thinking, remembering.*

She managed to slide off the chair, every joint rebelling. The wood floor of the porch seemed so hard against her knees.

I'm worse tonight. Why tonight? Why now?

She wondered if it could be the dampness.

Next Maggie had to bow her head, which brought painful protests from her stiff old neck muscles.

She knew she could stay in that position only briefly; otherwise she risked unconsciousness from the pain, from dizziness she had to fight against every second. And with the evening chill becoming more apparent, if she passed out and remained there for the night, pneumonia would surely be her newest companion in the morning.

We do so many things in our ignorance or our anger or . . . our grief. Please forgive me for this, dearest Lord.

Tears streaked the old, brittle skin of her cheeks.

It's just that I had never known a man before Randy. And I've not known one since he went to be with You, Lord.

Those last eight words felt bitter to her, strangely bitter.

Why, Lord? Why is that? What are You trying to tell me, precious Jesus?

She could not kneel any longer. The dizziness was quite a bit worse.

Good-bye, Lord. Good-bye for now. I await that moment, that most glorious moment, when I will bid this world farewell and take the hand of an angel who will lead me to Your throne of glory, and there I will stand and praise Thy holy name.

Maggie managed to stand, though a wave of nausea forced her to reach for the arm of the chair to steady herself.

She walked slowly to the front doorway and stood there for a moment, leaning against the frame, then went inside.

As she entered the hallway, she reached for a quilt she had earlier left on a chair, knowing she would be chilled when she came in. She wrapped it around her shoulders—and suddenly remembered others who had wrapped her in warmth and kindness . . . and love: Mama. Randy. That kind family that rescued them from the Mississippi. White Feather, saving her from frostbite.

All of them gone now. Long gone.

She moved on into the house and settled herself on the couch. Randy's face appeared in her mind. She smiled. Then, as though from a distance, she heard the sounds of young voices and imagined the touch of tiny hands, saw for a moment the smiles on young faces, eager to learn.

I lost my Patrick, but still, I had children. Many children. Oh, my darling Randy, they were not ours, but I made them happy . . .

Maggie, it's Mama. I'm waiting for you!

Had she heard a voice?

She strained her ears and was greeted only with the pronounced ticking of the hall clock.

Maggie, there's no more pain. It's wonderful! God really is so good.

There it was again.

Then there was another voice as well, equally familiar.

Papa!

We're waiting for you, Maggie . . .

And then suddenly she realized she had heard nothing, that those were voices she wanted to hear after so many years of cold, awful silence.

Maggie was partway up the stairs, heading for her bedroom.

She had been urged to sell the house Samuel Albertson had built for her and get something smaller, cozier, but she would not listen, would not discuss it at all. She also would not allow anyone to stay with her and compromise the independence that had come to mean so much to her.

She smiled as she thought of the truth, that for anyone nearly a century old, there was no such thing as independence.

I am a slave to my aches and my pains. I am chained to this frail old body. Where is the independence in that?

The stairs reached a little landing, and Maggie turned to go the rest of the way up.

I don't remember leaving the light on.

But there it was, light coming from her bedroom, very bright light. Even to Maggie's failing eyes, it was strangely radiant.

The door's open! Surely I didn't leave it—

Suddenly she was scared, scared to go to her room, and she turned around and started back down the stairs.

I do things and don't remember. I forget to eat. I go out to feed the squirrels and forget why I'm out there.

A dizzy spell overtook her, and she had to sit down on the landing, her heart throbbing erratically.

It's all spinning. Everything's spinning, like a whirlpool, and I can't stop it, can't get out.

She felt something wet below her nose, brought up her hand and wiped the back of it across the nostrils.

Blood.

She tried to stand but couldn't.

I need help. I—

Music.

She heard music.

And familiar voices singing.

Some children are outside. They're coming to see me. They can go get help; they can—

But it wasn't that.

Roberta!

Her sister had had an extraordinarily fine voice, operatic in quality. It was a distinctive voice, so clear, so—

Her strength returned abruptly, and Maggie took advantage of it by grasping the banister and pulling herself up. Slowly, carefully, she walked back down the rest of the stairs.

"Roberta!" she said out loud. "I thought you were gone. I—"

The voice faded, and there was no more music.

Sadness overwhelmed her.

"Don't leave, Roberta!" she cried. "Please don't leave. It's been so long now! Don't slip away from me like that!"

She knew she was becoming too excited over idle phantoms in the night, tricks foisted on her by the aging cells in her brain.

Maggie decided to go back outside, hardly remembering that she had just come in from being on the porch.

The clear ocean air will revive me, she told herself confidently.

She paused for a moment in the doorway, glancing back into the house.

Years . . .

Hundreds of needy people, many of them her former students. She had taught them, listened to them, prayed with them, laughed with them, cried with them for decades. Some of her students had returned to her as battlefield veterans, seeking encouragement after the stress and trials of the Spanish-American War.

"I was Your instrument, Lord," she said, her voice strained. "You led them to me and, in time, I turned them back to Thee."

Maggie remembered a certain young man named Timothy.

One of Roosevelt's "Rough Riders," he had become shell-shocked during the invasion of Cuba. When he returned home, a wasted ghost of his former vibrant personality, his family had brought him to Maggie after hearing about her amazing work with children. She had been surprised to find a grown man and his parents waiting outside the school that day and had explained to them that her work focused on children.

"But the goodness you do, it could work for our Timothy, couldn't it?" the tearful mother had asked.

"It's just love," Maggie had explained, "love, pure and simple."

"But we love Timothy very, very much," his mother protested.

"I'm talking about God's love," Maggie added intensely. "If we can just get Timothy to accept—"

"None of that," the father interjected. "That's pie-in-the-sky nonsense."

"Will you let me try, Sir?" Maggie asked.

Both parents were about to say no when Timothy, who had been standing silently behind them, suddenly spoke up.

"God's love," he said. "That's what I need to know about."

In a matter of weeks, Timothy improved though he would never become fully functional as a normal adult. He was, however, able to break out of the shell he, with his parents' unwitting assistance, had constructed around himself.

Other remembered faces and stories surfaced in her memory, and she rejoiced over them.

I've probably outlived most of them. They're probably waiting for me. They—

She returned to the old chair and sat down, rocking it gently back and forth.

The squirrel!

Sitting on the railing, silhouetted by the setting sun.

And beside the big one, two much smaller ones.

"I have no food for you, sweet friends," she said sadly.

They just sat there, studying her.

And then the chorus started . . .

The squirrels on the railing and others from trees nearby commenced a constant stream of chattering and barking sounds that went on for a minute or so.

That isn't like them, she told herself. *One or two chatter for a bit from time to time. But this—!*

And then the noise stopped.

But the little family stayed, quiet and unmoving. Watching her.

"Thank You, Jesus," she said, resting her head against the high back of the rocker. "Thank You for all these years."

She closed her eyes.

I'm ready, dear Lord. I'm ready.

She felt suddenly quite warm, no, not warm exactly but filled with some kind of radiating glow, a glow that touched every nerve in her body, every tired muscle, every arthritic joint.

There was no longer any sensation of the chair beneath her.

Nor the smell of saltwater, nor any awareness of the squirrels being there, none of that. Everything was gone, a curious isolation besetting her as though she was, for an instant, more alone than ever before in her life.

Though her eyes were closed, she could see!

She could see beyond flesh and blood, beyond the finite, as though a veil had been stripped away. It wasn't the mysterious lights and shadows she had heard others talk about from so-called near-death experiences but something quite clear, quite vivid.

Spread out before her was a city with golden streets and beams of something brighter than the brightest sunlight streaming through pure-white clouds, a city just a mere step or two beyond the most wondrous luminescent gates.

People were waiting.

People she recognized.

A very large group of them.

And at the front were three special figures . . .

She eagerly searched the multitude.

Scores of people with whom she had shared life . . .

A man stepped forward, his brown hair shimmering. He looked so very much like Randy—

"Mama!" he said, his young voice strong yet surprisingly tender, a smile of great warmth crossing his face.

She was flustered, briefly uncomprehending.

The man seemed to sense this as he added with great energy, "It's Patrick, Mama. It's Patrick!"

Her son, so strong-looking, so happy!

He was no longer wrapped in a shroud and covered with snow.

She shouted his name back to him, and he reached out his arms toward her.

My beloved Patrick, she thought. *And where is—Suddenly a being of unspeakable glory entered her vision. He had a radiant face.*

"It is time, Maggie. All of heaven is rejoicing for you," he said.

"Please . . . take me to Randy," she said.

The being disappeared, and she stood alone before the throng of happy faces.

But she could not find the one she sought. She could not find him at all.

Why not?

She was looking into heaven!

She was leaving that familiar old chair on that familiar front porch, leaving that home of hers!

She could feel her body being shed like a tattered old coat.

She was in heaven, surely she was. But Maggie could not find her beloved Randy though she was searching intently for him.

Seeing the angel again, she asked with joyous anticipation, "Where is Randy, Sir?"

She was nearly gone then, gone from that earthly body, nearly what those who found her later would call dead.

That weary heart of hers was barely beating. Her brain had stopped functioning. There was no more pain, no more—

"Randy is not here," the angel told her.

"No!" she screamed in futile protest. "That cannot be! I will surely spend eternity with my beloved, as I have been planning for so long."

"Randy is elsewhere, Maggie," the calm voice said kindly.

"Then I don't want to come here. I—"

She heard the sound of flames crackling, heard cries, ghastly cries, cries of pain, cries that would last through time without end—but not for her, wiped from her consciousness by a loving and protective Lord.

Randy was crying out to her.

"Randy! Dear God, my God, please don't let it be like this! I've waited all these long, lonely years to take his hand once again."

But Randy was wiser than she just then.

"Oh, Maggie, how can you say you love me?" he said, his voice weak.

"I *do* love you with all my being!" she cried out somehow through the steady tears.

"I have given you nothing but hell on earth."

"It's not true, Randy. With you I've known love and joy and—"

He reached out one hand, touched the tears on her cheek.

"Too many of these, my love, too many tears."

His body stiffened with some new pain.

His eyes opened wide.

"One more kiss, Maggie," he said.

She leaned down, her lips touching his.

And then he was gone.

She looked up. The crowd was still there in front of her.

"I want Randy," she said. "I need Randy."

"He refused the Son, Maggie," the angel said. "In the end, Randy Stuart turned his back on Jesus the Christ."

"But how can I go on?" she asked. "How can I go on, knowing that?"

Randy!

It cannot be, Beloved. It cannot—

"You will go on, Maggie. You will. Just trust, just obey."

The angel was smiling in so kindly a manner.

"Not just words have been spoken, sweet lady. They are—"

Maggie felt something on her cheek, something that seemed wet.

"—tears of joy from God Himself. They are being shed for you, Maggie Stuart, for you alone."

Suddenly, there was in her mind an image of her Randy standing out under the stars on a wind-swept prairie, looking up at the heavens, his fist raised in defiance, his voice shouting blasphemy.

"God is crying because of me?" she repeated, not quite comprehending, in part still captive to a senility-encrusted mortal frame.

"Yes, sweet saint, yes! You could have turned away. You could have stood, as Randy did, and mocked Him. But you did not. You cast your burdens upon the Lord, and He is now giving you rest for eternity."

"Oh . . ." she said, the last word she would utter in her dissipating finiteness, a word of sudden dying pain, then realization, and finally acceptance.

Maggie reached out her hand first with hesitancy, but then with growing anticipation, taking hold of the angel's hand, the angel who then shouted, "Thy will be done!" and lifted her the final distance. And then her limp, cold body of flesh was left behind, and she entered a new body, a body of light not unlike the angel's.

A quite rapturous sensation flooded over her, so total, so sublime, that she started to rush into the crowd. But then she paused for an instant but only that, the briefest flash of time that no longer could be measured in the face of eternity, and whispered words of farewell, for someone she knew was gone now, someone with whom she would never share the fulfilled promise of redemption, the reality of it, and the wonder of it.

And the incomprehensible wonder was that God would provide. She started singing "Hallelujah! Hallelujah! Hallelujah!" as first her sister, then her mother and her father and her son welcomed her, and they walked together through glory toward the throne, the blessed white throne and He who sat on it.

In a place so hot that bodies of flesh would have lasted only a second, a place wracked with endless and unfathomable pain, Randy Stuart wept for paradise lost and for imperfect love doomed amongst the unceasing flames . . .

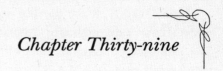

Chapter Thirty-nine

"Listen to that!" the handsome, brown-haired teenage boy said as he and his girlfriend approached Mrs. Stuart's oceanside house at the end of a foot trail leading from the edge of the Santa Monica Mountains.

The sunlight was fading, and the two of them needed to be careful where they stepped; the trail was makeshift at best, kept deliberately in that condition in order to make the sense of solitude all the more complete and also to discourage those with idle curiosity from bothering the legendary lady.

The house had been built several years ago by Samuel Albertson shortly before his death. He had built it specifically for the old woman, built it in such an isolated spot because he wanted her to be able to enjoy something of a retreat, a quiet place where she could be strictly alone or where her guests could find some rare and blessed peace and quiet.

"Squirrels!" his girlfriend remarked in a childlike manner. "More squirrels than I've heard before."

It was nothing less than an impromptu chattering chorus of sorts, and they marveled at the cacophony as they walked.

The quaint house was directly ahead, sitting on a stark bluff overlooking the Pacific Ocean.

Stopping for a moment, the young couple watched the brilliant, dying sun reflected off the sparkling water, which was the second reason he had asked her to go with him to that location.

"So beautiful!" the girl remarked.

"Yeah," her friend agreed, taking in the strong colors.

The first reason was that they had come with a present for the old lady, a shawl the girl had knitted for her but was too shy to bring on her own.

"She'll like it, Sue," the boy told her appreciatively as he reached out and put his arm around her waist.

"I hope so," Sue replied with obvious earnestness. "I love her, you know. I really love Mrs. Stuart."

The boy looked ahead, toward the house.

"So do I," he said softly. "Without her—"

Shawn had been pretty rebellious, a young man sowing his wild oats whenever and with whomever he could at any given moment. He was getting a "reputation" that would prove dangerous to his future.

She always seemed so fragile, this ancient human being, a face with the skin stretched tautly over sharp and brittle bones, twinkling eyes sunk deep into her skull, hair white, thin, a slight shake to her hand each time she extended it in welcome.

But there was love, love that showed through the fading shell that was her physical body, love deep and pure.

"She made me realize how foolish I was," he added. "She said I happened to be so much like someone she had first met when she was in her twenties back East and had known for many years; she said I was like him even to the color of my hair."

Sue reached up and kissed him on the cheek.

"Shawn, she changed me too, you know. I would never have started dating you if it hadn't been for her."

"Your parents were real upset at first," Shawn remembered.

"They threatened to kick me out of the house if I didn't obey them right on down the line as far as you were concerned."

He smiled.

"That old woman got me to give up all my other women for you, Sue," he said, smiling, though more serious than perhaps she realized.

Sue reached up and ran her fingers through his brown hair.

"So soft," she said, "almost like a woman's."

"That's what Mrs. Stuart said."

The first time they had met, Maggie Engebretsen Stuart had been sitting in the old rocker on her front porch. And Shawn was busy hiking in that area.

He had been alone that day, alone by choice on that afternoon of steaming West Coast heat. He had paused near the house, intending to drink from a battered old canteen his father had given him, a relic left over from the Spanish-American War, and then go on. But when he emptied the canteen he was still very thirsty.

Shawn had noticed the little house and Maggie Stuart sitting on the porch as she always did during those final years, and he had approached her to ask if she could spare him some water.

For a moment she hesitated, looking at him strangely.

"Ma'am . . ." he said, embarrassed, "if it's too much trouble, I'll be okay. Don't put yourself out now."

"Oh! For a minute I thought . . . You look like—" she started to say, but then her voice trailed off.

Then, waving her hand through the air, Maggie stood with some effort and asked him to follow her into the house.

As he was drinking a glass of water after sitting down on the bare wooden chair to which she had pointed, she came up to him and asked if she could touch his hair. It seemed an odd request, but he told her it would be fine.

"Oh, how soft it is . . ." she whispered as she placed one hand ever so gently on the top of his head.

"Are you all right, Ma'am?" Shawn asked, feeling more than a little awkward since he did not know how to treat the elderly.

"Yes, indeed I am," came her reply with surprising cheerfulness.

Then she stood back and looked at him.

Due to the heat, he had taken his shirt off.

And even at her age, she could not help but notice how well-toned his chest and stomach were.

"You pay some attention to your body, don't you?" she remarked appreciatively, noticing the arms and the well-etched stomach.

"Yes, Ma'am, exercises, that sort of thing."

"So did—"

Remembering Randy's fine build, Maggie had brought her

hand to her mouth and suddenly felt a little faint.

Shawn stood, concerned, and asked if there was anything he could do.

"Memories, young man," she told her new friend, "the sweetest, sweetest of a woman's memories."

Memories of their wedding night, Randy curiously nervous as he undressed, and Maggie feeling a bit guilty as her eyes roamed over his lean, strong body . . .

Shawn took her hand and helped her to another chair that had been placed a foot or two away.

"Thank you," she said. "What is your name?"

He told her.

"Thank you so very much for entering my life right now," Maggie told him with no little passion.

There were other visits in the weeks that followed, and eventually Maggie was to learn why he had been alone that first day, learned what was troubling him about life.

But you can change, Shawn. You surely can. God's strength is able to rout your weakness. Lean on dear Jesus. Let Him take the burden away.

"The squirrels, Shawn," Sue was telling him, breaking through those special thoughts of earlier moments with the old woman.

"Yes," he said, not quite aware of what she was trying to tell him, his memories having taken him back months before.

"There are so many of them," she remarked, "and they haven't stopped for a minute."

They walked the rest of the way to the house.

Mrs. Stuart was sitting in her old chair on the front porch. An identical rocker stood empty just an arm's length away. At least two dozen squirrels were there as well, squirrels that immediately skittered away into the undergrowth as the couple approached.

Except one.

It was on Maggie's lap, staying there until the young couple had come to within just a couple of feet.

This lone squirrel hesitated, seemingly reluctant to leave, its little nose twitching. But then it too followed the others.

"Mrs. Stuart?" Shawn said, looking at that old, old face, the eyes open, the mouth hanging open just a bit.

Then the young man touched her hand—cold and stiff and gray—and the mournful cry that escaped his lips would be repeated by him and by others through the long, sad days to follow until they came to accept, in the midst of their tears, a truth transcending all others . . . that Maggie Engebretsen Stuart's long journey had ended, and she was finally home.

For the many people who had known her, living their lives without having contact with Maggie Engebretsen Stuart would be strange and awkward at best.

The children she had taught.

Years later, they would remember her as they were passing through the area and inquire about her, only to be told what had happened.

"She influenced me so much," each would say in his or her own way, with one kind of accent or another.

"She always welcomed people around her, I guess, until the very end," another would remark. "And yet she always seemed to project a sense of loneliness."

"She was afraid," the answer would come, "afraid to reach out and love someone after so much loss in her life. But eventually, she got past that and loved anyway, because she knew the truth that it was better to have loved and lost than never to have loved at all. That sounds corny perhaps, but it really is true, you know."

Gone.

Maggie Engebretsen Stuart was finally gone.

And hundreds of souls, the souls she had touched, felt the void, felt it deeply, felt it always.

Christian faith is a grand cathedral, with divinely pictured windows. Standing without, you can see no glory, nor can imagine any, but standing within, every ray of light reveals a harmony of unspeakable splendors.

Nathaniel Hawthorne

Author's Notes

From *Angelwalk* to frontier dramas . . .

Now that is a switch, I must admit.

And if you consider that I also have written science fiction novels as well as espionage thrillers during the past few years, you will see that frontier dramas/westerns do represent a radical shift.

But in retrospect it seems reasonable.

Both involve dramatizing Christian principles. The time frame is different, but the purpose of this ministry of writing that I have had for nearly a decade remains the same.

Riversong represents yet another shift for me in the types of books I have written since 1988, which was when the first *Angelwalk* novel was published. (Now, so many years later, it is still selling well and has gone into its fifteenth printing, in fact.)

Many writers seem to specialize in one genre or another. They stake it out for themselves and go on churning out the books.

Take John D. MacDonald, a fine writer who wrote mysteries pretty much exclusively.

And Ed McBain, who did so-called "cop stories."

Ian Fleming created a popular spy-novel series.

The list of examples is a long one, to be sure.

Writers generally like the security of mining a genre for all it's worth and sometimes staying within it for longer than they should. Exploring new genres, new techniques, can be intimidating, but anything else seems, to me, nothing more than a prescription for looming artistic staleness.

I want my readers to feel as though what I write is as fresh as possible, that when I am in the process of writing, nothing is more important to me than the words the Lord enables me to put together into a cohesive narrative, and that what I write is truly from my gut, as the expression goes.

Even within the Angelwalk series, I have switched gears quite a bit.

The first book was from a somewhat rebellious unfallen angel's viewpoint, the second and darker novel from one of Satan's fallen-angel slaves. The third book was from a guardian angel's perspective. The style of these three proved to be similar, but the stories proved entirely different.

But with *Darien,* I did switch styles altogether, going from what was first person present tense to third person past tense, and this entry in the series was at least 125 pages longer than any of the others.

For me, it has been far more important to face a challenge each time I write a novel. And staying with the same type of story year in and year out is just not what I've ever found attractive.

So, early on, I deliberately decided to go on from *Angelwalk* (semi-allegorical) to *The Christening* (modern-day spiritual warfare/demonic possession) and then to *Dwellers* and The Wandering Bartlett Brothers series (action-adventure) and eventually to *Road to Masada* (a large-scale biblical/historical novel), then eventually to the recent *Ashes of Paradise* (a Civil War trilogy with an total of 2,000 or more pages), and *Without the Dawn* (a massive six-part work). In the future there will be others equally diverse in content and style, including those dealing with the fearsome aspects of the Year of Terror during the French Revolution, a future novel that deals with the occultic influence among the top Nazis before and during World War II, and a number of other subjects.

The change of pace has been invigorating to me.

But, at last, as it is turning out, I may switch genres substantially less in the future than previously.

The reason is not hard to ascertain: I have found that historical novels of one sort or another offer the greatest number of challenges to a writer such as myself, challenges that make each book exciting to tackle, and I don't expect that that will cease being the case for me anytime in the foreseeable future. As many historical periods as there are, that is how many challenges are ahead.

Surprisingly, as part of this new direction in my career, I shall be writing an increasing number of so-called Westerns, or prairie novels, over the next few years, surely a major change in direction for me by any reasonable guideline. One of these novels will be entitled *Under God's Spell* and will deal with the push westward of dedicated Christian missionaries eager to convert Indians to a saving knowledge of Jesus Christ. Be assured that the direction and motives behind the writing of this book will be wholly different from what, for example, James Michener surely had in mind when he started *Hawaii*, namely, tearing the worth and the integrity of missionaries to shreds.

Why am I doing this?

For one thing, the genre is very appealing to me.

You see, I have little respect for much of what we call the twentieth century, even with its revolutionary technological advances.

Along with the many blessings it has brought, there have been countervailing decreases in morality, ethics, and values.

The twentieth century has been witness to far too many steps down the road toward Big Brother and other manifestations of inevitable satanic control—inevitable, that is, from a biblical perspective.

This century has also seen at least one lifestyle that is abhorrent to Almighty God take giant steps toward political legitimacy. It has been a bloody century of wars and of tens of millions of murdered babies and of political purges in China, Russia, and elsewhere.

It is, after all, the century of communism and fascism and feminism and whatever else.

Westerns, in particular, take those who write them, as well as those who read them, back in time—but not so far into history that we feel entirely disconnected to the era being described. It was a time when abortions were surely being performed but were still considered by the vast majority of Americans for what they are: gruesome and murderous acts against those human beings least able to defend themselves—not anything a decent woman would allow, and the ones who asked for abortions suffer the utmost shame. It was also a time when gay rights were unknown, and gays themselves were shunned by a God-fearing society that did not want their unholy perversion even spoken of, let alone tolerated.

The era of the western frontier certainly was a bloody one, with much lawlessness, but respect for the unborn and scorn for perversion, by and large, gripped most individuals' conscience.

One man was responsible for getting me more and more interested in the Western and related genres.

The late Louis L'Amour.

There is no question in my mind that he was the catalyst. What an influence he would be on any writer!

When I first fellowshipped with Louis, I was just thirty-odd years old. And now I am in my fifties.

And nothing that this remarkable, principled man ever told me has lost its relevancy to my career.

Over the decades he wrote scores of classic Westerns . . . right up until the last few weeks of his life, and quite a few would be made into epic motion pictures starring such major Hollywood stars as John Wayne, Alan Ladd, Van Heflin, and others.

Louis told me that he stressed authenticity. That was at the core of everything he wrote.

The man's eyes widened with a hint of real passion as he spoke about this, for he regarded his readers with complete and unyielding respect, and he wanted them to know that he eschewed sloppiness when it came to descriptions of locales, moments in history, and a great deal else that really counted in each of his monumentally successful novels, which have sold, to date, more than 300 million copies worldwide.

Louis L'Amour wanted even the smallest details to be accurate.

He told me, "Roger, if I am describing a quaint little town in New Mexico, one that actually existed, I want to be as certain as I can that I am naming the streets correctly, that everything is down pat."

He paused, then added, "This is a point of honor with me, something that is absolutely inviolate."

And he worked very hard at this goal.

Before computers, it was so much harder to rewrite. But when he got his first word processor Louis rejoiced, because then he had the time and just the right equipment that would allow him to be even more careful, if that were possible. And he used the new technology with stunning zeal.

Louis L'Amour's approach meant that he found a great deal of traveling inescapable, visiting those locations that he planned to include in a particular forthcoming book.

The craftsmanship he revealed in each novel was memorable.

Anybody who got to know this man would be affected by him, inspired to listen carefully and absorb completely.

Writing Westerns, or what we might call frontier novels or prairie novels, fits in exceptionally well with what is becoming the emerging direction of my career as I find myself becoming more and more oriented toward historical plots as opposed to others that are of a modern-day variety. The latter are often fun to write, but I am constantly drawn back to history.

I like the idea of escaping today's excessively hectic, arrogant, and nihilistic society with its materialistic predisposition—and, in a sense, going back in time, probably the residual effect of my science fiction days and undeniably influenced by one of the finest science fiction films ever made: *The Time Machine,* starring Rod Taylor and Yvette Mimieux.

There are other books ahead, of course, and there have been many in my past, but none has been more emotional than *Riversong,* a novel that has the strongest female protagonist of any of my books except possibly *Circle of Deception.*

Technically, there is a surprise ending, but I hope it is taken as much more than that, mainly a commentary on how God sometimes deals with our expectations.

The climax was one that I had held firmly in mind from the moment I started the first chapter of *Riversong.*

It may be the most wrenching of any that I have done, with the exception of *Circle of Deception.* Both books involve an element of surprise that seemed completely natural as I came to the last chapter. Both have to do with the greatest love in the female protagonist's life. Yet they are such vastly different types of novels.

Well, frankly, I hope that thousands of readers of *Riversong* are going to have a brand-new box of tissues nearby, for as I was writing the last few pages, I myself cried, because what I was portraying was a transcendent, undeniable truth that is all too rarely dealt with by Christian novelists.

Truth?

That really is the only way to describe the last chapter of this book.

It is an unexpected truth and therefore a surprising one, and it will not be easy to take, but I believe that it is something a great many believers will be forced to face, however startling it proves to be.

Rewriting the history books.

How I hate it when so-called educators resort to doing this, unable to accept the verdict of history when it fails to support their anti-Christian agenda, which is most of the time, I might add.

How frustrating it must be to their kind!

They find themselves unable to change history, of course, so they stoop to changing the chronicles of history and brainwashing impressionable young minds into thinking that the "revised" material is historically accurate. But it is neither that nor moral or ethical either, for they have manipulated a skewed version of the truth into something that is essentially a lie.

That happens often these days.

Oh, it does, in major or minor ways, a line left out in a history book, a few words cut here and there, or else entire blocks of type omitted, to be replaced by politically correct material!

And falling under the editorial ax are usually references to the importance of the Christian faith in the lives of the early settlers of America.

They've even tampered with Thanksgiving!

Before the past few decades, the Christian base for Thanksgiving remained largely intact in the minds of American schoolchildren everywhere.

A time of pausing and giving thanks to Almighty God.

Thanksgiving.

The very name delineates what it is all about.

Nevertheless, the first Thanksgiving ends up, in many current textbooks, as sounding more like a New Age pantheistic ritual with little real spiritual content—or an excuse for yet another holiday—than anything of a Christ-centered nature. If that isn't disturbing to every Christian in the nation, particularly parents, then we had better start reexamining and realigning our family priorities.[1] Certainly, in fashion in more recent years is the revisionist propaganda that the American Indian of a hundred years ago was some sort of noble savage, a metaphor for downtrodden and oppressive people everywhere.

Baloney, plain and simple.

That is the plainest, most direct response I can give.

The truth, historically, is a different matter altogether.

Today they are called Native Americans, an obvious attempt to disavow any connection with the savagery of their past, a further example of rampaging "political correctness" at its most deceptive form.

After all, we can say, with certainty, that the average Indian a century ago really was, in Christian terms, patently heathenistic because of a lifelong, even generations-long, enslavement to a pantheistic approach to deity, which set him up as the forerunner of the New Age cults that are proliferating today.

Generation after generation.

I remember speaking with a veteran Indian actor on location with the "Dr. Quinn, Medicine Woman" television series, where the exteriors are filmed less than two miles from my house. He

---

1. The contradiction, hence the hypocrisy, is so blatant as to be almost a parody of itself. What is Thanksgiving supposed to be for if not to offer thanks to Almighty God for His gracious bounty? Such "political" moves surely reveal a certain and growing desperation on the part of the enemy of our souls and those who cause his policies to proliferate.

candidly told me, "Everything we are is New Age, the whole thing.[2]

. . . the whole thing.

And so it has always been since before the white man settled what was to become the United States.

Accordingly, you, the reader, should not expect to find, in any portion of *Riversong*, what might be called a spoon-fed portrayal of Indians as anything but what they historically were, not noble at all—far from it. In fact, while they were often abused by the reprehensible tactics of a cruel United States government bureaucracy, they proved completely capable of atrocities of their own and were often at war among themselves, one group fighting another, with even women and children not off-limits as victims. Annihilation of another tribe was, more often than not, the objective.

Bloodthirsty?

You can be certain of that, rightly earning for the various Indian tribes the identification as "savages," a word abhorred by the revisionists but utterly in keeping with the way Indians had been living for centuries.

On the other hand . . .

Do not expect to read this novel with the perverse hope of seeing these people depicted entirely as bloodthirsty killers, either. To say that they all were lost spiritually is to discount the work of the Holy Spirit and to refute the clear testimony of many Catholic and Protestant missionaries of the nineteenth century.

In this novel you will find some Indians who are every bit as ter-

---

2. The honesty of that response certainly is to be admired, but it also should chill the blood of any Christian learning of it. And yet it is not nearly as surprising as it might seem. The New Age movement specifically lists certain former Indian lands as important centers of the powers of nature and of the universe. These are where repeated mantras while holding "holy" crystals can allegedly cause the greatest response. Sounds like hokum, but not to New Agers, and if you realize that the arch deceiver is behind all of this, it should never be a laughing matter for any Christian.

rifying as they are supposed to be but, as well, others who definitely are not, especially in the case of White Feather, a prominent character, to be sure, and a solid Christian, someone who befriends Maggie Engebretsen Stuart and saves her life.

White Feather comes closest to a depiction of "the noble savage," but he is truly an exception to what various unfortunate settlers were forced to encounter as they pushed westward.

Many more examples could be offered of times when the unexpected shrieks of Indians in the middle of the night would chill the blood of any man, woman, and child forging a new world for themselves after leaving an altogether different life back East.

White Feather represents a determinedly realistic portrayal, one that is as balanced as possible.

He is an individual, period.

If other Indians had been like him, the United States government would not have had any excuses for the admittedly awful tactics it employed to bring these people under inhumane subjugation.

Sadly, it must be said that my extensive research suggests that relatively few Indians have ever converted to a saving knowledge of Jesus Christ despite the efforts of dedicated missionaries and for the same reasons as Christians' lack of success with converting people from the gay lifestyle today.

It seems that the "old ways" have been born into each successive generation, and it is a formidable task, usually ill-fated, to get them to give up all traces of their satanic past.

As a result, their eternal destiny is assured, and none of them will go to heaven unless they turn away from heathenism.

The various tribes worshiped only strange gods during the eighteenth and nineteenth centuries, gods as unsubtly satanic as any during the course of human history, and those that are "religious" at all today continue to do so though with a New Age sugarcoating, carrying on their participation in a corrupt and perverse belief system that is filled with all manner of abysmal demonic trappings.

The truth about all this is quite stark: The belief systems of

Indians today who have not converted to Jesus Christ remain as mired as ever in only slightly camouflaged evil, despite the so-called Great Spirit references, evil because nothing they believe permits the acceptance of Jesus as Savior and Lord, and yet Indian worship never stops there, as bad as that is, but goes to more bizarre and hellish extremes.

That may sound like a cruel thing to say and a judgmental one, but I have come to the conclusion that if sweet words and a New Age kind of love, together with liberal doses of insipid positive thinking, lead to spiritual delusion of one sort or another, condemning the unsuspecting to an eternity of punishment, then true spirituality must surely rest on an alternative platform, a platform of looking at the world and life and people strictly on the basis of what is indicated by the Bible, which is the inerrant and infallible Word of God, and that means doing so with realism and honesty, even if this hurts, even if it enrages the revisionists.

Those revisionists would have us believe that Indians are people with great dignity. Were that to be true, it still would not save them.

Dignity is not salvation.

The revisionists point to the injustices, already noted herein, that Indians have been suffering since the western expansion of the past century, with entire villages wiped out by United States government soldiers. Yes, that happened, undeniably so, and it is further evidence of the sin nature of human beings, whatever the color of their skin.

But tragedy is not salvation.

Finally, the revisionists say that Indians should be left alone to live the way their culture dictates, that no one on the outside of that culture has a right to interfere with anything in their lives, that there are many ways to God, and Indians have found one and should be free to pursue it.

But freedom is not salvation.

Roger Elwood